I0699647

THE SECOND SON

Dynastic Disasters and Political Intrigue:
England 1660

A LUKE TREMAYNE ADVENTURE

THE SECOND SON

Dynastic Disasters and Political Intrigue:
England 1660

GEOFF QUAIFE

ARPress
45 Dan Road Suite 5
Canton, MA 02021

Hotline: 1(888) 821-0229
Fax: 1(508) 545-7580

Ordering Information:

Quantity sales. Special discounts are available on quantity purchases by corporations, associations, and others. For details, contact the publisher at the address above.

Printed in the United States of America.

ISBN-13:   Softcover   979-8-89389-319-9
              eBook   979-8-89389-318-2
              Hardcover   979-8-89389-968-9

Library of Congress Control Number: 2024916231

The Luke Tremayne Adventures

Major Characters

Luke's Unit

Sir Luke Tremayne (Colonel)	Magistrate and special agent for Charles II.
Sir Mark Cowper (Lt. Colonel)	Royalist courtier and Luke's deputy. Newly elected member of House of Commons.
Miles Oxenbridge (Captain)	Former associate of Luke, captain of foot.
Mutton Johnson (Lt.)	Miles' deputy in quarantining Medlowe.
Matthew Hatch (Captain)	A former leading spy under the Protectorate, Luke's brother-in-law.

Other Royal Servants

Nicholas, Lord Ashcroft	Commander of the King's bodyguard.
Anthony Halford	Royal physician and alchemist.
Lady Jane Bohm	Dowager Marchioness of Nith, courtier to the Queen, Luke's friend and associate.

Royalist County Elite gathered at Medlowe Abbey

Algernon, Earl of Medlowe	Lord Lieutenant, master of Medlowe Abbey.
Lord Ranald Medlowe	Son and heir of the Earl of Medlowe.
Lady Caroline Medlowe	Ranald's wife.
Dr. Adrian Ravenscroft	Chaplain to the Earl of Medlowe.

Dr. Hector Gregory   Lawyer, steward of Medlowe Abbey.

Lady Veronica Petty   Widow of Sir Julius Petty, sister to Phineas

Nathan Petty   Veronica's son.

Sir Phineas Leigh   Leading rival to Petty before the Civil Wars.

Alexander Kemp   Uncommitted ambitious conspirator.

Elspeth Kemp   Alexander's predatory wife.

Lord Edwin Symes   Aristocrat, obsessive opponent of a standing army.

Sir Winston Finch   Baronet, corrupt and violent, newcomer to the elite.

Lady Lucy Finch   Winston's wife, and Edwin Symes's sister.

Piers Carey (esquire)   Friend of the King, immoral but tolerant and able.

Cassandra Ramsden   Piers's distant cousin, twin sister of Hyacinth.

Hyacinth Ramsden   Piers's distant cousin.

Sir Orlando Hall   Devoted long suffering Royalist with marital problems.

Lady Ursula Hall   Orlando's Papist, Welsh, estranged wife, herbalist and midwife. Accused witch.

Sir Job Elliott   Unhappy Royalist with high expectations.

Charity Elliott   His niece, whose property he administers.

Others

Sir Septimus Ingle   Former leading republican magistrate.

Wilfred Mills, (Captain)   Former Cromwellian officer, later local militia.

Blackie   Publican at The Blue Dog.

Little Johnny   Poacher.

Lionel   Head coachman.

Bryan   His deputy.

Samson   Medlowe Abbey gatekeeper.

Bettina   His wife.

Reginald, Lord Vaughan   Lady Caroline's cousin.

Referred To

Sir Julius Petty	A leading local former and would-be powerbroker-deceased.
James, Lord Medlowe	Algernon's eldest son, disappeared—presumed dead.

Real Historical Characters

Charles II	Recently restored King of Great Britain and Ireland.
James, Duke of York	His brother, and heir.
Henrietta Maria	Queen Mother.
Edward Hyde, Earl of Clarendon	Lord Chancellor (Chief Minister).
George Monk, Duke of Albemarle	Former Cromwellian general, who restored the King, and now commands Royal Army.

Prologue

Sir Luke Tremayne, was a former secret agent, head of military intelligence and latterly ambassador to the Islamic states of North Africa for Oliver Cromwell. He spent the two years since the Lord Protector's death as a magistrate and landowner in North Yorkshire. During this period, which saw the collapse of the English Republic, and increasing demands to recall the King from exile, Luke avoided high politics, and concentrated on his magisterial responsibilities.

In the beginning of 1660 he accepted a surprise assignment in this role from the exiled King to investigate a dysfunctional family whose activities had concerned the soon to be reinstated monarch. Luke completed this mission in early May and returned to his estate just in time to welcome the birth of his two children—unexpected twins. The eldest he diplomatically named Oliver Charles, and the younger by just a few minutes, Maud, a variant of their mother's name Matilda.

The King entered London on May 29th and immediately continued with putting together a new administration. Within the month Luke was in London in response to the King's request that he join the new government in a position that was similar to that which he held in military intelligence under Cromwell.

1

Luke waited in a small antechamber for his initial discussion with the monarch. Luke had met the then young King in-exile in Scotland in 1651 where he saved the young man's life from obsessive fanatics, and again in 1653 at his court in exile in Paris. On both occasions the then staunch republican had a favorable impression of the young royal. This positive impression had been strengthened by the first month of the new administration in which Charles had carefully balanced positions in his new government between Royalists who went into exile with him, Royalists who had stayed in England during the republican rule, leading republicans who had opposed Cromwell, and leading Cromwellians such as his new head of the army, George Monk, and the deputy head of the navy, Edward Montague. The King aimed at reconciliation—not revenge.

Eventually a brightly liveried servant entered the antechamber and asked Luke to follow him. They entered a large reception hall where Luke saw the empty throne, and a dozen or so men standing around awaiting the King's appearance. To Luke's surprise the servant led him across this large chamber, and through a door on the far side.

Entering this second room Luke realized he was in the King's dressing room. Charles clapped his hands and all the servants left the room. The King was wig-less, and had not yet applied the cosmetics that was to become a feature of the Restoration Court, especially for men who wished to emulate the French. He signaled for Luke to draw up a chair.

He was blunt. "Tremayne, I wished to see you alone before I began my morning of audiences. Given the nature of the position I offered you, you will often remain in the shadows and our meetings must be like this—early in the morning or late at night."

"Am I to head military intelligence as I did under Cromwell?"

"No, you will not be part of the army establishment. George Monk, now Duke of Albemarle will head that body, most members of which will be quickly demobilized, except for my household guards, a few garrisons in key cities, and two regiments for overseas service. You will have nothing to do with Albemarle."

"Not civilian intelligence, I hope?"

"My Lord Chancellor, The Earl of Clarendon is currently constructing an intelligence service for the government. In fact I have spared Cromwell's chief spymaster, John Thurloe, from the gallows to assist him in that enterprise."

"If I am not part of military intelligence, or your general intelligence service, am I part of Lord Ashcroft's personal security group?"

"Yes and no. Let me explain! Bearing in mind the death of my father and my years in exile, I vowed that should I ever be returned to the throne, I would create a situation where I would never suffer the same fate. In order to retain the confidence of my people, my government would need to be open, transparent, tolerant and ready to compromise. This open approach is evident in everything I have done since returning to London. You,Tremayne will not be part of this open government."

"Then what am I part of?" asked an intrigued Luke.

"I once told a friend during the depths of my exile that the government I would create on my return to England would be open—but devious. You will be an essential element in the devious aspects of my new administration."

"I am not sure I quite understand."

"Tremayne, there will be matters concerning the security of the state, or my personal safety that I as King cannot be seen to be involved in, and for which my open instruments of government, and other overt agencies are not capable of dealing with within the law. You will not only provide my own personal intelligence group with power to execute whatever remedies to a situation I think fit, but you will be the extra-legal arm of my administration. You have no superior, other than myself. I have allocated you an apartment just along the corridor from here, and as far as the Court is concerned your team will be part of my many Gentlemen of the Bedchamber, and for outward appearances only, attached to Ashcroft's internal security group."

"How many men will I have?"

"You will know what you need once you become active, but initially I suggest yourself and two or three deputies, whom I would need to approve. When you need a body of troops to effect any of my decisions, Ashcroft will release the required number of men for your service from my household guard. For this I re-commission you as a full colonel. As you will not be involved in any large scale army exercise, your republican rank of major general is not appropriate. I have already validated your knighthood, and the grant of your Yorkshire estate, but unlike many of your former comrades, I am not raising you to the peerage, or adding to your assets. Ideally few should know of your existence, especially the councilors and administrators in my open administration. After all they will probably be the prime object of your enquiries. In addition, to help you in your work I will gazette you as a magistrate not only for Yorkshire, but for Middlesex and the other home counties. Do you formally accept my offer?"

Luke nodded agreement. The King clapped his hands and once more the room was immediately flooded with servants. "My man here will show you to your apartment. Send me the names of the men you wish to be part of your unit. We will meet again in four weeks, and I expect that you will be ready to act."

A servant led Luke out through yet another of the many doors leading into the dressing room. A short distance along a gloomy corridor he was presented with a gigantic key and taken to the door which it fitted.

Within a fortnight Luke, after he had located them and obtained their approval, submitted the names of three of his former comrades to the King. The first person he named was John Thurloe's top spy, Luke's brother-in-law, Matthew Hatch. The second was the man who had commanded the soldiers on Luke's ship *The Cromwell* during his Mediterranean mission, Miles Oxenbridge. For the third, in the spirit of the new administration, he chose his deputy on his most recent assignment on the island of Nith, the royalist courtier, Mark Cowper.

He then returned to Yorkshire and discussed the situation with his wife Matilda. It was agreed that when fully recovered from childbirth, Matilda and the children would move into her brother's house in Kent—and the one that she had lived in before she married Luke. From there any trip up to London was manageable. The Yorkshire estate would be left in the capable hands of its steward, and Luke's deputy on his Portugal mission, Peter Frost.

Luke's apartment within Whitehall became the office of the new and hopefully secret arm of the King's administration. Early in the following month as arranged, Luke was summoned to the King's bedchamber at six in the morning. In exile the King had a reputation of being an early riser, but since arriving in London his nightly debauchery had meant that now he usually arose much later.

On the morning of Luke's meeting he reverted to his earlier habit. Luke directly entered the King's bedchamber along a secret passage and was immediately praised, "I approve your choice of deputies. Your selection of Cowper is inspired. It is in line with my policy of reconciliation. You are learning fast to adapt to my ways. I have a suggestion as to how you could employ Cowper. As he is well known to many of the courtiers from his days with me in exile, he could be your source of courtly gossip. In addition since we last met, Cowper has been elected to the Convention Parliament. I am already facing trouble from some of those parliamentarians, and his information from that quarter is invaluable. While I wish the rest of you to remain in the background, Cowper can play a more overt role as an active courtier and Court-supporting politician. Should any of you need to appear socially in public, you can be introduced simply as one of his friends."

"We are all assembled ready to serve. Do you have an assignment, sire?" asked Luke, anxious to be employed.

"Yes, openly my loyalist gentry are reestablishing their control of county administration, but in some areas they are experiencing unexpected difficulties. Bitter feuds have erupted for almost every position. Gentlemen who went into exile with me are resented by those who stayed behind and suffered in my name. Many who sacrificed much for my father and myself are unhappy that my compensation has not reached their expectations. These individual concerns could coalesce into threats against the government, and my person."

"Surely a royal hint would be enough to put an end to these problems?" said Luke.

"Very true Tremayne, but among the competing Royalist families within the counties I do not always know which families to discard, and which to support. I have only been back in England a few weeks, but the rumors I hear from some areas alarm me. Although some who were in exile, and some who remained here will serve me well, there are very unsavory rumors that some Royalists in the home counties are being traduced by London merchants whose loyalty to me has always been suspect. Get to the truth of these rumors! And then recommend to me which of the warring factions I should elevate, and which I should reject."

"This conflict is between fellow Royalists, and does not involve those gentry who supported Parliament?"

The King smiled, "Neither of us are naïve. The former Parliamentary gentry, are waiting to throw their weight behind which of the warring families they find least obnoxious. In other counties I have been forced to reappointed some of the current Cromwellian magistrates as the least destructive compromise."

"How am I to be introduced to this conflicted gentry environment?"

"My father's old Lord Lieutenant in one of the home counties is Algernon, Earl of Medlowe. He is into his seventies and not long for this world. Nevertheless he has organized a ball at his manor, Medlowe Abbey, for all the county's aristocratic and gentry Royalists to celebrate my return."

"Isn't that the county where there was some serious trouble in the period between the downfall of the republic and the imposition of royal rule? The leading republican magistrate, Septimus Ingle, his wife and some fifteen government soldiers disappeared without trace."

"Apparently, according to Ranald, the Earl's son and heir, Ingle saw the imminent dominance of the old Royalist families and migrated to the Dutch Republic. Now back to your mission! The gentry and aristocracy of the country will meet at Medlowe Abbey for a few days before and few days after the ball to reorganize the administration of the county following the disruption of the last two decades, and also to agree on their Parliamentary representation. Overtly you will attend as my special envoy to advise on the reorganization of the county militia. The only person there who knows of your real role is Ranald, who was with me for a year early in my exile in Paris in late 1651."

"If you have such a loyal and trustworthy person in the center of the imminent discussions, why do you need me?"

"Is Ranald still trustworthy? It is nine years since he was close to me. Since then I believe he and his father have fallen out. Ranald probably has very different views to his father who was a loyal servant to my father and myself. Consequently my actions in this county will depend on what you uncover. Even if loyal, a future Earl Ranald may not be able to rectify all the situations that I find need redressing, but you will. It is a pity that Lady Matilda has not yet come south. It would be useful if you were accompanied by a lady, both for your own convenience at the ball, but more importantly to elicit information from the fairer sex."

"Matilda will be here in a couple of weeks."

"Good, but in the interim I have made arrangements to assist you in this matter. I have arranged a female associate for you. She is a person whom you got to know on your recent assignment on the island of Nith. It is Jane, the Dowager Marchioness."

"I thought she was content to live out her life on the island with her least troublesome step son, the new Marquess."

"Come Tremayne, Jane is still a relatively young woman. When my mother, who will soon be in England heard that Jane had recently been widowed, she asked that I bring her to court to take up a position she once held as one of the Queen's Lady-in-waiting."

"What exact role will Jane play in my investigation?"

"The darker side of many families is their treatment of the womenfolk. Jane may be able to elicit more information from such women than you or my more overt investigators. Your association with her in this joint endeavor will remain a secret. Not even Ranald is aware that she too, is acting for me."

2

Luke arrived at Medlowe Abbey the day before the week-long meeting of the Royalist county elite was scheduled to begin. He was immediately shown into the Abbey's library where Lord Ranald Medlowe, heir to the title and estates of his father Algernon, Earl of Medlowe, awaited him.

Luke was surprised. Lord Ranald was a small man with the stature of a young girl rather than that of a mature male—no doubt an unfortunate by-product of dynastic inbreeding.

The diminutive peer was effusive. "Welcome Tremayne! I never thought I would be in a position to say that. For several years during the Cromwellian rule your name was constantly on our lips. Every plot that we hatched, if not infiltrated and aborted by his spymaster Thurloe, was thwarted by the elite military intelligence unit led by you. Your involvement was most feared by our people."

"I was hardly in a position to strike fear into Royalists," replied an embarrassed Luke.

"Don't indulge in false modesty. Unlike Thurloe who largely operated within the law, you stopped at nothing to achieve your ends. You were ruthless in protecting the security of the state—that is why Charles has appointed you to a similar position in his administration and why you are here. I must always act within the law to curtail any problems that arise within this county that might threaten His Majesty, but there may situations where that may not be enough."

"Do you anticipate many such problems, my lord?"

"There are bitter divisions within our Royalist camp. Rival factions will spend the coming week trying to gain the advantage over the other. There is no telling what the losers might do, as there is much at stake."

"What is the basis of this division—behavior during the Interregnum?"

"In part. Those who remained in England during the republican and Cromwellian rule and suffered for their loyalty to the King, believe they should be rewarded now with all the perks of office, while those who went into exile, and usually suffered much more material loss in property and income than those that remained and are now struggling to reassemble their estates, claim the moral high ground and demand the limited number of perks and positions available. All of this is complicated by family feuds, and the intrusion of ambitious newcomers into the county elite during the past two decades who are clearly determined to replace the traditional leadership."

"Surely the King and yourself can solve this by dividing the spoils between the opposing groups? There is no need for high powered intervention by any secret agencies of the state."

"It is not that simple. The members of each group are themselves a diverse group and some will not accept the decisions of their own leaders if it goes against their family interests. There are rumors circulating about many of the leading gentry, which if true, would rule them out of any royal appointment or parliamentary nomination. On the other hand if these tales are untrue, not to appoint such a person, might seriously harm the King's standing in the area. It is hoped that you will clarify these issues for us. The situation in some counties has been so fraught that the King found it least divisive to reappoint the existing Cromwellian magistrates rather than decide between the warring factions of his supporters."

Suddenly the door burst open and a liveried servant entered the room. "My lord, forgive this intrusion, but Lady Veronica Petty has arrived with a large entourage, and is causing an unpleasant situation. She demands that she be taken immediately to her husband. Her husband, Sir Julius, has not yet arrived."

"Would you take this gentleman, Sir Luke Tremayne, to his quarters. I will speak with her ladyship. Luke, I will brief you further before most of the guests arrive. Julius is the leader of those gentry who remained in

England. He and his wife have clearly become confused regarding each other's movements."

The servant led Luke from the library to his accommodation.

In the afternoon Luke retrieved his horse from the stable and trotted around the expansive Medlowe Abbey estate noting the fertile soils of numerous fields of wheat and the rich pastures for fattening cattle. He was greatly impressed by the magnificent and ancient trees that dominated the woods which made up about a third of the estate, which had a sizeable deer population. Luke was intrigued by a large rectangle depression between the furthermost field, and the beginning of the woods. A massive hole had been dug, and its refilling was now almost complete. He would asked Ranald for an explanation. Luke was impressed by the number of outbuildings and separate cottages that were found throughout the estate, occupied no doubt by various out-servants of the manor.

The Earl of Medlowe was indeed a very wealthy man.

Next day Luke was summoned to the library where he found Ranald and a petite, lavishly dressed woman.

"Tremayne, this is Lady Veronica Petty. I explained to her ladyship that in addition to being an expert on the militia, you have had experience in investigating disappearances and murders. Her husband seems to have gone missing. I have to return immediately to a meeting, but I am formally asking you to use your magisterial and royal authority to investigate Sir Julius's non-appearance."

Ranald left, and Luke asked Veronica, "Why did your husband leave his home a day or so before the rest of your household, and well before today's meeting was scheduled to begin?"

"He said some time ago that given the current volatile situation he would meet the Earl on the eve of these crucial county discussions to plan their strategy."

"He would have known for some time that this was no longer possible. The Earl has been seriously ill for weeks and confined to his town house in London. Ranald does not expect him to survive the summer. If your husband had an assignation for the evening in question, it was not with the Earl. Who was it with?"

"You are blunt, if not rude, Tremayne, but I reached a similar conclusion—although knowing Julius it would not have been with a woman. It was probably with one or more of the participants in these meetings. He was determined to bolster his position and destroy that of this opponents."

"Do you know any of your husband's movements since he left home?"

"Yes—and it is disturbing. I sent my servants around the local area to discover if he had been seen. Apparently he arrived at The Blue Dog late in the evening. His horse had gone lame, and he had walked it for several miles. He told the publican that it was too late to reach the Abbey and he would stay there that evening. Next morning he was gone, leaving behind his lame horse apparently in lieu of the unpaid bill. No one here saw him arrive."

"So he disappeared between The Blue Dog and Medlowe Abbey?"

"Or at either of the places you mention. The Blue Dog has an unsavory reputation and Medlowe Abbey has had its scandals."

"Was Sir Julius carrying any valuables with him? Could he have been the victim of a random robbery?"

"No, not from our perspective—although to an impoverished footpad his neck chain might have appeared a veritable treasure."

"Would it be easily identified, if found?"

"Yes, I have never seen another one like it—alternate links of gold and silver."

Within the hour Luke was in The Blue Dog. He explained that he was the magistrate investigating the disappearance of Sir Julius Petty. He quickly established a rapport through an extensive and prolonged drinking bout with the solidly built, raven haired and bearded publican, known to everybody as Blackie.

"You have met Sir Julius before the night in question?" asked Luke.

"Dozens of times. During the exile of the King, he often visited the old Earl as the two were the pinnacles of Royalist resistance in a county then firmly in the hands of the republicans and Cromwellians, a position their opponents maintained through the proximity of the anti-Royalist London militia. Sir Julius often spent a night here before going on to the Abbey."

"Was he usually alone?"

"He always came alone, but on most visits it was to meet someone."

"A woman?"

"Never! He usually met with other leading Royalists who are now just coming out of the woodwork. For the last decade or so many Royalists found it inconvenient and dangerous to meet with each other in their own homes. There were Cromwellian spies everywhere, except here."

Luke could not conceal wry smile and wondered if that was true. He continued probing, "Sir Julius had such an assignation on his last visit here?"

"He certainly did."

"You seem emphatic about that?"

"Yes, his would-be companion caused quite a stir when Sir Julius had not arrived by the time they had apparently scheduled for their meeting. Julius had been delayed because his horse went lame, and he had to lead it for several miles."

"Do you know who this person was?"

"Yes. He was one of the young Royalists who spent many years on the continent. Since his return he has spent much time up at the Abbey. He and Lord Ranald are close companions. Rumor has it that both were friends of the King when his court was in Paris."

"For a young Royalist who left the county during the Interregnum to have a secret meeting with the leader of the Royalists who remained behind before a gathering of the county elite to divide the perks and positions that a return to power might offer them, seems a reasonable approach for both parties?" commented Luke.

"I do not understand the ways of my superiors, but as a simple tavern keeper I assumed it was attempt by Lord Ranald to get Sir Julius onside for whatever he and this young gentleman planned. Youngsters without the restraint of more experienced men will create chaos and endanger the monarchy once again."

"Who was this dangerous young man who met Sir Julius?"

"The drunkard, Piers Carey, esquire."

"Tell me more about him?"

"According to some of my customers, he is a serial drunkard and whoremonger. He certainly showed his ability in the former category. He was very wobbly when he left here."

"He left before Sir Julius?

"Yes, around midnight. I had to open up to let him out. His own manor is just over the nearest rise."

"He left alone?"

"Yes."

"When did you realize that Sir Julius was also gone?"

"Next morning. One of the maids told me that his room was empty. I assumed he had left early for the Abbey, but I had my doubts when I found his horse was still in our stables."

"Was it usual for him to leave without paying his bill?"

"You know the custom. It is almost a tradition that the superior classes never pay us humbler folk at the time. Sir Julius always paid what was due, even if it took a while. I expected that he would drop in on his way home and settle his account, as he had done countless times before."

"Could he have been robbed on his way to the Abbey?"

"There has been a breakdown of law and order on some of the outer reaches of an expanding London, but the old republican militia and its temporary Royalist replacement have kept this part of the county reasonably secure. I have not heard of any robberies in recent weeks—except that at the same time as Sir Julius left here, a leg of mutton that was being roasted disappeared from my kitchen. I suspect Sir Julius took it."

Luke pushed a pile of silver coins in the direction of Blackie.

"If you think of anything else that may be useful to me, you will find me at the Abbey for the next week at least. I will drop back in a day or so to savor more of this magnificent amber ale."

Early next morning Luke visited Ranald who asked, "Any news on Julius's disappearance?"

"Before I answer that my lord, tell me about Piers Carey!"

Ranald looked at Luke quizzingly, almost in disbelief, and replied with a tinge of irritation, "Piers is a good friend. As boys we went to the local grammar school which my father had founded. We spent most of the early war years there together. On the execution of the old king we were both sent to the continent where eventually in the early fifties we joined the King and his brother at the royal court-in-exile in Paris. The four of us were boon companions for about a year. I left, but Piers remained a courtier for a few more years. I am surprised that given so many shady characters here you should ask about Piers. He is one of the few gentlemen in this county that the King could entrust with great responsibilities. Unfortunately his lifestyle is anathema to the traditional God fearing conservative elite of this area, and consequently a potential liability to His Majesty. Those god fearing old timers must have already spoken to you. Piers is more suited to the new Court than county administration."

"What's Pier's main liability?"

"Drink—he is almost continually drunk. And he is a whoremonger."

"As you imply I cannot see these as a worry to the King. Women and excessive consumption of alcohol are a trademark of the new Court."

"True, and the Royal Court is a far different place to the rural manors of this county's gentry and aristocratic elite, even if we ignore the Presbyterian and Puritan landowners, who may have lost power centrally, but still form a sizeable minority of the elite. They could make life for an unreformed Piers very difficult."

"There are plenty of places at court where King Charles can find a place for Piers, and avoid a potential problem for you here," suggested Luke.

"I have to admit that it is I who want Piers to assist me to control this county. Despite his weaknesses, he has four virtues that the county needs. He is very tolerant. He believes that none of your former comrades should be punished for what they did in the wars, except for the regicides. Even here he thinks they should be imprisoned or exiled, but not executed. He is charming, even charismatic. He could win over the most vengeful Royalist to accept such a policy. Thirdly, he is very able. A thinker with a practical bent. And lastly he is very compassionate. Since he has been back in the county he has spent a considerable fortune on helping the unfortunate and dispossessed. He even gave the soldiers of your New Model army that were disbanded in this county, a small allowance to help them settle back into society."

'A perfect renaissance man!" said Luke half seriously.

"I think so, but why with so many dubious gentlemen gathered here did you want to know about him?"

"Did you send Piers to meet Julius on the night he disappeared?"

Ranald tensed and looked Luke in the eye, "Of course not! Why would you think such a thing?"

"A witness identified the man that Julius met at The Blue Dog as Piers."

"Did they meet for long?"

"Several hours."

"Did they both stay there over night?"

"No, Piers left at midnight, and Julius before dawn. Why would Piers want a secret meeting with Julius? From what you tell me they had nothing in common."

"Your basis assumption may be faulty. Perhaps it was Julius who wanted to see Piers—a much more likely proposition than the reverse."

"Why?"

"Piers is not ambitious. He much prefers the good life to that of service, although when he did act in the public interest, he was very effective. Julius on the other hand is a long time traditional politician, who before any meeting would want to ensure he has the numbers."

"To achieve what?"

"To reestablish the power he exercised with my father before the late King's death. Pier's recently acquired wealth makes him a strong force to be reckoned with at the local level, and Julius would be anxious to get him onside."

"What should I know about Julius?"

"Before the civil wars Julius and my father controlled this county. Father was the wealthiest aristocrat and Lord Lieutenant, and Julius was the largest gentry landowner who with his clients dominated the bench of magistrates and parliamentary representation."

"Julius was your father's lackey?"

"Not at all. It was a partnership rather than a master-servant relationship. Father treated Julius as the son he really wanted. My much more personable older brother disappeared. I am the second son. Mother died in giving birth to me. Father blames me for the loss of the love of his life and has always been disparaging of my physical appearance. We have never had a real relationship. I have seen very little of him throughout my life. I was sent to boarding school at a very young age, and then into exile as a teenager eventually to join the royal court-in-exile. Julius remained here throughout the Interregnum, and continued to work closely with father. They were the leaders of the Royalist cause for the last two decades."

"Did Julius's possible desire to meet Piers have something to do with you and your father?"

"In what way?"

"Power within the county! Your father is dying. Within weeks, if not days, you will be the Earl. Your best friend in the county is not the old power broker, Sir Julius Petty, but a maverick yet able Piers Carey, who also has the King's ear. This meeting could have been a desperate attempt by Julius to prevent the development and possible dominance of a Ranald Medlowe, Piers Carey alliance—or a desperate attempt to become part of it."

"You could be right. Question Piers! I am intrigued as to his explanation. I will come with you."

Luke and Ranald made their way to Piers' apartment and informed a servant that they wished as a matter of urgency to speak with his master. After being led through several rooms they finally reached Piers who was seated around a small table eating oysters in the company of two of the most beautiful women Luke had ever seen.

"Colonel Tremayne meet my cousins, twins—almost identical, but not quite, Cassandra and Hyacinth."

The latter asked, "Do you wish to speak to cousin Piers alone?"

"That is entirely up to your cousin, but you ladies may be able to help our enquiry as well," replied Luke diplomatically.

Piers turned to his cousins, "Colonel Tremayne is not just one of Ranald's guests. He is now a special agent of the King, but spent most of the Interregnum as Oliver Cromwell's head of military intelligence. His presence here suggests that the King has problems within the throng gathering in the Abbey."

Luke wanted to put an immediate end to speculation about his attendance. "At the moment, Piers, I have a simple task to investigate, on my authority as a magistrate, the disappearance of Julius Petty."

"And how can I help with that?" answered Piers.

"You were probably the last person to see him alive," Luke replied.

Piers was momentarily shaken, but quickly realized that denial would be useless. Nevertheless he hesitated, and after a sustained silence finally answered. "You are very efficient, colonel. Yes, I saw Julius the night before he disappeared. We engaged in almost four hours of useful discussion."

"Who initiated that meeting Julius or yourself?"

"Both of us. We needed to meet, and Julius suggested The Blue Dog on the eve of our gathering here at Medlowe Abbey."

"And the nature of these discussions?" asked Ranald who appeared irked, if not furious that his friend had not discussed such a meeting with him.

"Land! A year ago I inherited my father's estates, but last month on the death of my mother, several other large properties came into my possession on reversion. Many of these had been leased to Julius. He sought to discuss those leases with the new owner, and ascertain my attitude to our tenant owner relationship in general. I made it clear I would not be renewing any leases of property close to my manor house, and I was interested in obtaining some of Julius's land that was adjacent to these. We discussed the transfer or selling of several parcels of property that would be in our mutual interest."

"Was Julius happy with the result?"

"There were a few matters that remained unresolved, but in general he seemed content."

"You never raised the subject matter of this week's meetings with him."

Luke thought Piers was too ready to answer, "No, not at all!"

Luke aggressively continued. "I do not believe you. I suspect Julius was desperate to regain his control of the county which he shared with the Earl of Medlowe before the war. However things had drastically changed. The old Earl is on his deathbed, and the incoming Earl is not a close friend. In fact the new Earl's best friend is now a powerful landowner with strong connections to the King. Ranald and yourself are on the verge of replacing the old Earl and Julius. Ranald will use this week's meetings in favor of a new alliance that would destroy Julius's influence for good."

"There is only one thing wrong with that assumption, colonel. I am not interested in county politics. I want to consolidate my estates, marry and produce a dynasty. Ranald certainly faces problems in maintaining the Medlowe dominance of the county whether of his new or his father's old model. His aristocratic status even with the assistance of the King might not prove enough. Although he inherits the goodwill of some of those that supported his father and Julius, there are many more anxious to destroy the Medlowe influence. As someone who left the country during most of the troubles he now struggles to become the leader of those that remained. There is a major problem brewing here. Look into the activities of the five or six gentlemen who plan to meet secretly before every open meeting! And leave me alone," pleaded Piers.

Luke had no desire to become embroiled in the factional politics of the Royalist gentry, all determined to benefit materially from the King's return. He remained focused. "When you left Julius around midnight, what sort of a mood was he in?" asked Luke.

"Tired. He said he was going straight to bed, and would leave for the Abbey around dawn the next morning."

Just as Luke and Ranald were leaving the two girls who had been quietly chatting, turned their attention to Luke. It was Hyacinth who spoke, "Sir, Piers can only take one of us to the grand ball on Wednesday. Will you take the one he leaves behind?"

"I would be more than delighted to take one of you to the ball, but unfortunately the King himself has chosen a partner for me—and I could not disobey the King," he teased.

Luke on his way back to his apartment decided to take advantage of the mid-morning sun, and sat on a garden bench at the entrance to the maze.

His heavy drinking of the previous night caught up with him.

He dozed.

He was awakened by the voices of young women gamboling around the lawn. They were the laundry maids returning from the surrounding hedges, having placed the Abbey's washing out to dry. One girl immediately gained Luke's attention. She had a very low cut cleavage that as she pranced around revealed her more than ample breasts.

Luke's lust was suddenly curtailed. Around the girl's neck was a chain of alternating metals—possibly silver and gold.

Luke jumped to his feet, followed the playful women and called out to the girl with the low cleavage, "My girl, can I ask you about that magnificent chain that you wear. From where did you get it?"

"It is a valueless trinket sir. My sweetheart found it in the pig pen. He gave it to me last night."

"What your sweetheart's name?"

The girl giggled. "He is well named. He is a swineherd and his name is Joe Bacon."

"Where would I find him at this time of day?"

"He takes most of the pigs to graze on the lower reaches of the hills to the east of the Abbey. He will not return until dusk."

Having examined the chain more closely as he spoke to the laundry maid he was sure that it was made of alternating silver and gold links, and was most likely that which Julius had worn.

Luke ascertained from the girl where Joe Bacon had taken the pigs. The rough ground was on the way to The Blue Dog. He would question Joe, and then move on to the ale house and continue his questioning of Blackie.

4

Luke found Joe under a chestnut tree as his pigs foraged happily amongst the blackberries, gorse and nettles. Luke introduced himself as a magistrate investigating a case of a missing person. To break the ice Luke asked, "How did you spend the last few years?"

"I spent the last six years in Scotland serving under General Monk. I was on garrison duty at Scone castle for most of the time. It is probably not wise to admit such a thing now with the return of the King."

"Don't worry lad, I too served in the Parliamentary army until the death of Oliver Cromwell."

"You have clearly survived the change of government better than I," he commented. "Why does a magistrate want to see me?"

"You gave your sweetheart a nice two metal chain. Where did you get it?"

"From one of the pig pens."

"Tell me more!"

"Some pigs remain confined in a large pen for several days for various reasons, while the majority are brought out here each day by me. When we finally let those confined to the pens out, they leave behind a scene of devastation that requires considerable remediation every couple of days. Whatever has been thrown into that pen over those several days is ripped up and consumed, or half buried in the mud. I saw fragments of clothes, numerous bones and then something glistening in the fading light. It was a chain. I washed it, and gave it to my girl last night."

"The chain you found belonged to my missing person, Sir Julius Petty."

"My god, talk to Rob Taylor, one of the herdsmen. His cattle are just below me in the nearest meadow."

"Why?"

"Several mornings ago as he drove the cattle through the main gate he found scattered along the way bits and pieces of what could have been a human body. It had been so savaged and ripped apart by dogs that he doubted its human origin. He despaired of every being able to recognize the pieces and wishing to preserve any family from such a horrendous experience, Rob collected the pieces in his cart and brought them home to the Abbey. After consultation with the steward, it was decided that they were not human. The collected bones and pieces were fed to the confined hogs. Clearly they made a terrible error."

Luke confirmed with Rob Taylor his activities on that fateful morning, and concluded that Julius was dead, and his remains consumed by the ravenous Abbey pigs after being ripped apart by marauding dogs. But the real problem remained. Had the dogs killed him? If so had they been the agents of a human killer who directed them towards the victim? Or another possibility was that the dogs had been fed an already murdered body?

Luke joined the other guests for the early afternoon meal. He informed Ranald. "My lord, sad news. Some remains of Julius have been found."

Luke explained in detail the horrendous circumstances of the discovery, and the state of the completely dismembered body.

"Most unfortunate! I will take Veronica out of the room and inform her. I will also order a search for every possible remnant of Julius that we can find. I will introduce you now to the assembled guests. You can break the news about Julius after Veronica and I leave."

He returned to his seat at the head of the high table and called for order. "Ladies and gentleman, I would like to introduce to you formally, Sir Luke Tremayne, special agent of the King, and here with us to help reorganize the militia. Unfortunately he has spent his whole time so far looking into the disappearance of Sir Julius Petty. He wishes to say a few words regarding that investigation."

Ranald gathered up Veronica and both left the room.

Luke spoke, "I have waited until Lady Veronica has left to inform you that Sir Julius Petty is dead. Although the investigation is not complete it appears that early on the morning when this gathering began, Sir Julius on his way here from The Blue Dog was savaged, mauled, killed and dismembered by wild dogs. Various pieces of him, believed at the time not to be human, were ultimately consumed by pigs into whose pen these remnants were placed and where some of his possessions were identified."

An involuntary shudder went through the group. Luke sat down, but one of the audience asked, "There are countless savage dogs, usually carefully controlled by their masters. I have not heard of any wild dogs in this area. Was Julius the unfortunate victim of a random animal attack, or did someone let their killer dogs loose to attack him?"

"A good question. It is too early to say, but there is some evidence that Julius left The Blue Dog in possession of a roasted leg of meat. That may have incited a wandering pack of dogs to attack, but I have certainly not ruled out murder, and will seek your help as I probe further."

Ranald returned to the refectory alone, and immediately informed the gathered group. "Lady Veronica has asked that we suspend this afternoon's meeting out of respect for Sir Julius, but also to enable his heir, now Sir Nathan Petty to take his place amongst us."

After the meal Luke followed Ranald to the library where the latter announced, "It time you began questioning several of the gentlemen here especially as to how the death of Sir Julius might hinder or advance their political ambitions. You have already considered Piers. There are five other persons that the King and I want to be sure of, before they are offered positions of importance, or are asked to share power in the county"

"All of them Royalists during the interregnum?" asked Luke.

"Yes, and unlike the King, the Royalists of this county have little desire to forgive their opponents, let alone share with them positions of power. But as you will discover being a Royalist in the past may mean very different things to each of these men now. Quite frankly a few of them have no desire to share power even with their fellow Royalists. Talk first to the most orthodox of Anglicans and Royalists, but who is not without his problems and idiosyncrasies—Sir Orlando Hall."

"What do I need to know about him?"

"His strengths are his absolute loyalty to the King and to the Anglican church of Archbishop Laud. He sacrificed a lot for the King's cause in the early days of the war, but surrendered on the battlefield under conditions that did not lead to any further loss of property. He nevertheless wants all officials under the previous republican and Cromwellian regimes to return their salaries, and demands that all the regicides be executed. He is not happy that people of your background are here. However he is most concerned with re-establishing the High Church Anglican clergy in every parish in the land by increasing the stipends, and removing all those Puritan and Presbyterians usurpers from their livings. His problem is his wife. She is a Papist, a herbalist and an accused witch. In recent years she has provoked Orlando into extreme positions regarding women and Roman Catholicism. Neither obsession will help him in the eyes of the King. Orlando demands ruthless persecution of Catholic priests whose insolence he believes knows no bounds, wants Parliament to force the King to marry a Protestant, and to prevent the Catholic peers returning to the House of Lords. All are very controversial topics. On a personal level he supports the current move to prevent marital separation without the consent of the male. At every opportunity he declaims that during the absence of the King, society has been destroyed by the ridiculous attention by women for place."

Later in the afternoon Luke approached Orlando. "Sir, may I ask you a few questions about the situation regarding the death of Julius?"

"You are a special agent of the King?"

"Yes, but to be honest with you we would not have crossed paths in the past. I served the late Protector as head of military intelligence. The King has appointed me to a similar role, on the basis that during his exile the then government uncovered almost every plot he devised through its superior intelligence."

"As long as those that remained loyal to the King and his father do not suffer by the retention of Cromwellian officers like yourself, who am I, as a humble county gentleman, to complain," replied Orlando unconvincingly.

"Were you close to Julius?"

"Yes, very. The three leading Royalists in this county who suffered most under republican and Cromwellian rule were the Earl of Medlowe, Sir Julius and myself. We were the three leading Royalists within the county during almost two decades of Parliamentary, republican and finally Cromwellian rule."

"Did you have discussions with Julius about these current meetings and how you could re assert your old influence?"

"Yes, of course. These meetings were originally designed by the Earl of Medlowe so that the loyal local gentry could put their house in order and come up with an united front against Presbyterians, Puritans, religious extremists and Roman Catholics—and an unexpected group of socially inferior Royalist landowners who rose to prominence in the last twenty years. We need to compile an agreed list of the right people for the parliamentary elections due soon, and from which the King can appoint a new bench of magistrates."

"Was Julius worried about any particular recent developments?"

"Yes, the illness of his best friend and our political leader, the Earl of Medlowe has created confusion and increasing fear and concern that the proper people will not be recommended. Young Ranald is from an entirely different generation and spent much of last twenty years abroad. He only returned to England on his marriage five years ago, and did not move into Medlowe Abbey until about two years ago. No one expected him to be thrust into a position of leadership for this meeting. After all, he is not the Earl. Algernon went downhill very quickly and was moved to everybody's surprise to his town house by his daughter-in- law who is the real power at Medlowe Abbey in the absence of Algernon. Ranald remains closer to the King than to the county, and within the county probably closer to those that went into exile than to those like me who remained. I now hear that he is not as close to the King as he claims, but your presence here might suggest otherwise."

"Or exactly the opposite?" countered Luke.

He continued probing, "What was Julius going to do about the developing situation?"

"He thought that he and I should talk to as many of our fellow landowners as we could."

"And did you?"

"No, unfortunately I had to confront some personal problems over the last week, but Julius said he would talk to that drunkard Piers Carey as a way of influencing Ranald towards our position."

"That meeting took place."

"And Carey probably murdered Julius," was the surprise response.

5

"**N**o evidence of such. Unfortunately, the issue is not so easily solved. On the evidence at hand, Piers left The Blue Dog hours before Julius set out for the Abbey," replied Luke.

"Carey is now the wealthiest landowner in the county. He inherited from his father a year or so ago but more than doubled his estates by the reversion of several properties through his mother who died a few weeks back. Julius wanted to discuss with Piers some of the estates that now belonged to Piers which the previous owner had leased to him."

"That does seem to have been the subject of the discussion at The Blue Dog rather than county politics," admitted Luke.

"It looks as if it is up to me, and I hope with your help to stop Piers Carey taking over the county. It is not good for the county that its wealthiest landowner is a known drunkard and worse. He has several mistresses and is known to frequent the London brothels. He has the audacity to bring two such women with him to the Abbey."

"You will find that those women are his cousins," suggested Luke.

"Come Sir Luke, a man of your experience should not believe in fairy tales. If these girls are related to him, you can add incest to fornication. I had no time for your murderous Protector, but at least he tried through those obnoxious major generals to impose a strict Christian morality on the nation. In the future this King is not likely to do so, therefore the Parliament must take the lead. That is why this county must return people like myself, rather than Carey and his ilk."

"On one issue we may agree—your concern about the influence of Roman Catholics."

"Are you married Sir Luke?"

"Yes."

"Then I trust you may never have my experience. Some time ago my wife tired of me. She is a Papist and decided to enter a convent on the continent to begin life as a nun. She requested most of the furniture in one of our houses as a dowry for her acceptance into that religious house. I was reluctant to agree to all this, but seeing her dedication and devotion to her new religious life, I went along with it, and even wished her the best."

"What went wrong?"

"I have yet to find out, but some months ago she returned to England and assumed that she could return to my manor as my wife, as if nothing had happened. I refused her access and now she has employed lawyers who demand that I readmit her as she is still my wife, and I am obliged to do so. She even has members of Parliament moving motions to force my hand. This is an intolerable interference in the rights of a head of household. Women are out of control."

"Did anyone encourage your wife to become a nun?"

"Not that I could discover. You may uncover the culprit. There are no overt Catholics in the area, but I have always wondered as to the real beliefs of a fellow strong, but unstable Royalist, Sir Job Elliott who you should question next."

"Why? Tell me about him!"

"A deceitful and vain man who expects the King to restore his family to a preeminence they never had. He is a disaffected and dangerous cavalier who wants all of your sort punished severely, all regicides publicly executed, all Presbyterians and others removed from the Church of England. He briefly controlled the local militia when the Parliament summoned back the King. Under his leadership some local Royalists committed atrocities against the leading Parliamentarians and Cromwellians. Ranald had to remove him. His real problem is that he badly managed his estates, and he is heavily in debt—probably to one of the money rich newcomers, Kemp or Finch. He blames the previous regime for all his problems. He hates you."

"What you tell me about Job and his attitude to the Church and former Cromwellians is exactly what another witness said about you."

"That was probably Ranald who has all the weaknesses of a second son. He sees the only way of climbing the political and social ladder is by pulling down those who have already made it."

"I am also a second son," explained Luke. "Our system may preserve the family assets by giving everything to the eldest, but it makes it hard for the younger siblings."

"The Civil Wars have exaggerated the problem. Almost half the landed families in this county are now presided over by a second or later son, the eldest having been killed in the conflict. Lord Edwin is a good example, as I believe also is Finch."

"Second sons have received a bad deal over the last two decades. Some were forced to fight on the opposite side to their father and eldest brother to protect the family assets whichever side won. Many, as you imply, were forced into estate management for which they were ill prepared. Others were sent into exile so that the whole family would not be wiped out, only to be considered cowards by many," confessed Luke with some emotion.

"What's your story, Tremayne?"

"I was sent to join the Dutch army in my teens because the daughter of the local aristocrat and I were becoming too friendly in the eyes of both our parents. I enjoyed army life and only left it when Oliver Cromwell died. Father would have preferred I could have taken up law or entered the church. Now let me return to my questions!"

"What do you see as the major issues confronting the new government in extending its effective control in this county?"

"The replacement of Algernon with his incapable son, Ranald would be a disaster. The lack of firm and decisive leadership will allow all sorts of troublemakers to emerge. If you have the authority close this meeting down and send everybody home before dangerous alliances are formed. Bringing everybody together without Algernon to preside is a major mistake with possibly disastrous consequences."

Luke only partially updated Ranald on his questioning of Orlando. The young peer agreed with the latter that given Luke's past, and Sir Job Elliott's demeanor that it would be more fruitful to first question the other three land owners who were jockeying for pre-eminence—Lord Edwin Symes, Alexander Kemp and Winston Finch.

"They are a mixed bunch all with more demerits than virtues. And I am sure no one will support going lower down the social ladder, after the county's experience during the Interregnum. Finch and Kemp hardly make the grade themselves."

"If I remember correctly this county was well and ably represented in the various Parliaments of the republic and within its Council of State," replied Luke a little too aggressively. "Perhaps the King should retain some of these existing magistrates and parliamentarians?"

"A situation father once admitted—but it's not a sentiment that can be raised in the current environment," countered Ranald.

"Tell me about Lord Edwin?"

"The lordship is a courtesy title. He is the heir apparent to Kenrick, Baron Symes whose vast estates dominate the neighboring county to the east. However there are sufficient properties in this county to make the Symes substantial landowners here as well. The concentration of their land in the south of the county make them the dominant family in that area. Edwin lives in this county, and has been made by his father the family's senior representative here. In addition there is a borough electorate in that part of the county returning two members to the Parliament, control over which the Symes wish to maintain."

"What about Edwin himself?"

"His strengths are his industry, ability and ambition. He is a man of wit and learning. It has been said he is afraid of nothing. He is strong on law and order and he has proved a dangerous enemy. He wants all regicides executed."

"And his problems?"

"He is full of obsessions, and has a deplorable history with women."

"Which obsession currently dominates his thinking?"

"The militia. He hates the standing army, and is delighted in seeing it disbanded although he does not think demobilization has gone far enough. He sees the country's future in the militia which he wants to see permanently mobilized to maintain law and order. He is overly concerned about the spread of urban settlements and wants towns prevented from expanding into the surrounding countryside. He often pursues vested interests above the county interest such as his desire to drain many of the low lying regions of the county and to expand the hemp industry—all to the advantage of the Symes family."

"And the problem with women?"

"In his youth he killed a young woman he was living with, apparently while in a rage. He was never charged and has gone on to marry three times with two of his wives dying unexpectedly. He is currently a bachelor."

"A complex personality!"

"And with a near fatal flaw. Despite all I have said that is positive Edwin will stick at nothing, and has an inability to focus—a condition attributed to a fall from a horse in his youth."

Luke was surprised at Ranald's ambivalent comments on Edwin. He must question the rival aristocrat immediately.

Luke found Edwin sitting on a stone bench in the Abbey's orchard reading. "My lord, I need to question you regarding the death of Julius."

"And I want to talk to you about your plans to reorganize our county militia."

"I have none. Parliament is about to determine its structure in The New Militia Act currently under discussion. I do not see much change to the current legislation. I am more concerned to see that this county can raise an effective force within hours without any major problems. Do you have any constructive ideas?" asked Luke.

"You may have heard that I am resolutely opposed to a standing army. The lessons of the last twenty years should be well heeded, but army rule was not all bad. The availability of armed forces on the ground to support law and order was a good thing. With expanding cities and increased violent crime the traditional watch is ill equipped to handle urban crime, and our village constables need to able to call on more effective support than poorly armed parishioners. I would like to see the militia mobilized on a semi-permanent basis. Then this locally controlled, gentry-led militia could act against traditional crime, and be considered a special force only to be raised in the case of riot, rebellion and invasion."

"I totally agree with you. The biggest change I had to adjust to on ceasing to be in military intelligence was trying to enforce my decisions as a magistrate, without a body of troops. Did you remain in England during the absence of the King?"

"No, as a young man my father sent me to the continent. Given the gossips who are gathered here you will undoubtedly have heard that I killed a young woman, and father thought it wise that I leave England until the matter was settled."

"So you were another exile at the Royal Court?"

"Not at all! I was never a courtier."

"How did you spend the twenty years away- in scholarship and study?"

6

"That is what father intended, but I joined the French army and like you served as a cavalry officer. Most of the time I fought alongside your English republican troops against the Spaniards in the Netherlands."

"Did you know Julius?"

"Not really. The Earl, my father Kenrick, and Julius were close before the wars, and dominated these adjacent counties. Father gave me instructions a few days ago to support whatever Julius wanted at this meeting as long as it did not affect our end of the county and the interests of the Symes family."

"Even if what he wanted may have been contrary to the wishes of the man soon to become Earl? Lord Ranald has very different views to his father. What in particular did you father want you to preserve?"

"Put bluntly the influence that the Earl, Julius and my father exerted before the death and exile of the monarch. Rumors have already spread that Ranald will appoint himself or recommend to the King or yourself a new group of leaders—for example the unknown Kemp, the corrupt Finch, or the womanizing drunkard Carey."

"I am sure Orlando and yourself retain Ranald's good graces, but Sir Job Elliott seems a problem."

"And Sir Phineas Leigh."

"Sir Phineas Leigh. I have not heard of him. Is he here?"

"Inexplicably he is not. Phineas was the figurehead of those county gentry who opposed the interests of the Medlowes. It was expected with the return of the King, Phineas and his supporters would dominate this meeting and take advantage of the illness of the Earl, the inexperience of his successor and the bevy of new generation talent to gain control of the county. He has not turned up."

"Have his supporters?"

"I don't know who would support him. Finch, Kemp and Elliott maybe potential supporters but equally they may be his bitterest opponents."

"My lord, the situation does seem more complex than Medlowes against Leighs. For example, I gather that Ranald has alienated many of his father's supporters and is gaining backing from many of those whom in the past were loyal to the Leighs. Traditional alliances have crumbled. Do you think there are any groups within the county who would go as far as to murder Julius?"

"Ranald claims to be a reformer ready to abandon the policies and alliances of his father. Those who were discontented with Medlowe, Symes, and Petty, the power triumvirate of the prewar years, may seek change through the Earl in waiting. In many ways Petty was already a has-been. So why kill him?"

"So you think his death was an accident? He was the random victim of rampaging dogs?"

"Not necessarily! Your years in intelligence has trained you to look for the political and security aspects of any death, but in my world the first thought is family, and the second, women."

"Julius had problems in those areas?"

"You should mix in with the other guests more, particularly the women. They know more than their menfolk. If I were the magistrate investigating Julius's death I would first interrogate his wife, Lady Veronica. She is not the docile traditional wife you would expect of a county power broker."

"What are your views on Kemp and Finch?"

"Their wealth exceeds their abilities. Their families made a fortune in London trade and they are only second generation landowners, lacking the refinements of the traditional landed classes. Kemp is a devious bastard and Finch the most corrupt man in England. The King must not have anything to do with either—other than to destroy them."

"Harsh words!"

"But deserved! Finch is a frivolous young man, constantly dueling to the neglect of any position he held. He lives betwixt knavery and foolery and is simply not of sufficient quality to be one of us. He has bribed his way to any position he may hold, and lies constantly. Most of what he does is underhand and in the shadows. He is involved in the illegal export of wool and the illegal import of Irish cattle. He is the most unpopular landowner gathered here. He is in constant conflict with his neighbors and tenants over enclosures, and has treated his own family abominably. He has a violent temper. Provoke him into a duel and remove his unpleasant presence from this earth!"

"Come Lord Edwin, your tirade against Finch suggests some personal vendetta. What has he done to incur such wrath?"

"He is my brother-in-law. While I was abroad he lied his way into my parents good graces and father accepted his very hefty bribe to marry into the aristocracy. My sister now leads a terrible life but she will never admit it. As a dutiful wife she continues to defend her husband."

"Given what you say, why has Ranald invited him here?"

"There are rumors that Ranald is heavily in debt to Finch or Kemp as the Earl never releases much of the family money for his use, but ask him directly. Let me ask you a question. Why are you here? The King would not appoint one of his enemy's most dangerous agents to some highly secret unit and then send him into the counties to advise on the militia. You were in intelligence. You know less about the militia than I do. What really worries the King about Medlowe Abbey that needs your intervention?"

Luke was momentarily flustered. Edwin's question had struck home. They were his own thoughts. Giving advice on the militia would convince no one who had any inkling of Luke's background. The covert reason that he was to advise Ranald and the King on the personalities gathered at Medlowe Abbey was hardly more convincing. He must seek immediate clarification from Ranald or perhaps the King himself. And he would come clean with Edwin.

"I agree, I could not have been sent here for the reasons the you have been told. Perhaps Petty's death is part of what the King feared—a bloodbath between competing Royalists or is it completely irrelevant to my real mission, whatever that may be?"

"Talk to Veronica. You could offer to escort her to the ball."

"Surely the widow will not attend the ball."

"Most women in Veronica's situation would have already left Medlowe Abbey to mourn, having escorted the remains of her husband home. But not Veronica. She appears determined to take Julius's place, at least until the arrival of her son."

"I cannot take her to the ball as I am already spoken for. The King personally has provided a lady for me."

"Another spy?"

"I doubt that Jane, the dowager Marchioness of Nith and now lady-in waiting to the Queen Mother would consider herself an agent."

But she was.

During his long interview Luke warmed towards the young lord. He saw no signs of the instability indicated by others. Although Edwin was obsessed about not retaining a standing army, he saw the value of a military force to maintain law and order, provided it was controlled by the local landowners in the form of a militia. Given his military experience Edwin would be a perfect active commander of the county militia, under the nominal future leadership of Ranald, once he acceded to the Earldom of Medlowe and was appointed Lord Lieutenant Luke was intrigued by Edwin's suggestion that any problems surrounding the late Julius were most likely related to family and women, rather than politics and religion. He was equally engrossed by Edwin's verbal assassination of Finch. Both were interesting leads.

As a result he faced a dilemma. Would he interrogate Julius's widow Veronica, or first test Edwin's assessment of Finch?

He did neither immediately.

A servant informed him that Jane, Marchioness of Nith had arrived at Medlowe Abbey, and that she wished to see him immediately.

He gave Jane a passionate hug which was returned in equal measure.

"How is this assignment for the King progressing?" she asked.

"To be blunt—what assignment? On reflection the purported reason for my presence here is too trivial for the King to engineer, and for me to execute. He and the county leaders can determine the local magistrates and parliamentarians without any ultra-legal help that I might provide. In fact I have spent all of my time using my magisterial position to examine the death of a former leading power broker. Maybe the King anticipated such an event ? Who knows?"

"After your experiences on Nith, you know that the King does not initially reveal his real purpose. Your comments actually put my recent discussion with His Majesty into perspective. It appears that I am to help you narrow your investigation. I was told that I should focus my attention on a Lucy Finch and elicit whether she needs any assistance from the King. Have you met this Lucy?"

"No, but you could be right. The King's suggestion to you to concentrate on Lucy might assist my imminent investigation of her husband, a thoroughly obnoxious character."

Luke suddenly gave a loud drawn out groan, "Jane, is the King using me to progress one of his affairs of the heart—to uncover the dirt on the husband of a woman he seeks to seduce?"

"Not likely! Charles has solved several such affairs without the recourse to ultra-legal help. If only the rest of the aristocracy treated their former mistresses and illegitimate children as generously as the King, England would be a far happier place for women. His concern for Lucy involves more than a past passing affair or future dalliance."

"Was she a former mistress?" asked Luke.

"I don't know. Most of the women who claim to be such have never been within miles of Charles, but he too readily accepts their claims."

"Perhaps that is the nub of my mission—to see if Lucy's claim, if she has made one, is genuine. How are you enjoying your new role as a lady-in -waiting to the Queen Mother, after an absence of twenty years isolated on the island of Nith?"

"Not at all. The Queen has only just arrived from France and has little time for her English born ladies, most of whom have been forced on her by Charles. As soon as she feels her son is secure on the throne, she will return to France without any of us. The King is prepared for this eventuality. He has offered me the position of the senior lady-in-waiting to his future wife."

"Is he likely to announce such a choice in the near future?"

"The Spanish, Portuguese, French, Danish and several German envoys are busy bribing the Council of State to influence the King towards their candidates. I do not think a decision will be made until England sorts out its foreign policy priorities—perhaps earlier next year. The Queen Mother having married off her daughter to Louis XIV's younger brother would love her eldest son to also marry a Bourbon. This very pressure from his mother will probably lead to the opposite result. I must now pay my respects to Lord Ranald."

"And I must continue my investigation. I will talk to Lady Veronica."

An hour later Luke was in Veronica's apartment, apologizing for his intrusion. He was surprised at her warm welcome, and calm demeanor. She was not the shy and mourning widow he had expected. While he contemplated his approach, she took the initiative. "You seem to be the only person interested in the death of my husband. Our neighbors do not seem to care. After the decades of service he gave to the county, and the personal assistance he has rendered to so many families during the King's exile, it is a disgrace."

"My lady, did Julius discuss his expectations of this assembly with you. What was he hoping to achieve?"

"Yes, he talked about it a lot. He was increasingly depressed. Initially with the return of the King he expected that the situation of the early forties would be reestablished with the Earl and himself controlling most of the county, in alliance with Viscount Symes whose family dominate the southern parishes."

"And this dream was shattered?"

"Abruptly! So many of the next generation have inherited their family properties without Julius recognizing its possible effects on the balance of power. The most obvious change is that the old Earl is dying and young Ranald has very different ideas, and friends to his father. Viscount Symes has already transferred his influence in the south of this county to his son Edwin, another relative youngster with some disturbing attitudes. What is even worse is that a number of young Royalists who had spent the last twenty years on the continent have made it clear that they want a direct say in the nomination of magistrates and parliamentarians. Ranald and Edwin will have great trouble in consolidating power in the hands of the elite few, even if that is what they want. They are already making concessions to the demands of the pushy Johnny-come-latelies."

"What did Julius intend to do?"

"He had a three pronged program—win over some of these young ambitious types to his side. He believed that Carey was a possible convert. Secondly he would make peace with his age-old rival Phineas Leigh around whom all the anti-Petty families had gathered in the past. Julius believed he had more in common with the old enemy than with the younger generation of nominal friends. And thirdly he would hold out an olive branch to some of the Parliamentarian families that dominated the county during the King's absence. These families are not present at this meeting, and several may find themselves in gaol, heavily fined or even executed. Julius had astutely picked up on the King's policy to reward enemies as well as friends as your presence here confirms. He never had a chance to explain, elaborate or execute such a program at this gathering."

"He certainly met Carey. Did he speak to Phineas?"

"I don't know. I was amazed that Phineas, who is my own brother, had not visited me to pass on his condolences. Now I have been informed that he has not arrived. Is it not strange that the leaders of the two rival gentry groups of the pre-war period failed to make it to this vital conference to reshape the future of the local community? Were they both murdered to ease the transition to the next generation?"

"I have just been made aware of Phineas' absence. Are you suggesting that a group of young Royalist fanatics on their return to England have united to seize control of the county from the traditional families to the extent that both Julius and Phineas have been killed?"

"There is certainly a loose alliance of the younger extremists who are more Royalist than the King himself. I only hope that Phineas has been delayed, and that you will soon uncover what really happened to my dear Julius."

"Who, at this conference, belong to this alliance to unseat the traditional county elite?"

"The would-be-leader is Finch. According to Julius that upstart hoped to win over Kemp, Carey and my dear friend, but the perpetually unhappy Sir Job Elliot."

"Surely our two aristocrats Ranald Medlowe and Edwin Symes have the weight to stop this coup occurring."

"Rumor has it that a lot of out of county money is pouring in to assist these young troublemakers. London mercantile interests are at the bottom of all this. The expanding city is the real disruptive force."

"And that is not in the interests of the old county elite?"

"Nor might it be the interests of the King. Nor would I put much store on the young aristocrats Ranald and Edwin to protect such interests. They probably have more in common with the newcomers than with Julius or Phineas. Even the location of this meeting was a test of strength. Ever since the days of Queen Elizabeth meetings of the county gentry have been held in Medlowe Abbey, but a letter from Finch signed by a number of his fellow conspirators asked that they meet on neutral territory—the semi derelict manor of one of Cromwell's recently evicted officers."

"How did the Medlowes react to what on the surface is a reasonable request?"

"Ranald was quite happy to go along with the idea, as was Edwin Symes, as the designated manor was more convenient to the majority of gentry."

"Surely the well-respected Earl was still capable of making a decision in favor of his own home. Julius would have alerted the old man to Finch's plan, even if his son was happy with the new venue?"

"He tried to. Phineas went to London to see him but was turned away by his daughter-in-law on the grounds that Algernon was too ill to receive visitors."

"Then how was the Finch relocation plot foiled?"

"Pure chance. The King who clearly knew nothing about these county machinations simply assumed it would be held here, and issued invitations to that effect. That the King was sending a close confidante to the gathering, that being you, has helped overcome some initial unhappiness. I am surprised that these restless agents of change have not tried to influence you. The whole group is now aware that despite your long history as a Parliamentary soldier, and a head of Cromwell's military intelligence, you once saved the King's life, and have been appointed by him to a secret unit responsible only to him. Your very presence here is raising a lot of speculation. Are you here to influence the local decisions in favor of the King, whatever that means on specific issues?"

"Nothing so sinister, my lady. In essence the King wants an up to date assessment concerning the men he will entrust with the governance of this county. You have raised one of the obvious questions yourself—will young Ranald be a capable successor to his father, or had your husband and his generation retained the ability and attitudes to serve the current King, as they had his father?"

"If the King endorses the likes of Finch or Kemp he will rue the day. They lack the quality to lead the county," announced Veronica with unexpected pomposity.

"What can you tell me about Finch that might help me destroy him?"

"Finch's grandfather bought his title of baronet from James I but until recently the family did not have enough assets to maintain the title adequately. However Winston astonished the county when on the death of his father, this previously impoverished heir married Lucy, the only daughter of Viscount Symes. Her dowry brought him several wealthy properties."

"Why would Symes agree to such an arrangement? Edward has no time for his brother-in-law," commented Luke.

"Finch is a charming almost charismatic young man who is also a completely untrustworthy liar, and readily corruptible. He seems to be much wealthier than gossip implied, and may have bribed many of the participants at this gathering. Who knows what lies he told the Symes family years ago?"

"Have you seen much of Lucy, his wife?"

"They were married a decade ago on the continent and returned here soon after. Finch until recently spent most of his time with his London friends. During the republic there were few social occasions for the Royalist gentry wives to socialize. I did meet her once at an illegal horse racing meeting held on one of her father's properties, but Finch quickly put an end to any social intercourse between his wife and others. I have not seen her here. Has she come? There are stories that Finch beats her on a regular basis."

"She is here, but I have not spoken to her."

"What about Kemp?"

"Whereas Finch is a lying corrupt knave, Kemp is difficult to fathom. He is a professional conspirator. Julius said Kemp's political methods were those of the back stairs, and his attacks on his enemies never exceeded the whispered sneer. He seems uncommitted on most issues—except for his own advancement in obtaining office. He has major personality flaws. He often shows a complete lack of judgement. His tactless manner in addition to his lack of commitment has created many enemies. The man is totally unfit for any position within the county. Cement your ruthless reputation! Eliminate both of these parasites!"

"You misjudge me your ladyship. I have always acted within the law, except where the security of the state required an extra-legal intervention. A corrupt wife beater and a devious conspirator both of whom want advancement within the system, hardly meet that criteria."

At supper that evening Luke excused himself from the high table. He sat with Alexander and Elspeth Kemp and Sir Winston and Lucy Finch. He made it clear that he would question each of them on the following day as part of his investigation into the death of Julius.

Kemp took the opportunity to influence a man he had been told was a personal confident of the King. He diverted every question regarding himself and continually encouraged his wife to flirt outrageously with Luke. On the other hand Finch bombarded Luke over which issues he thought the King might support. He suggested if Luke lent support to his scheme to make the county's rivers more navigable, he personally would benefit financially. Luke was uncertain as to whether this foreshadowed a bribe to back such a scheme, or a simple statement of the profits he might make in getting involved. Finch's other major contribution to the supper small talk was to prevent his wife Lucy from making any comments at all. Every time Luke directed a question to her, Finch answered in her place.

As the evening drew on both men focused in on the same subject. Finch was the more direct. "We all know your history and your current position as a special agent for the King. Why has His Majesty sent such an experienced investigator to this informal meeting of Royalist gentry? We might recommend whom we want on the bench of magistrates, but it is the King who ultimately will decide. We may put up candidates for the next parliament but the King's influence would determine most results. Lord Ranald who lacks any experience in these matters is simply going through the motions of pretending we are deciding our future, but your advice to the King is probably more decisive than anything we recommend. For that reason I look forward to talking to you tomorrow to give you a forward looking view as to what this county really needs."

Elspeth's over passionate farewell to Luke was curtailed by the arrival of the marchioness, Jane, who had come down from high table to confront him.

Jane immediately teased him. "Shame on you Luke! All the time we were on Nith together you resisted my advances, claiming that the notorious womanizer of the past was now a happily and loyal married man. Having rejected me, you are clearly falling prey to the predatory Elspeth."

"It may help my investigation. Finch embarked on a charm offensive. He believes what I tell the King about this assembled throng will be much more decisive than what they decide themselves, whereas Kemp is clearly using his wife, and my outdated reputation to advance his cause. Both are living up to their reputations."

8

Luke escorted Jane back to her apartment where they indulged in a little Irish whiskey which Jane knew was his favorite drink—and in short supply at Medlowe Abbey. There was no doubting Luke's affection for Jane, but he was saved from any lustful temptation by frenetic knocking on the door. It burst open. A highly agitated Ranald entered the room.

He hardly noticed Jane, "Sorry for this late night intrusion. We have a serious problem. There is an outbreak of the plague in a small area of London. The valet of Sir Phineas Leigh arrived this morning, and explained that his master and mistress have been delayed there as the local magistrate has quarantined the area in which they were staying. The valet was given the all clear, and expects Phineas and his wife to arrive here tomorrow or the following day at the latest."

"What is the problem if the valet and I assume his master are considered clear of the plague?" asked an irritated Luke.

"Unfortunately that was a premature assessment. Luckily I put the valet in one of the outlying cottages, awaiting the arrival of the full Leigh entourage. He did not turn up for the evening meal and one of my servants discovered him on his bed in a feverish condition—and disastrously, with lumps under his arms. He has the bubonic plague. Then half an hour ago the gatekeeper informed me that Phineas himself had arrived. I have put him in another cottage having explained the condition of his valet. I have asked our family chaplain Adrian Ravenscroft to join me here immediately."

"Why? The clergy's only answer to this scourge has been that it is a punishment from God, and its prevention is the closure of all alehouses, theatres and brothels," commented an unimpressed Luke.

"Not Adrian! In the last major epidemic in thirty six, he had a parish in London that was badly affected. As a result he has practical experience in dealing with it, and in the last twenty five years he has made study of its intermittent occurrence across Europe."

A gentle knock was heard and Luke opened the door to a wizened up old man whose hair above the ears appeared to grow horizontally, divided by a bald patch across the top of his head. Introductions over, Luke ignored the cleric and turned back to Ranald, "By law, you know what you have to do. Quarantine the entire estate! No one in or out!"

"And how am I going to enforce that with the county's most powerful gentlemen? As soon as they hear the news they will be out of here, and I am in no position to stop them."

"But the law is—but we need troops to enforce it. I will ride immediately to London, and ask the King for a company of soldiers to supervise the quarantine. I will also ask that the county be advised next Sunday in every church of the situation here. Your own men must make sure that there is no contact with Phineas or his valet. How many of them know the real situation?"

"Only the servant who went to check on the infected valet—and he has been told to say nothing. If questioned as to the non-appearance of the Leigh's valet, we will say that the man has influenza."

"Good! Do not inform anyone else until we have troops in place!"

"Is all this necessary?" asked Adrian. "The plague is an urban phenomena and since the thirties has killed no more than a handful of people in England each year. It is caused by foul air concentrated in the filthy alleys of the capital. In the clean air of the countryside it does not spread. Do not create unnecessary fear! Even if infected, a significant proportion, despite common opinion, recover."

Luke was surprised at this confrontational intervention by the chaplain. "What do you suggest? That we break the law?" responded Luke.

"No. We can obey the law, insisting on quarantine, without involving the whole estate and the assembled gentlefolk. Across Europe victims are quarantined in two ways—within their houses, or sent to a designated quarantined location. This is a large estate and there are several isolated areas with suitable accommodation that could be used as a temporary pest house or hospital."

"I am inclined to follow Adrian's advice. I will inform everybody of the true situation and encourage them to leave before any contact is made with the infected. If we are all quarantined together for several weeks, the chances of being infected will increase," announced a slightly rattled Ranald.

Luke was silent for some time. He finally commented, "Even though it ignores the procedures set down when the plague is discovered, I agree with you both. You cannot risk the entire county elite. Arouse everybody! Ask them to leave immediately, and tell them why. Put a guard around the pest houses. Their inhabitants must stay where they are."

Luke turned to Jane, "You must leave immediately. I will stay until Ranald has completed the evacuation."

There was another knock on the door and one of Ranald's servants entered, "My lord, Sir Job Elliot wishes to see you urgently."

"Can't it wait ?" replied an agitated Ranald.

Before the servant could answer, Job burst into the room, "My lord, woe is me. I have to report a dire development. Three of my servants have taken ill. At first I thought it was simply a common cold but they are now revealing lumps under their arms. It is the plague. Two of them spent a week in London before they joined me here. And they have mixed socially with the retinues of the other guests. My niece and I are departing now before we too are infected."

"I'm afraid that will not be possible," remarked Luke now aware how this changed the situation.

"And who will stop me?"

"If necessary, I will arrest you in the name of the King. You are well aware of the law regarding what must happen on the notification of the plague. Your servants are not the only victims on this estate. We could be experiencing a major outbreak. We cannot have you spreading it throughout the county."

Luke turned to Ranald, "Given this latest development we have to isolate the entire estate. Job must join Phineas in his enforced isolation, and his three servants can join Phineas' valet. You have two pest houses, one for the gentry, and one for their servants. I will ride immediately to London. Jane, come with me! There is no reason why you should put yourself in danger."

"No, I will be needed here. When the news breaks there will be a lot of distraught women. And if the victims remain isolated, I will be in no danger. I will be able to comfort their relatives. Panic, not the plague could be our major enemy."

Luke rode through the night and arrived at Whitehall well before the King's regular early morning briefing. When he entered the room Charles expressed surprise, "What are you doing here Tremayne ? I thought you were at Medlowe Abbey assessing potential political powerbrokers on my behalf."

Luke explained the situation at the Abbey, and was shocked at the King's immediate refusal of his request for troops. "Tremayne the plague is an urban phenomena. As soon as victims reach the country it rarely spreads beyond the immediate contacts. Medlowe Abbey is a large estate and Ranald can easily create effective pest houses to accommodate any suspects without endangering the rest of the guests. The outbreak in London is confined to five adjacent houses on one of the filthiest lanes in the city. The authorities there have it controlled. What was Phineas doing there? That is the interesting question. Now, on a more important subject, have you isolated any potential troublemakers among my allegedly loyal gentry and aristocracy?"

"I have negative feelings about Sir Winston Finch, Alexander Kemp and Sir Job Elliot, but my interrogation of those three has not yet begun."

"You need more time?"

"As much as possible."

The King's face lit up as if suddenly inspired. He could give Luke almost six weeks to complete his investigations with a captive audience.

"Luke on second thoughts you shall have the troops. According to the law, if plague is notified the location must be isolated for forty days. I declare Medlowe Abbey plague infected, and a company of troops under your comrade Captain Oxenbridge will march there immediately. In addition your deputy, Sir Mark Cowper will return with you to Medlowe Abbey to assist you and the Marchioness in your mission."

Luke smiled and commented, "As someone once said, your administration is both open, and definitely devious."

The King chuckled. "One additional piece of advice, do not forget the women, especially Elspeth Kemp, Lucy Finch and Charity Elliott."

"I hope Your Majesty that this advice is due to some issue of national security, and not to matters of the heart?"

"Tremayne, I will forgive your impertinence, but you must realize that in the case of a monarch one can easily involve the other. I leave it to you to inform Cowper and Oxenbridge of their new assignment. I will have a secretary draw up the paper work needed to quarantine Medlowe Abbey. Ranald will need evidence of my decision to convince the recalcitrant gentry. Also ask Hatch to consult the relevant authorities dealing with the outbreak in Offal Alley! I want to know why Leigh and those servants of Elliott were in the area. My people tell me there is nothing there except butchers and brothels—and the latter not of the class to be frequented by gentlemen."

Luke went to his Whitehall apartment from which he had been absent for over a week. Mark and Miles were pleased to see him and delighted that they would now become part of his Medlowe mission. Matthew was not as happy having to investigate the situation in plague ridden Offal Alley.

The men breakfasted together. Suddenly Matthew clapped his hands, "I knew I had heard of Offal Alley before. When I worked for Thurloe we sent one of our agents to investigate a strange group of religious fanatics who had taken over a semi-derelict church located nearby. I can't remember the details but it was deemed they were not a threat to the government of Oliver Cromwell, but if they still exist, they may be a real threat to the King. If Leigh belongs to a secret cult, he may be a clandestine enemy of the state."

"At the moment Leigh is not a problem. He is isolated in a pest house, and may even die. Maybe Elliott's men were not frequenting the brothels, but engaged in some underhand mission for their master," replied Luke. "If Leigh and Elliott are enemies of the King and plotting against him, they could cause serious disruption at Medlowe Abbey. I may need those troops for more than simple guard duty."

Mark and Luke arrived at Medlowe Abbey late afternoon, and immediately reported to Ranald, who expressed disappointment that they were not accompanied by troops.

"The situation here has been difficult to contain. Finch has been stirring the guests, suggesting that I and my supporters have staged a coup, and have imprisoned Job and his servants. My explanation that Job and his men have influenza, and are simply in isolation has not been universally accepted. In addition he has now discovered that there may be another gentleman imprisoned with Sir Job. I have promised that you would give a full explanation at supper tonight. Without troops the situation cannot be contained."

"No problem, my lord. A company of the King's own guard will arrive at any moment, and set up camp on the green outside the Abbey gates. A detachment of them will also guard the two pest houses, relieving your men of that unpleasant chore. I will explain all tonight at supper, emphasizing that we must obey a direct order from the King."

At supper Ranald spoke first, "Good friends some of you are concerned about the fate of Sir Job. Colonel Tremayne has just returned from an audience with the King and will explain the situation."

Luke was direct. "I bring you grave, but not necessarily fatal news. I have in my hand an order from the King. Certain persons within the Abbey have the plague."

Uproar followed with women screaming and fainting. Finch jumped onto his table. "Then we will all leave before the contamination spreads."

"I am afraid you will not. In applying the law, His Majesty has imposed a forty days quarantine on the Abbey. As Lord Ranald has already isolated those suspected patients, the rest of us should not be in danger. Some of Sir Job's servants have the plague and given his closeness to them, Sir Job has been isolated with Sir Phineas Leigh, who arrived late the night before last, also exhibiting possible symptoms."

9

inch moved to the elevated platform on which the high table stood and turned towards the rest of the gathered guests. "There is no way I will remain here. All of us must leave at once, and there is nothing that Medlowe and his cronies can do to stop us. I ask that you all regather at my manor in three days to continue the discussions that must be curtailed here."

As Finch spoke, a servant approached Luke, who after listening to his message, hammered the table with the hilt of his sword to gain attention.

"I would not be so foolish Sir Winston. To defy the King would end your political ambitions, and I will send you immediately to The Tower."

"To save my wife and friends from possible infection, I will ignore what you say is an order from the King. If it is a genuine order then you, Colonel, must have misrepresented the true situation here."

"Calm down Sir Winston and let us all enjoy supper. If you continue to disrupt, I will arrest you in the name of the King."

"I would like to see you try," challenged the serial duelist.

Luke walked down the refectory towards the table to which Winston had returned. The gathered assembly believed that they were about to witness a sword fight. To everybody's surprise, Luke walked past Winston towards the room's large double doors. He opened them to reveal a unit of red coated soldiers. He turned back into the room, and simply announced, "To ensure compliance with his orders, the King has sent a company of his household guard to enforce the quarantine. To leave this room you will pass through the troops. Already the outer perimeter of the Abbey is surrounded, as are the two pest houses. One of the cellars of the Abbey is now a prison for those who defy their King."

Luke glared at Finch. Should he provoke the man? The corrupt businessman would be no match to Luke's sword fighting prowess. Caution prevailed. He did not want to make a martyr of the man.

Meanwhile Matthew Hatch with a small cohort of soldiers arrived at Offal Alley to assess the plague situation, and to uncover what might have attracted Phineas, and the Elliott servants to the area.

Offal Alley was a very narrow lane in which many of the upper stories overhung the street, and were so close to each other that light was almost excluded from the path below. Dark and dirty summarized the environment.

The alley was long and Matthew was pleasantly surprised to discover only three houses in the middle of the pathway that was hardly wide enough to take a horse and cart, had a red cross painted on their door. This indicated the presence of plague. On the doors of two of these such indication had been almost scrubbed away. Only the middle house exhibited a fresh sign.

Matthew deduced that it was the only premises in which the plague was still rampant—one house rather than the five originally reported was good news. The outbreak was contained.

A buxom wench leaned out of the overhanging window of the still condemned house. She shouted at the soldiers, "I'm Dolly. Don't believe that sign, my loves. The city watchmen refused to remove it because my sister and I did not offer ourselves for free. Look at my armpits! No sign of the alleged plague!"

She pulled off her blouse not only revealing her healthy looking armpits, but ample naked breasts.

Matthew replied, "Good woman, we do not seek your services, but I will reward you much more highly than any customer would pay. I want information."

"I'll tell you whatever you want to know—when I see the color of your money."

Matthew threw two silver coins through the window. "Thank you, good sir," replied a smiling Dolly.

"When was the last time a customer visited you?"

"At least a month ago. Our forty days quarantine has another week to go."

"You have had no visitors in the last fortnight?"

"No."

"I have information that at least one gentleman, and three or four servants came this way in that period."

"Yes, those people did come this way. With nothing to do all day I have spent most of my time hanging out of this window, making conversation with anybody who passes by. My only entertainment, apart from conversation with such people is to watch the horde of local cats attack the rats that scavenge continually amongst the filth."

"What did the gentleman and the servants want?"

"They tried to enter next door, but were initially physically restrained. Eventually my new neighbors admitted them after a bit of money passed hands."

"How new are these neighbors?"

"Very recent. They are a large family that have just moved into the city from the country. The men work from time to time in the fish market. My long term neighbors who offered similar services to myself, although the husband did a bit of butchery, moved away as soon as their quarantine was lifted."

"Did these old time neighbors attract many gentlemen? Such men would not make up your normal clients."

"You would be surprised, kind sir, but my friend Betty appeared to attract a considerable number of the superior classes—learned folk as well as fops."

"Did you ask her what was her special appeal to the superior classes?"

"Yes. She made up a pack of lies to emphasize her superior charms over mine. Then one day after too much ale she confessed that they did not come to see her."

"What, they came to obtain meat from her husband? I don't believe that. Most gentlemen would send a servant, especially into such an area as this," commented Matthew, who was finding the stench of rotting vegetables, and faeces, animal and human overwhelming.

"No, her house has access through some secret tunnel to the wealthy properties that back on to us, but front the more salubrious Newchurch Road."

"The street with a semi derelict church which is almost as large as a cathedral at its eastern end?" asked one of Matthew's men.

"Yes, but despite its appearance, it had an active congregation during the period that the king was in exile. They were a strange bunch. One of my clients claimed they were a coven of witches and wizards. Some people still meet there from time to time."

"You can access that church from your neighbour's place?" Matthew repeated.

"So I have been told."

"Why not access it directly from Newchurch Road?" Matthew probed.

"Fear of discovery. Both the current city authorities and those of the Old Protector kept a close surveillance on those who attended that strange church. Apparently by gaining access through Offal Lane, the gentlemen could conceal their presence."

Matthew thanked the woman and tossed further coins through her window. He knocked on the neighboring door. A small woman, smelling of stale beer and nursing a baby—and with two other small children hanging on to her aprons, answered the door. She was terrified. "Sir, we have done no harm to anybody."

"Do not fear, good woman. We simply seek access to the hidden passage that leads to the next street."

"There is no secret passage. Our back door opens within feet of the backdoor of an adjacent building which fronts Newchurch Road. Several times a year I have been told gentlemen enter that building by coming through our house. My husband receives a few coins for allowing them access."

Matthew and his men moved through the tiny house and left by the back door. They were immediately confronted by another door which led into the property that fronted Newchurch Road.

It was a different world. This house was relatively clean with large rooms. They had recently been used but they appeared to be a series of meeting rooms rather than a residence. Eventually they found the front door which opened onto the church grounds. Matthew assumed that the house they continued to search was probably the old vicarage for the church. Perhaps now it was a meeting place of a mysterious cult?

Matthew and his men searched the premises for any evidence that might indicate what had gone on within its walls. He hoped to find symbols of witchcraft or magic that might confirm the rumors that Dolly had advanced.

Suddenly the quiet was broken. Four armed men burst through the door and the only person armed with a sword demanded to know who the intruders were. The force of his query was dented by his discovery that they were uniformed troops. Matthew quickly explained, "We are a detachment of Royal troops who were on an assignment in Offal Alley and surprisingly found ourselves here. Who are you?"

The swordsman answered, "I am the steward of this establishment and my cudgel-armed assistants are servants of this house."

"But what is this house? It is not a residence."

"It was a residence until recently when the owner died. He left it to a group of alchemists and scientists who call themselves, The Invisible College. It is now their meeting place and for some of them a location to experiment."

"Some of neighbours think it and the adjacent building house a cult of diabolic wizards," explained Matthew.

"I can see how such a view arose. Before the owner of these premises died, the college, did meet in the semi derelict church, using the crypt for their experiments. To keep the inferior sorts away they cultivated that diabolic image. Not to arouse too much suspicion many of the members entered this area following the course you have taken from Offal Alley."

"Can I have the names of those who attend these premises?"

"No sir, not because I wish to defy an agent of the King, but I do not know."

"Surely you have picked up some information in this regard?"

"No, they all use aliases, many of them take the names of the planets but I do know their meetings are chaired by Mercury."

"You must realise that in the current environment with the return of the King and the array of groups aligned against him, any gathering, especially a gathering of gentlemen who use fake names and meet in secret, needs to be investigated. When do they meet again?"

"I do not know. Mercury informs me a week before any gathering."

"When he does, you will inform us. Send a message to me, Captain Hatch at the barracks of the Household Guard, Whitehall."

Matthew took his leave of the steward, and with his men entered the derelict church, making their way to the crypt. It was pitch dark. He sent one of his men back to the house to request several tapers.

Matthew was surprised to find an additional altar in the crypt and above it, engraved into the stone wall was the outline of a cross. This was not unusual. However on closer inspection he noted an unusual detail. In the centre of the cross was a carefully incised rose bloom.

Luke covered his clothing with sprigs of rosemary, and stuffed his pockets with raw onions. The latter soaked up the foul air that surrounded plague victims, and the former replaced it with a sweet smelling aroma. He now felt protected enough to interview Phineas—but at a distance. Phineas sat in the door of the pest cottage, while his interrogator stood several yards away.

Luke explained, "I am Luke Tremayne, agent of the King who was sent here to assist with the reorganization of the county's militia, but who has been seconded to examine the death of Julius Petty, and now the infection of yourself, and some of Job Elliott's servants with the plague. How are you feeling now?"

"My lumps have burst and my fever seems reduced. Thank Lord Ranald for providing me with such a comfortable cottage."

"He did ask his family's physician to visit you, but that gentleman refused. However I recently returned from London where I discussed the situation here with the King. He is sending one of his own physicians who was infected with the plague himself some years ago, and recovered—Anthony Halford."

Phineas face lit up. "I know Dr. Halford very well. I was with him only a few weeks ago. It was probably on my journey to a meeting that we both attended that I became infected."

"That was to be my first question. Where were you infected?"

"I attended a meeting of learned scholars, alchemists, astronomers and mathematicians. They met to decide whether to petition the King to transform them into a Royal Society by issuing a patent. It was lively meeting, but the details by mutual agreement are secret to the membership."

"With due respect Sir Phineas in preparing for this visit I examined your background. You have never showed any interest in the fields that you mentioned. Why did you, a racehorse owning and fox hunting rustic squire attend a meeting of esoteric scholars?"

10

"Your research is accurate. I am completely ignorant of any scholarly pursuits, but my late father was not. He was an eminent astronomer whose best friend's life work was usurped and claimed by another. I attended at the invitation of many of father's old friends to seek redress on this matter."

"And was this intervention successful?"

"No! My father and his friend worked together for many years and the friend who was also a mathematician gathered all the evidence to show that he had discovered a new comet. Unfortunately he fell on hard times and sold the essential proof to an entrepreneurial gentleman, who has already presented these necessary documents and claiming that the learned group name the comet after him—Kemp's Comet."

"Not the Alexander Kemp who is with us here?"

"The very same."

"What is your next step?"

"To buy back the supporting documents from Kemp."

"You may be able to exert other pressure of Kemp, given his political ambitions, but how did attending such a learned group of scholarly gentlemen expose you to the plague?"

"They met in a part of London where a row of respectable houses backed onto filthy hovels. In order not to be seen gathering for a meeting, which might invite unwanted attention, entry could be made through one of the hovels located in this filthy alley."

"Why did these gentleman not want to be seen meeting together?"

"They are uncertain about the attitude of the new administration to their activities. That is why seeking the King's approval for their activities is the main subject on their agenda. I cannot tell you more as I took an oath not to reveal anything I saw or heard—and I was excluded from much of the meeting as I am not a member."

"That satisfactorily explains your unfortunate situation. Perhaps you can help me regarding Julius. You were in London at the time Julius died, but did you have any discussion with him earlier regarding this current gathering of the Royalist gentry."

Luke was pleasantly surprised at the answer. "Yes, we spent a day together in the fortnight before Julius came here, and I left for London."

"Who instigated the meeting?"

"Julius."

"Given your past relationship, were you not surprised?"

"No, we had been great rivals for dominance in the county for both the list of magistrates and parliamentary representation twenty years ago. Since then power has rested with a new breed of parliamentary and republican families who are just relinquishing their dominant positions as we speak. The purpose of this gathering under the auspices of the Earl of Medlowe was to ensure that the appropriate Royalists took their place."

"What was Julius's reason for talking to his old time rival?"

"Fear that the new breed of young Royalists, who hardly sacrificed themselves during then King's exile, might try to obtain dominance over the more traditional families. I agreed with him. We had similar interests, and agreed to work together."

"Surely you both had the support of the Medlowes, which would be decisive?"

"No, that was Julius's great fear. The old Earl was solidly with us, but he appears to be on his death bed. Ranald, Julius thought might as easily side with the newcomers as with us. He is of their generation, and he has views very different from those of his father. It's a pity James disappeared. There could be serious problems when old Algernon dies."

"What is the problem?"

"James is Algernon's first born who when he became of age just disappeared. He renounced his position in the household, and told his father and younger brother that he was embarking on a great adventure. There has been no communication from him since."

"So as the law stands, James is still the heir apparent despite his renunciation to the family. In such circumstances Ranald's accession to the title remains problematic."

"Precisely! That is why I believe Ranald asked the King to send a representative to this meeting. He needs to impress you so that with your favorable report to the King, His Majesty on the death of Algernon, will declare James dead, and Ranald the rightful heir. That was Julius's assessment of the situation."

"So I could reasonably deduce from what you say that Ranald and his comrade in arms, Edwin Symes, are happy with Julius's non-attendance."

"Yes, and doubly pleased that I have also been sidelined."

"You have little time for Ranald?" probed Luke.

"I do not know the tiny lad that well. All I will say is that I would be much happier if Algernon recovers and resumes control of the Abbey, and thereby the county. Algernon has been steadfastly loyal to the King, and lost a lot by staying here during the republic. He should not be cast aside now."

"What are you suggesting?"

"I tried to see Algernon when I was in London. I have visited the Medlowe town house on many occasions usually to complain about Julius. Now I wanted simply to pay my respects to the senior aristocrat in the county. I was refused entry by some rather aggressive bodyguards. As the King's representative you need to establish that Algernon is indeed very sick, and that he is not being held against his will on the orders of his second son?"

Luke was astonished at the explicit allegation.

"That is a serious suggestion. Do you have any evidence that led you to make such an assertion?"

"The older generation stayed in England during the King's exile, the younger flocked to the Royal Court in exile. Julius had heard some of these young blades, when in their cups, boasting that while on the continent they had planned to take over county government on their return."

"Maybe they simply meant a return to the rule of Royalist gentlemen after the aberration of republican and Cromwellian officials—not the removal of traditional Royalist leaders," suggested Luke.

"Maybe, but Kemp and Finch are ambitious and unscrupulous men. Frankly I would prefer that some of the retiring republicans and Cromwellians stayed on the bench rather than this new breed of fanatical, but self- interested Royalists. The King has rewarded many former enemy officers, including yourself in his new administration. Perhaps he might include some of your former comrades in our county hierarchy."

"He has already done so in some counties. His latest list for Devon is hardly different from that of Oliver Cromwell's two years ago, but in the Welsh counties not a single republican or Cromwellian remains. The King has an open mind on this issue, and will listen to the voice of the county. This meeting is not a waste of time."

Luke continued, lowering his voice, "What can you tell me about your fellow guest in this cottage, Sir Job Elliott. Is he with you the traditionalists, or with the Finch-Kemp faction? Was he with you at the meeting of scholars? Do you know why his servants were in the area?"

"Elliott was not at the meeting, and I do not know why his servants were in the area. His background and attitudes were once very similar to those of Julius and myself, and he formed part of the traditional leadership, but he has viewed developments since the return of the King in a very different light to Julius and myself."

"I have heard him referred to as Jeremiah Job. He appears an unhappy soul."

"He believes that he should be handsomely rewarded by the King. His family certainly sacrificed a lot in the royalist cause, but he has become quite irrational in his attitude to the King's disposal of favors and positions. He hates you—a leading republican Cromwellian soldier rewarded with a significant position in the new government. I honestly thought he was demented given his reaction to the news that the new head of the King's army was a former Cromwellian general, Monk, and the deputy head of the Royal navy a Cromwellian admiral, Montague. Job just cannot accept this. He wants to severely punish our local friends and neighbors who sided with the Parliament, republic, and eventually Cromwell."

"How does he propose to severely punish us former Cromwellians?"
"Confiscate your lands and reallocate them to loyal Royalists like himself— and execute as many of you as the law will determine."

"I had better interview Sir Job. Can you call him to the door?"

"I can't. He sees me as a plague victim, and himself as an innocent thrust into the same environment for no reason. He lives in the back half of the cottage, and our paths do not meet. You will have to go to the back door."

"Thanks Phineas you have certainly enlightened me on a number of issues."

Luke made his way to the back door of the cottage. It was open and Job stood on the doorstep.

"I heard most of what you and Phineas discussed, I don't think I can add much."

"My simple question to you, given the fate of your servants is how they became infected, and what were you doing in Offal Alley?"

"I can answer the first, but the second is completely irrelevant to your enquiries. My servants, unbeknown to myself visited a brothel some weeks ago. Unfortunately they were inside these premises when the city watchmen painted a red cross on the door and imposed a forty day quarantine. I was informed, and went to the area to obtain their release from such a restriction."

"How did you manage to persuade the local authorities to release your men after no more than a week?"

"Those city officials were Cromwellian appointees, and given their imminent dismissal were willing to accept a financial inducement to release my lads."

Luke ignored the deliberate provocative remark, and then dropped a bombshell—in fact a complete fabrication. "Come Sir Job, you have not explained how you and your men became aware of the Offal Alley location. It is not the normal area frequented by gentlemen of your class, or by servants of such elite. You followed Phineas."

Job was visibly taken aback. His initial thought was to deny the suggestion and bluff out any possible consequences. He had second thoughts. What he had done was not illegal, immoral or in any way incriminating. He would come clean.

"Sir Luke, you must have excellent sources or a brilliant technique in extracting the truth. Yes, I followed Phineas. I saw him in the center of the city and decided to approach him in order to discuss the coming meeting here. His movements surprised me. He took a coach so I decided to follow him. He left the desirable parts of the town and alighted from the coach at the beginning of a narrow alley way. I did the same and saw him enter premises half way down a dirty lane way. I was not sure which house he entered. I sent my men into one, apparently the wrong one. As I stood outside, the city watch came past and affixed their notification that the area was declared plague ridden. I left, leaving my men locked inside one of the cottages."

"Why did you follow Phineas?"

"Initially simply to catch up with him, and ask him to support any requests I might make at this meeting. As he moved into a strange part of the city, I thought I may catch him out in an activity that I might use against him, unless he supported me."

"Blackmail! Visiting a brothel would hardly destroy him."

"No, and my men told me afterwards that Phineas had not been into the house where they were trapped."

Luke decided on another lie. "I accept what you say is true, but you have unwittingly put yourself in a position where you could be suspected of treason. Phineas would have led you to the meeting place of a cult, some members of which may be a threat to the security of the state."

Job took a deep breath suddenly realizing the dangerous situation that was emerging. "What will you do?" he asked in a very strained and anxious manner.

"Other members of my unit are investigating this cult, and I should have a report in the next few days. When you are released into the general community of Medlowe Abbey will you be supporting the old guard that was once led by Julius whose remaining adherent appears to be Orlando, or are you with the younger aggressive gentry such as Kemp and Finch?"

11

"I will support whoever can get my case before the King. I deserve massive restitution in the form of lands, money and positions. Ranald appears a better proposition than the youngsters, but I am no fool. You are closer to the King than either local group. I need your help."

"I am surprised at your attitude. I was told that you hated former Cromwellians such as myself."

"I do, but I am not going to cut off my nose to spite my face. You are my best route to obtaining justice. I will give you my petition to present to the King."

"I will present your petition, but I am not here to take sides."

Luke left the pest house quite buoyed. Both Phineas and Job had been helpful.

During supper Luke was given a letter by Ranald, which given its seal was from the King, or one of his leading officials. He opened it in the isolation of his bedchamber, and then as arranged met Mark and Jane in the marchioness's apartment to review the situation.

Luke immediately revealed the contents of the letter to his colleagues. "It is a letter from Matthew outlining his investigation of Offal Alley and its environs. He confirms what I was told by both Phineas and Job. A significant piece of new information is that the meeting place where these learned men meet has inscribed on the wall a cross with a rose in its center. The King has added in his own hand, that this is a symbol of the Rosicrucians who are a secret society who believe the world should be ruled by the learned, rather than by monarchs or republics. He wants us to discover from Phineas who attended the meeting. Many leading scholars have already approached him to give them a corporate identity as The Royal Society of London. I assume he would like us to discover who are dedicated Royalists, and who harbor thoughts of a scholarly coup."

Mark turned to Jane, "You were married to a scholarly type for twenty years. Did he ever mention the Rosicrucians?"

"My husband rarely discussed the esoteric aspects of his endeavors with me. He never mentioned the Rosicrucians, but I do know that many of his learned friends were Masons."

"Why would an alchemist and astronomer have any dealings with the Masons?" asked Mark.

"Since the 1620's the Mason's Company of London has been admitting people who have nothing to do with the mason's trade. My late husband called these non-artisan members, Freemasons."

"Tomorrow I will see what Phineas can tell us about these two clandestine groups!" remarked Luke. He turned to Jane, "Did you discover anything of relevance from the women?"

"Not so far, but I have built up a friendly relationship with Elspeth Kemp and Lucy Finch, both very unhappy women."

"And what particular charms did you exert to win their confidence?" teased Luke.

"These women whose husbands are very ambitious and driven obsessively to climb the social ladder were probably ordered by their spouses to cultivate the highest ranked woman here, myself, a marchioness," answered the practical Jane.

"Why are these women unhappy?" asked Mark.

"Probably for opposite reasons. Elspeth's husband is so jealous he gives her no freedom at all except to use her sexual charm to further his political ambitions, whereas Lucy suffers a philandering spouse who I suspect mistreats her."

"I'll question both of them after I see Phineas again in the morning."

Luke's desire for an undisturbed night was shattered somewhere around four in the morning. Not one to lock his door he was awakened by an attractive woman wearing nothing but a chemise, gently shaking him. It was Jane.

"Enough my lady! Desist! Return to your room!" muttered a half asleep Luke.

"Be quiet, Luke—and listen. I am not here to seduce you. I was awoken about half an hour ago by a serving girl sent by Elspeth Kemp asking me to inform Ranald or yourself of an event that is about to occur which you must prevent."

Luke still half asleep struggled to comprehend. "What could possibly happen at dawn that needs my intervention?"

"A duel."

"Between whom?"

"Finch and Carey."

"Who has challenged whom, and why?"

"Finch claims, incorrectly according to the servant, that Carey engaged in inappropriate behavior towards his wife, and demands satisfaction."

"Stupid young royalists. The law is clear, but with the King back in power, it may not be enforced. Traditionally a man's honor had to be satisfied, and if one party should die the survivor would be exonerated in terms of self- defense, or at the worst charged with manslaughter, but never murder. During the Civil War, the Parliament implemented an extreme position—the summary execution of duelists. What am I expected to do?"

"Talk them out of it, or at least supervise it to prevent any deaths."

"You want to make me complicit in this illegal, but apparently acceptable activity.?"

"I want you to stop what may be a clever excuse for the murder of young Piers. With him, a known favorite of the King's out of way, Finch's chances of being a Royal appointee are greatly increased," pleaded Jane.

"That is pure supposition. You women are infatuated by the charm of Piers Carey, and equally repelled by the unfortunate personality traits of Winston Finch."

"Stop talking, and get dressed. Dawn is almost upon us."

"Where is the duel to take place?"

"In the pear orchard."

Luke accompanied by Mark, whom he had awoken by tipping a mug of cold water on his face, arrived in the orchard as the two combatants and their assistants prepared to duel. Luke was not surprised to find that the gentleman presiding over the combat was Alexander Kemp. Kemp was initially flummoxed by Luke and Mark's appearance, but quickly recovered ."I trust you gentlemen are not here to prevent a question of honor being resolved?"

"Not at all, but as a soldier who has participated in many a duel I am here to ensure that it is conducted fairly, and that the satisfaction of honor, not the death of an opponent is the prime consideration," said Luke.

Kemp's rules for the combat were simple. Carey and Finch would commence the conflict from the center of a cleared flat piece of ground between the trees. Should in the course of the duel they move too close to any of the trees they were to cease and return to the starting position."

Both were able swordsmen. Finch's strength and reach were countered by Carey's nimbleness, but eventually the former drove the latter backwards towards one of the fruit trees. Finch completely ignored Kemp's instruction and continued a flurry of strokes with such intensity that Carey retreating backwards tripped over a protruding root. Finch moved in for the kill. To Luke it appeared that he was about to plunge his rapier into Carey's chest before he could regain his feet.

Luke shouted, "Desist, or you will answer to me. Honor is satisfied."

He turned towards Carey, "Piers, I shall talk to you later. Return to your quarters! Sir Winston I gather you were defending the honor of yourself and your wife. While I do not question your right to do so, it is not the most positive way to win the King's favor. If you do become a courtier, or one of King's top men in the county, another avenue for settling such disputes must be found."

"Why did you intervene?" asked an obviously irritated Finch.

"To save your political career. If you had killed Carey, you would have killed one of the King's favorites. That would have not have helped your cause. Secondly, given the precise situation of this duel, if you had thrust your rapier into the prone Carey and killed him, I could not claim on your behalf that it was self-defense or manslaughter. It would have been premeditated murder, and you would have hanged for the crime."

"If Carey offends again, I will kill him," shouted Finch.

"Be content! You won. Your honor is satisfied. Return to your lodgings!"

When everybody had left the clearing Mark asked, "Would Finch have stabbed Carey, if you had not intervened?"

"Certainly. He should have taken a pace backwards, when Piers fell, but instead he did the opposite. A step forward and a plunging movement towards the victim—but I prevented that."

"From what I hear Lucy is given no freedom to be indiscreet, and Finch resorts to the duel at the most trifling of alleged insults," remarked Mark. "Perhaps you should provoke him and dispatch him. For a regular duelist he is not very competent."

"We need to know what the incident trivial or otherwise was that Finch used as an excuse to fight Carey? I will talk to Piers after breakfast, and later in the company of Jane have a word with Lucy and Elspeth. It was the latter that warned us of the duel. It is going to be a busy day."

Later in the morning Luke confronted Piers. "I am surprised that you endangered your life by provoking a duel with Sir Winston."

"I did nothing of the sort. The alleged incident was a figment of Finch's imagination. He claimed that I had inappropriately touched his wife at supper. Lucy and I have had our liaisons in the distant past, but nobody can get near her since we have been at Medlowe Abbey. Finch keeps her imprisoned."

"Why should I believe you?"

"Lucy's demure reputation is as well-known as is Finch's constant recourse to demanding satisfaction of his honor through a duel. This was nothing more than a deliberate attempt to kill me."

"Why did he want to get rid of you in particular?"

"Of the younger Royalists I have made it clear that I will support our aristocratic leaders, Ranald and Edwin, and I have persuaded many of my generation to do so. Finch and Kemp want a more extreme change in the balance of power, leaving them as the dominant force in the county. I have been actively advising most of the guests here that to move away from the Medlowe patronage would be a mistake. Consequently Finch and Kemp want me silenced."

Over the midday meal, Luke who had not been able to talk to Elspeth, Lucy, Phineas or Kemp as he had planned, discussed the situation with Mark.

Mark raised an additional issue. "Since I arrived here, perhaps with a set of new eyes, I have been intrigued by a matter you have not mentioned. You came here under the belief that your role was to help Ranald prepare a list of county gentry to fill the various offices on behalf of the king—the list of magistrates, candidates for election to Parliament, and officers to control the militia. Knowing how the King works, I wonder if all that was a cover, a smoke screen."

"For what?"

"The King's real concern is with his two county aristocrats. The post of Lord Lieutenant, now that military power resides in the local militias rather than a standing army, is the most critical position in the county. It is always held by an aristocrat. In this county he has a poor choice. He may have to appoint an outsider, perhaps from his Privy Council."

"Do you have any evidence that Ranald and Edwin are the real targets of our Royal investigation?" asked Luke.

"No, but don't you find it as odd that the hostess for this gathering of the county elite is the recently widowed Lady Veronica? Where is Ranald's wife, the soon to become Countess of Medlowe, the Lady Caroline? This is the biggest gathering of the county Royalist establishment for decades. Every wife in the county would give their eye teeth to host such an event— and Caroline does not even attend. Lord Edwin is between wives."

"I see nothing sinister in Caroline's absence. Perhaps it is simply class snobbishness. These aristocratic women may find little joy in mixing with the lowly gentry, some of whose wives have been drawn from even lower down the social scale," countered Luke.

"You know full well that the main task of an aristocratic woman apart from bearing a male heir, is to offer hospitality across the social spectrum. Where is Lady Caroline?"

"Where do you think she is?"

"A prisoner of her husband. No woman, especially one about to become the leading aristocratic female in the county, as the new Countess of Medlowe, would pass over an opportunity to meet those who will seek her patronage. She is not here, because she cannot get here."

"That is the second attack I have heard on Ranald. Phineas thinks he has his father imprisoned in their London town house, and you think his wife could be under similar restraint. It looks as if I must go to London," announced Luke apparently concerned by Mark's assertions.

"You can't. You must set the example. You are quarantined. You cannot leave Medlowe Manor for several weeks. Matthew will have to assess the situation of the Earl and his daughter-in-law."

12

Luke would now question the younger women—Lucy Finch, Elspeth Kemp, Charity Elliott and the Ramsden sisters, Cassandra and Hyacinth. Both protocol and common sense demanded that Jane should accompany him.

They were received with simmering hostility by Winston Finch who clearly had not forgiven Luke's humiliation of him at an earlier dinner, and his decisive intervention in the duel with Piers. He was not going to leave his wife alone with the investigative duo. Luke started politely but firmly.

"Her ladyship and I would like to talk to your wife alone."

"It is not seemly for a married woman to be questioned on any aspects of her life without the presence of her husband," replied a truculent Winston.

Luke failed to control his growing irritation and expressed a scarcely concealed threat. "It is in the interests of seemliness that the marchioness is present. If I alone were to question Lady Lucy, I can understand your position, but in the present circumstance I can only consider your refusal to leave as an obstruction of royal justice—another black mark in my imminent report to the King. Please leave!"

Finch incandescent with rage stormed from the room, not before glaring intently at his wife, a glare that Jane interpreted as an order not to co-operate with them.

Lucy received her husband's message. Then she began to tremble. Jane diplomatically took up the questioning while Luke strode to the door to ensure that Finch was not eavesdropping on the other side.

"My dear, Colonel Tremayne and I are simply investigating the death of Julius Petty and are seeking the help of the county community to understand any situations within that community that could have led to his death. Can you tell us anything that might be useful?" Jane asked gently.

"I can't. I spent most of the last fifteen years abroad at the various locations where the king in exile held his court. I know little about the local community since I left it as a schoolgirl, and since my return to England I have lived in London."

Jane was not impressed. "Now, Lucy that is a lie. The whole county knows that you spent only a few years on the continent, and returned just under nine years ago with your husband, who certainly pursued his business career largely out of London. But you had several estates within the county were you stayed often, as well as the properties controlled by your parents. These were often extended stays in the country, but admittedly you were not seen by the local gentlewomen. This led to rumors that you were kept a prisoner by your husband and that he regularly assaulted you. Why does an aristocratic woman of your breeding put up with such treatment by an inferior oaf?"

Lucy did not respond and Luke asked, "Surely your husband, who has an intimate knowledge of what is happening in the county, discusses issues that concern him. These may be relevant to our enquiry. What does he hope to achieve out of this gathering at Medlowe Abbey?"

"My husband does not discuss any issues with me. It is not the place of a woman to concern herself with such matters," was the reply, as truculent as any of her husband's.

Jane changed the direction of the questioning. "How did you find yourself on the continent at such an early age?"

"My father sent my brother Edwin to the continent where he joined the French army, and I went to the exiled King's court in Paris.

"How did you survive? The court-in-exile was often a lawless and dangerous place especially for young girls without a protective male."

"In those early days Charles shared his court with that of his mother. The Queen Mother insisted on a degree of decorum and morality. Nevertheless father asked a friend of a friend who was with the King to look after me."

"Who was that ?" asked a reinterested Luke.

"He is also here. Piers Carey."

"And did he fulfil that role effectively?" Jane said.

"Yes, he became, and continues to be a big brother to me. Far better than Edwin who still ignores me, and continues to undermine my marriage to Winston."

"That marriage must have raised eyebrows—a peer's daughter marrying into a family that continues in trade. How did it come about? asked Luke, perhaps a little too abruptly.

"That is a personal matter that does not concern your investigation other than to paint Winston in a better light."

"To do that would help. The Colonel has not developed a good picture of your husband," said an encouraging Jane.

"I got myself into trouble at the court and Piers acting on behalf of the King persuaded Winston to marry me, a decision strongly supported by my father, Piers and, I understand, the current King."

"That may explain his current concern about you. He asked me to especially see that everything was alright with you. Were you close to Charles a decade ago?" probed Jane.

"Yes, but not as his mistress. He, like Piers was a big brother to me and in my time of need came to my aid. I am delighted that he is still concerned after all these years."

"Is there anybody from those days in France in addition to Piers and Winston present here today?" asked Luke.

"Yes, it has been a pleasant reunion—Cassandra and Hyacinth Ramsden were part of the group that also included our host Ranald for a short period."

Luke and Jane thanked Lucy and as they left they were confronted by a glowering Finch whom Luke dismissed with the comment, "You have a loyal wife, who wasted our time saying nice things about you."

As Jane and Luke wandered across the grounds in the direction of Elspeth Kemp's residence she asked, "What did you make of Lucy's comments?"

"I am surprised. She obviously feels that Winston saved her but from what. It was a too sensitive an issue to pursue. How much her defense of that scoundrel her husband comes from fear, I do not know," answered Luke.

"There is little doubt about the trouble Lucy found herself in. She must have become pregnant and marriage to Winston, failing the real father doing the right thing, saved her honor. That explains why the Symes acquiesced in their daughter's marriage so far beneath her status," suggested Jane.

"If that is the case Lucy lied to us again. She gave the impression that her role in the group was as a little sister to the males, not their sexual toy. Who was the father? Both Ranald and Piers are real possibilities."

Jane suddenly looked very serious, "Do not forget the other two important members of that group, the Stuart brothers—our current King Charles and his brother James Duke of York."

"And that could explain the King's directive to you Jane, to see that Lucy was alright. What happened to the child?"

"It must have died. The Finches have no children, much to Winston's chagrin. With his current wife he is unable to produce an heir. Perhaps the circumstances of the child's birth rendered Lucy unable to have any more children," added Jane.

"A fact that Piers may have kept secret from Winston which might account for the latter's antagonism. Winston desirous of a large family is tied to an infertile wife. No wonder there is also antagonism by Winston against his wife. Perhaps the King, in alerting you to Lucy's possible situation, suspects that Winston may try to get rid of Lucy."

"Have her killed?" asked an appalled Jane.

"Possibly."

"How can we protect her from such a fate without removing her from her husband? And we have no legal grounds to do so."

"She could be abducted," whispered Luke." And if it becomes necessary I shall not hesitate."

As they approached the Kemp residence Luke said, "Jane, leave this to me. The predatory Elspeth will be more forthcoming trying seduce me, than in the presence of the woman whom she thinks is my mistress."

Jane blushed, "I trust she will not have any success." She gave Luke a gentle kiss on the forehead and continued on into Medlowe Abbey's large pear orchard.

Luke knocked on the door of the Kemp apartment. It was answered by a servant who indicated that Alexander was not at home. Luke asked that he be announced to the lady of the house.

Luke waited some time before he was ushered into a chamber where Elspeth was ready to receive him. He quickly assessed why he had been kept waiting. Elspeth was dressed, or rather undressed to seduce.

She was an inviting woman—ample breasts, rampant nipples, large and sensuous lips and a tiny waist.

She did not hang back. She hugged Luke and began to kiss him lasciviously. Her tongue invaded his mouth, and one hand began to explore his body. Luke's defense was his imagination. Pictures of his twin children and his wife Matilda were summoned up as he gently disengaged from Elspeth. "You are a most desirable woman, but for the present I cannot deviate from my mission."

Elspeth was unabashed, "You may change your mind after several drinks."

Luke noticed that on a small table were several carafes of wine and two glasses. He compromised, "I will drink with you, while you answer a number of questions I have."

"And I will answer all your questions, if you join me on this most comfortable bench."

Luke obliged and began his questioning as Elspeth placed his hand on her breast. "I am investigating the death Sir Julius and need to understand as much about the local community as I can. You are one of the few women present who stayed in the county over the past decade and a half. Did Julius create enemies over that period, or did problems only arise with the imminent return of the King?"

"Julius was the master politician. Even his enemies respected him. His problems were largely domestic. He and his wife became increasingly estranged. She began to spend more time with his political enemy, her brother Phineas."

"That sheds an unexpected light on my investigation. Phineas' behavior may have been strongly influenced by his sister, who had a growing dislike of her husband."

"Yes, Veronica was apparently beside herself over some recent action of Julius's. She sought everybody's support which was difficult because she refused to tell anybody except perhaps Phineas what had actually happened."

"What can you tell me about the tensions and alliances that developed amongst the families in the county over the past decade, and particularly about people who are here?"

"No, Luke, ask me about my life, and my possible contribution to the problems brewing here at Medlowe Abbey. I am more important than you think."

Luke freed his hands from Elspeth's grasp and location on her breasts, rose and refilled their glasses and said, "Tell me all! What are these tensions brewing at Medlowe Abbey and how are you involved?"

"My contribution is seducing both Edwin and Winston, brothers-in-law who hate each other."

"Apart from your recent sexual conquests, how can your activities help my enquiries?"

"You would not have known that I was brought up by Sir Orlando Hall."

"You were not his daughter?"

"No, I was adopted and brought up in his household. It was a very happy time. Orlando and Ursula were devoted adoptive parents. Unfortunately this changed for Orlando when Ursula absconded to a nunnery. He is not the same man now. Fortunately for me, I married Alexander soon after Ursula left."

"Were your parents killed in the wars?"

"No, my father is still alive but only just and I do not know who my mother was."

"Who is your father?"

"Algernon, Earl of Medlowe. I am the illegitimate half-sister of our host Ranald.

Luke was stunned. "Is this widely known ? How does Ranald react to it?"

"He doesn't. He ignores me completely, but he will have to consider me when Algernon dies."

"In what way?"

"The Earl has included me in his will, and I will benefit immensely from his generosity. He constantly provided for me, through generous support to Orlando."

"When did you know that you were Algernon's daughter?"

"He and Orlando told me when I was about nine, and the Earl explained why I could not live with him, but he promised to look after me. I have received an allowance from him ever since."

Luke decided he had heard enough, "Thank you Elspeth. If you can think of anything else summon me."

He gave her a gentle kiss, and exited as fast as he could. The presence of an illegitimate Medlowe could certainly complicate the situation.

13

Jane was left to question Charity Elliott, as Luke thought she would have nothing to offer.

Jane explained that she was helping Colonel Tremayne investigate the death of Julius, and to establish the issues and understand the tensions that consumed the local community.

"Charity, you are one of the few women here who remained in England during the exile of the King. Many of those gathered in Medlowe Abbey spent several years on the continent, either in the center or on periphery of the Royal court-in- exile. You are in a position to tell me about the Royalist community who stayed behind."

"Power remained firmly in the hands of the Earl and Sir Julius. The only major issue was the degree to which people openly supported the King or co-operated with the government. The Earl and Sir Julius argued for a quiet acceptance of republican and then Cromwellian rule, as the time was not right for a Royalist uprising. A few local gentry such as my uncle disagreed. He was willing to give open support to the King despite the consequences for the rest of us."

"You were brought up by your uncle. What happened to your parents?"

"Both were killed when Parliamentary artillery bombarded our manor house. A collapsing wall and roof crushed them both to death. Father was uncle's older brother so Job inherited the lands that will become mine when I marry. They will go to my husband. Uncle's desire to retain my inheritance as long as possible explains why he has rejected so many suitors, and why I still remain a spinster. I need help to overcome this problem. This is why I came to Medlowe. I came to appeal to the Earl, but he is not here. Rumor has it that your Colonel has direct access to the King, perhaps he can solve my problem?"

"In what way?"

"If the late King had controlled this area on the death of my parents, I could have been made a ward of the Crown, which would have protected my estate. Colonel Tremayne could persuade the King to declare me as such, and the Crown could free me to marry. It has now become very urgent."

"You and your uncle are in dispute?"

"Increasingly so since I became of age, and his fortunes at the same time decreased. He is a very unhappy man and something occurred in the last month to infuriate and depress him."

"Do you know what it was?"

"Something to do with Veronica."

"Why do you think it relates to Veronica?"

"He received an urgent request to meet her in London. Uncle is usually very slow to act on anything, but on this occasion, he headed for the metropolis on receipt of the message. His comment when I asked what was the trouble, was that Veronica was distraught, and needed his help."

"What link has Job with Veronica?"

Charity smiled, "The strongest of all! She was his first love. Job was betrothed to her. At the last minute her father decided that in the interests of political harmony, she should marry into the family's traditional opponents for control of the county, the then heir to the Petty influence, Julius."

"Did you uncle take it badly?"

"I was not around at the time, but years on he still grieved for his lost love. That is why he never married. And probably why he tries to undermine Petty at every opportunity, while being equally antagonistic to the Leighs."

"Charity, you seem keen to marry. Is there a suitor in the offing?"

"That is the other reason I came to this gathering."

"Your potential husband is present?"

"Yes."

"And who might that be?"

"Piers Carey."

Jane took a deep breath, "You are aware my dear of Piers' reputation?"

"Very much so, but he is a very wealthy man in his own right, and is not after the wealthy estates that I would bring to any marriage."

"Have there been others who you suspected of lesser motives?"

"Only one, and he is also here and still prosecuting his case—Sir Winston Finch."

"But he is already married."

"Yes, but in his suit to me, he claims that now that the church courts are back in operation, he is seeking an annulment of his marriage on the grounds that Lucy is unable to bear him any children—and he is desperate to start a family and establish a dynasty."

"Is there anything else that will help the Colonel?"

"Since I have been here I have renewed my friendship with Lucy Finch who I knew as a school girl, and with the Ramsden twins. All three surprised me by being very positive about Winston Finch. He apparently helped Lucy out of a heap of trouble, and she is well aware, in fact complicit, in his attempt to dissolve their marriage. When I suggested she should fight such an attempt she claimed that Winston married her unaware that she could not bear children. It was not a deliberate misrepresentation according Piers who arranged it. Nobody knew of that problem at the time."

"Earlier you mentioned that your uncle Job rode posthaste to meet Veronica in London. When was this?"

"The day before this gathering commenced."

"So Veronica came here from London, probably with Job?"

"She did, but Job arrived back at our manor mid- morning of the first day. I was annoyed as I wanted to be here at the very beginning."

"Had he spent the night with Veronica ?"

"No, he stayed at the local tavern, The Blue Dog where he was seen and spoken to by Piers."

"Do you know what this means, Charity? The Colonel may recreate a scenario that has Veronica asking Job to eliminate Julius. She knew he would be at the Blue Dog that night."

Charity simply smiled, and Jane wondered whether this last revelation was a deliberate attempt by her to incriminate her uncle. She may not be the innocent that Luke had assumed.

Luke was surprised by Jane's information and readily admitted his erroneous perception. "I thought Charity was a nobody, who would have no worthwhile evidence to present. Now what she says could completely overturn my previous preconceptions."

He immediately went to see Piers hopefully to confirm some of Charity's statements where he asked, "When you went to The Blue Dog to talk to Julius, did you see Sir Job Elliott there?"

"Yes, he stayed the night. He had hoped to go straight on to Medlowe Abbey, but had to return home to escort his niece here. It was a fortuitous meeting, as I am now courting that beautiful woman."

"His reaction to this development?"

"Alarm. Almost panic."

"Why?"

"At the time I had no idea, but Charity explained to me later that he would lose almost half the property he controls. They belong to her, and would transfer to her husband on marriage. So it was not me in particular he objected to, but all suitors to his niece."

"Charity has already sought my help to have the King remove her from Job, and become a ward of the Crown."

"Good, I have already written to Charles seeking similar help."

"Have you received a reply?"

"Yes, but only so far as to say he was delighted that I intended to settle down, and this would greatly enhance my standing in the local community."

"In my investigation into the death of Julius, and the tensions and interests of the local community in which it took place, I am increasingly convinced that some of the tension originated ten years ago in the early days of Charles exile first in Paris when Ranald, Winston, Lucy and your cousins were very close to Charles and James Stuart."

"Winston was never part of that group. He was very much an outsider. I brought him into the group to solve a particular problem—an act I have lived to regret."

"I believe that was to save the honor of the then Lucy Symes. Whatever happened to her child?"

Piers looked astounded, "What do you mean? There was never any child."

"Then what was her problem that you had to rescue her from by marriage to that scoundrel Finch."

Piers was silent for some time. He then said quietly, "On your word as a gentleman this must go no further. Lucy was raped by a hooded man whose identity has never been either known or revealed. Lucy was passing in and out of consciousness and has limited recall of the event."

"But there must have been a limited number of possibilities?"

"Within that tightly knit group, it could only have been one of the royal brothers, Ranald or myself, but we are all ruled out. The royal brothers did not need to recourse to such an act. Most women threw themselves at Charles, and I treated Lucy as a little sister. She was still so young. We decided it must have been an outsider, but in recent times Lucy herself has wondered whether it was Ranald or Winston."

"Would Winston Finch be devious enough to destroy a woman's virtue so that he could then redeem her, and climb the social ladder through the consequent marriage?"

"More than a possibility, knowing that jackanape," Piers acidly remarked.

"So why does Finch hate you?"

"None of us realized that the rape had so damaged Lucy that she was unable to bear children. Finch believes that I knew that in advance, and I had tricked him into marrying a barren wife. It was another reason he provoked that duel."

"I would like to speak to your cousins. They are both beautiful women who spent time at the court-in-exile. How is that they are still unmarried a decade later?"

"They have had many disappointments with aristocrats and gentry promising all, and delivering nothing. So much so, and this is another confidence that I wish you to keep, they now prefer the company of women. I believe they have become close to the notorious Elspeth—and I had to warn them off my future wife, Charity."

The two women confirmed what it was like in the early days of Charles's Parisian exile. Luke asked, "Were you aware that Lucy had been raped?"

"Yes, she confided in us immediately after it happened."

"Who did it?"

"At the time we had no idea. While the group around Charles was small, there were always new outsiders trying to break in."

"Such as Winston Finch?"

"Yes."

"What will you do when Piers marries Charity?"

"He has already allocated to us a substantial manor house with appropriate income. We cannot wait for that happy day."

To assess the latest developments, Luke, Mark and Jane met Miles in the gatehouse, which had become the headquarters for the troops. Luke issued new orders as to their deployment, and gave Miles a number of letters to send to Whitehall.

The death of Julius was the major item on the agenda. Luke suggested that there now appeared to be three possible explanations. Julius had been the victim of a random attack by feral dogs, or he had been murdered at the instigation of his wife either by her former lover, Job Elliott who was in the vicinity at the critical time, or by her brother Phineas Leigh who appears however to have been in London.

More evidence was needed to reach any reasonable solution.

The meeting was interrupted by a courier from London carrying a bundle of documents for Mark who as a new member of Parliament was expected to attend the next session. Mark perused a document, jumped to his feet and exclaimed, "Julius was murdered, and I think I know why. At the next parliamentary session there is bill before the House to declare Nathan Petty a bastard, and ineligible to inherit Julius's title or property, on the grounds that Julius is not his father."

"That is the development that must have sent Veronica, Job and possibly Phineas into a spin," noted Luke.

"This may have been the motive, but it does not identify the actual murderer," commented a practical Jane.

14

Luke and Mark accepted Ranald's invitation to participate in a game of ninepins. The bowling alley had recently been constructed as an addition to one of the wings of the expanding manor house. Already present were Ranald, Edwin and Alexander Kemp. They played for an hour when Alexander announced that he had to leave before noon as Elspeth needed him.

With Kemp's departure, Luke decided to ask the two aristocrats a couple of sensitive questions. He turned to Ranald, "Is Elspeth Kemp your half-sister?"

"Father sowed a lot of wild oats, but Elspeth needs to provide some evidence."

"Doesn't that exist in the regular payments your father paid to Sir Orlando Hall over a twenty year period, the generous allowance he now pays her, and the provision in your father's will to provide for her?"

"I do not wish to appear cold and harsh but should all that Elspeth claims be true, I will nevertheless try to have that part of father's will put aside. It is not common for English aristocrats to virtually legitimize bastard children in this way."

"The King does," interjected a cheeky Mark.

"And that is true. Monarchs have traditionally looked after their bastard offspring, but it has not been the custom of the aristocracy. Elspeth does not need help from the Medlowes. Her husband who just left us is a wealthy man."

Luke turned to Edwin, "Were you aware that your sister had been raped a decade ago, and that Winston volunteered to marry her to save her honor?"

"And to get himself an aristocratic wife. No, I was unaware of those circumstances until very recently when Finch informed my father that he would be seeking an annulment of the marriage due to Lucy's infertility, a result of that assault."

Ranald interrupted, "To put the record straight Finch did not volunteer. The now King was distraught at what had happened to Lucy, and asked Piers to quickly find a husband for her. He then made us all take a vow of secrecy. Piers found Finch who hovered about the court, but was never close to the King or the rest of us."

"All this certainly explains why your aristocratic family accepted an ambitious inferior gentlemen as their son-in-law family," said Luke.

"Piers negotiated it all with my father," added Edwin.

"Let's get back to the game," declared Mark who was showing considerable bowling prowess.

"This is a new alley?" asked Luke.

"Yes, it was only recently added to the wing. It was deliberately built over the coal cellars that were very unsightly. If you look out the windows you can see three trapdoors in the lawn against the wall of the alley. The coal is now simply unloaded from the wagons into the three holes," Ranald explained.

Luke who was not doing well sought an excuse, "I have played ninepins in taverns across England. It varies considerably. These wooden bowls are unusually small."

"Yes, in this form which we call London skittles, the balls are smaller than the gap between the pins. That is why a lot of your efforts Colonel have gone through the ninepins without disturbing any," remarked an amused Mark.

"I much prefer the version where you throw projectiles, even a round of cheese at the pins. You don't need such a long alley in those cases," added Edwin, another loser.

Luke suddenly took a deep breath and momentarily froze. "Gentlemen, get out of here. I smell burning cordite."

Edwin was about to pour scorn on the suggestion, but his military experience led him to reach a similar conclusion.

No one made it outside.

A terrific explosion shattered the windows and most of the outside wall collapsed. Half the roof disappeared and there was a gaping hole in the floor.

Four bodies lay in various positions around the perimeter of the demolished alley.

All four began to show signs of life.

Luke recovered quickly. He was able to direct a host of servants to smother the smoldering coal beneath the missing floor, and to carry Mark and Edwin to their rooms. Ranald had stirred, and apart from a sore head and a bruised arm seemed reasonably well, if a little shaken. Luke who had experienced several explosions in his lifetime was immediately concerned with the motive of the perpetrator. He put it to Ranald, "Which of us was the intended victim?"

Piers who arrived on the scene took charge, "Neither of you are well enough to discuss that now. Both of you should return to your quarters."

Piers was intrigued. He had received a note purporting to come from Luke to meet him in the bowling alley at noon. He was late. Otherwise he might have been killed. Was he the intended victim?

Next day Luke, Ranald, and Edwin gathered around Mark's bed. Mark had several shards of glass removed from various parts of his body and had been bled by Ranald's physician. Miles arrived, who in complete disregard of the quarantine had with several of his men who had experience with explosives, come to examine the scene of the incident.

He reported to those gathered around the bed, "The explosions were caused by three modified mortar bombs in which the wooden plug that controlled the timing was replaced by medium length fuses that enabled the perpetrator to leave the scene in plenty of time. The fact that small mortars were used, probably saved your lives. The iron mortar shell is reasonably thin and therefore the impact and quantity of the fragments are much less than if a bomb designed for demolition had been used."

"Thank you Miles," Luke responded.

Miles turned to Ranald, "Your armory contains several mortar shells, and plenty of gunpowder to fill them, and saltpeter in which to soak the fuses. If you have an inventory of what the armory contains I will establish if those used in the attack came from there."

"Unless some unknown bombers have penetrated your perimeter guard they must have come from there. It is less than a hundred yards from the bowling alley," replied Ranald.

"I repeat my key question, who was the target?" asked Luke.

"The most obvious target is Mark and yourself. Your investigation is discovering many unflattering facts, and more than one person wants to stop your enquiries before you discover their potentially destructive secrets," suggested Edwin.

"Or it could be personal attack against you, Luke. You have upset at least one of my guests. Sir Winston Finch makes his feelings known at every opportunity. And your probing and personal questioning could have upset others. Husbands do not respond well to another man questioning their wives alone," added Ranald.

Mark winced with pain as he spoke, "Or it could be a gentry attack on the aristocracy. If Winston had his way, power in the county would rest with the gentry not the aristocracy. Or it could be an attack by the old guard who fear that the two of you will side with Winston and his cronies, and not carry on the policies of your fathers."

"Ranald, who would personally dislike you to the extent they would want to blow you up?" probed Luke.

"Nobody."

"What about Elspeth? Does she know you intend to remove her inheritance?"

"Yes, but she is a woman. She has no experience of explosives."

"She could have use her charms to persuade an experienced male to act for her. What about you Edwin?"

"I have upset numerous people, but not I believe to the extent that they would want to kill me."

"The target may not have been any of us. Piers saw me earlier. He had received a note from me to meet him in the bowling alley at noon. I did not send that letter, and if Piers had not been late, he too would have been caught up in the blast."

"Between the five of us, almost everybody currently at Medlowe Abbey could be a prime suspect," announced Mark with an air of despondency. "Let's forget motive for a moment and concentrate on opportunity. Ranald, who knew that we would be in the ninepin alley at that particular time?"

"Everybody. As a matter of courtesy I invited all our male guests."

"When would the invitation have been received?"

"Forty eight hours before the event."

"Unfortunately we have to reach the same conclusions as regards motives. Almost everybody knew the timetable, and could have planted the bombs," said Luke.

"Kemp was lucky. He left only minutes before the explosion," remarked Mark.

There a long silence and then Luke stated quietly, "Was it luck? What if the bomber had warned him that there would be an explosion around noon?"

"If Kemp knew that there was a bomb, why did he come in the first place. Most of the males declined my invitation. He would not have stood out."

"If he was warned, an obvious informant could have been his wife," muttered Edwin. "Maybe it was directed at you after all, Ranald."

Later that morning Luke visited the coal cellars from inside the house. He was led through the spacious kitchen and then downstairs to a sequence of cellars containing foodstuffs, wine and finally coal. Stopping in the kitchen he made it known to the staff that he was investigating the explosion of the previous day. He asked had they seen anybody in the area who should not have been there.

A brazen scullery maid who clearly wanted to gain Luke's attention spoke up. "No sir, none of us saw anything but that doesn't mean no one was in the cellars. There are other ways of getting there without coming through the kitchen."

"Do people risk being seen opening the coal trapdoors and entering from the outside?" asked a skeptical Luke.

"No, sir. There is a narrow staircase from the upper floors that leads directly into the cellars. It is often used by couples wanting a secret cuddle without much of chance of being disturbed."

"Undoubtedly it is well used by most of you," said Luke with a knowing smile. "But do those upstairs use it?"

Another plump serving girl added, "They certainly do. Since the visitors arrived for the meetings, I have seen the same lady climbing up the stairs at least twice."

"Could you describe her?"

"No, it was dark and these canoodling couples extinguish their tapers as soon as they reach the staircase."

"If that is the case, how do you know it was the same woman?"

"Just before the taper was put out, it reflected a pair of silver shoes as the lady clambered up the staircase."

Luke thanked the servants and led by the more brazen of the females he was given a tour of the cellar area. After an examination of the area which revealed nothing of significance he left his guide and clambered up the narrow staircase and emerged into one of the main corridors of the house. To find a woman with silver shoes would not be easy. Given the long gowns worn by most of them, footwear would on most occasions be well hidden.

In any case anyone could have entered the coal cellar down the narrow isolated staircase and planted the bombs.

Meanwhile back at Whitehall, Matt received Luke's instructions to investigate the condition of the Earl of Medlowe. As he left his apartment he recognized the figure walking towards him. It was his former superior, and Cromwell's right hand man, John Thurloe.

Matt was surprised. "Of all the people in the previous regime I thought the head of intelligence, and chief minister would at least be imprisoned, if not executed. Yet he is freely wandering around the King's inner sanctum."

"You were always impertinent Hatch. It was the very success of our organization that has saved my life. The King was so impressed with our ability to undermine every Royalist conspiracy that I have been spared to help the Earl of Salisbury create a similar body for His Majesty. How do you explain your obvious survival?"

"Very similar to your own. The King was also impressed with Luke Tremayne as head of military intelligence, and has set up a small special unit with Luke as its head, responsible only to the King."

"Do you have any work to do? The King is so popular that I doubt that at the moment there is any threat to his person, or to state security."

"My comrades are assessing the aristocrats and gentry of one of the home counties for the King, before he makes a number of appointments. Unfortunately the gathering of Royalist landowners at which they are present has been disrupted by the outbreak of the plague. Luke and his assistants are quarantined there for forty days."

After being told the exact location of Luke's mission, Thurloe smiled. "That shire gave us little trouble. The Earl of Medlowe was outwardly co-operative, but I always suspected he was nevertheless secretly funding

Royalist activity. One of our best agents, probably better than you Hatch, nevertheless kept us informed of every Royalist move."

"His name?"

"I never knew it. His code name was Exodus. He was highly placed in the community given the information to which he had access. And I am not sure if it was a male. This excellent agent may have been a woman."

"That information will assist Luke. Someone tried to blow him up a day or so ago. Maybe that agent is not able to distinguish between the civilian intelligence led by you, and Luke's military endeavors. He or she may be terrified that their past association with the Cromwellian government is about to be revealed."

"Give my regards to Tremayne. The old Protector thought very highly of him, although both of us know he is not the easiest man to work with."

Later that day Matt arrived at the town house of the Earl of Medlowe with a warrant from the King demanding entry so that he could ascertain the Earl's real condition. Acting as Matthew's deputy was one of the King's doctor's—a former soldier who combined the practical outlook of a military surgeon, with the academic theories of a university trained physician. He accompanied Matt into the Earl's bedchamber where they were gently confronted by a very tall aristocratic woman with flowing strawberry blonde hair. She was soberly dressed in brown with masses of golden thread highlighting her bodice and dress.

"I am Caroline, daughter-in-law of the Earl. Gentlemen please leave us. He is very ill and cannot talk. I fear he is at death's door. Why this unwarranted intrusion?"

"We regret our untimely visit, but the King is anxious to establish that everything that can be done for his father's most loyal servant is actually occurring."

"The doctors have bled him several times, but he seems to get weaker and weaker. He sparks up only for his meal of special mushrooms gathered from his beloved Abbey woods every day."

"Lady Caroline, the King wishes his own doctor, here with me, to examine your father-in-law so that he can rest contented. The doctor will examine the Earl while you and I discuss other matters in the next room. You must be aware that a great assemblage of the Royalist landholders of the county are gathered in your home, Medlowe Abbey, yet you, the obvious hostess, are not there."

"The recently widowed Veronica Petty is delighted to take my place," was the instant reply.

"According to my commanding officer, who is in attendance as the King's representative, it has led to unhealthy speculation that you are a prisoner here, or even more absurdly that you were confined to the crypt of your chapel."

"Ranald should have explained that he sent me here to be with the Earl in his last days. The Earl and I became closer as he and Ranald drifted apart."

"How long have you and Ranald be married?"

"Five years, nearly six."

"Ranald was in exile for most of the King's absence, so were you married on the continent?"

"You are mistaken. Ranald was exile for only a few years. In the early fifties he was a boon companion of the King in Paris, but he returned here during the Cromwellian Protectorate, and we were married soon after."

"By your accent I gather you are from the north. What stand did your family take during our civil war ?"asked Matthew.

'Father was an ardent Royalist and a great friend of the Earl of Medlowe They attended the House of Lords together. My marriage was arranged by those two peers. I had not set eyes on Ranald until a week before the wedding. I was staggered by his unimposing presence. My brother, and subsequent heir to the family title and estates was a strong supporter of Parliament and latterly Cromwell. He was the last garrison commander to pledge allegiance to the now Royalist commander, George Monk. Up until the last minute he sided with John Lambert, believing that the Republic could be saved."

Matthew wanted to ask the most pertinent question, but considered it inappropriate. Did Caroline have views similar to her father or to her brother? It also struck him that given Caroline's five years in the county during the Republic that she might be Exodus."

Instead he pursued a line of questioning that had been suggested to him by Luke. "Lady Caroline, you know of the tragic death of Sir Julius Petty. Initially it was believed to be an accident, but there are now suggestions that he was murdered. Over the last five years have you become aware of any enemies he may have created? Of any reasons why anybody would kill him?"

"Many possible suspects, I could have done the deed myself."

"What did he do to so alienate you?"

"He was only being his pre-war self, advocating the views of a much earlier generation. He was the main cause of the rift between Ranald and his father. Unfortunately despite my closeness to the Earl, I could never persuade him that Julius's views were outdated, and that he should listen to his son."

"Did others feel the same way and would they have taken steps to remove him?"

"Over the last couple of years tensions have increased between Phineas Leigh and Julius over the alleged mistreatment of the latter's wife, Veronica. Even more pronounced was the growing coldness between Job Elliott and Julius over the same issue. Job was betrothed to Veronica, but pushed aside at the last minute for an arranged marriage between the Leighs and the Pettys. This reached crisis point just before I came to the town house when a rumor circulated that the Petty's son Nathan was fathered by Job."

"So both Job and Phineas had reasons to act against Julius?"

"Captain, don't forget the woman in this situation. The harm done to Veronica's reputation when branded by her husband as an adulteress, and to Nathan now considered a bastard could be devastating. Mother and son in my eyes must have developed a bitter hatred of Julius. They would be my prime suspects."

"In the current session of Parliament there is a bill to declare Nathan illegitimate."

Caroline gasped, "How horrible for Veronica! Julius has a vicious streak."

"Your views about others who are currently at Medlowe Abbey would be very helpful."

"Of two of those that I have come to know after five years, Sir Orlando Hall and Sir Job Elliott, I have vastly different assessments. Both men have and continue to suffer from a major trauma. Job lost Veronica, and has never been reconciled, refusing all other offers of marriage. Orlando has a Papist wife who left him to become a nun, and then returned expecting to resume her marital position. Despite their difficulties they treated the young women in their care in very different ways. Orlando was a perfect surrogate father for the Earl's bastard daughter Elspeth. Despite her

16

"Jane, any luck in tracing the silver shoes during your informal socializing with the women?" asked Mark.

"No, I bungled that. I showed off my golden shoes, hoping the women would show me their footwear. Most assumed I was showing off my superior status as a marchioness to wear gold, while they as mere wives of the gentry had to be content with silver."

"Didn't a decade of republican rule destroy such archaic rules?" remarked Luke.

"No, the reverse. As people lost real power they concentrated on aspects where their superior status could still be asserted, such as food and dress. I had more success though when I raised the question of canoodling in the cellar."

"Elspeth?" asked Mark.

"She openly admitted unbridled canoodling, but seemed genuinely aghast that any gentlewoman would disappear into the servants area of the cellars."

"How did others react?"

"Veronica wanted to know how I knew so much about these activities, and those cheeky Ramsden girls suggested that you, Luke had ventured into the cellars with me."

"Charity Elliott seemed disinclined to believe that anybody in the room would engage in such activity in such a dark environment. That girl is either naïve or too clever by half. The light hearted nature of the conversation suddenly changed when in answer to why I seemed obsessed with canoodling on the stairs I said that whoever it was, was a prime suspect for detonating the bombs."

There was a knock on the door. A soldier entered and spoke to Luke who responded, "Take a seat, trooper! You have information that we all might find useful."

"Yes, sir. Since we have been on duty surrounding Medlowe Abbey, a group of us spend our free time in The Blue Dog. Some of the locals have been antagonistic especially where their womenfolk are concerned. Others have been very friendly. One man in particular whom everybody refers to as Little Johnny became very talkative after a few drinks. Eventually he revealed that in addition to being a laborer on one of small holdings nearby, he is a poacher."

"And where did he poach?" asked Mark, anticipating the answer.

"Medlowe Woods, it is overrun with rabbits and deer."

"Did he confess his poaching activities to you for any reason?" queried Luke.

"Of course. He claimed that our cordon around the estate had prevented him carrying out these activities, and that he and his family were suffering—not far removed from starvation. If we could turn a blind eye and let him enter the estate, he would be grateful."

"One of our number, not me, asked what would we get in return if we let him in. I said we could not accept the product of his poaching as we would find it difficult to conceal it from our officers who would view such an arrangement most unfavorably. His reply surprised us. He said he had information which if passed on to our officers might hold us in good stead. The rest of my comrades were not interested, and moved away."

"But he revealed all to you?" asked Jane.

"Yes, my lady, he told me a story that I knew would interest the colonel. One night while he was poaching in the woods he heard a commotion as a body of horsemen, and several wagons arrived at the edge of a large pit that had been dug to bury infected cattle. What struck Johnny as strange was that the horsemen except for their leader were clearly not locals. They spoke in a broad West Country accent, similar to yours Colonel. Johnny pointed out this pit was dug to cater for the surrounding parishes only, not distant parishes, let alone other counties. He was also intrigued that there were so many horsemen. Normally local herdsmen brought in the infected cattle, buried them under a layer of lime and soil. In this case none of the horsemen dismounted. A couple of waggoneers did all the work."

"What did Johnny suspect was happening?"

"He thought that the horsemen were out-of-county brigands who were burying their stolen loot. He even suggested that I should do a little digging, and if I came across any loot to share it with him."

"It could hardly have been valuable loot. A lime pit would be a damaging hiding place for most goods," remarked Luke.

"Did this occur on the evening when Sir Julius Petty disappeared?" asked Jane.

"When did the disappearance occur?" asked the trooper.

"About a fortnight ago."

"No, this happened months ago when the republican government was collapsing and the maintenance of law and order was fragile," concluded the soldier.

Luke dismissed him, and announced to Mark and Jane that he would see Ranald immediately to clarify some of the issues the soldier had just revealed.

Ranald's comments deflated any significance that Luke had begun to give to the story. "Luke, I was not living here at the time. Father was in charge but when I took over our steward made me aware that there was a rumor circulating at The Blue Dog that a fortune in stolen gold and silver had been buried in the infected cattle pit. I put a guard around the pit at night in case the villagers wanted to try their luck and dig into it. Not surprisingly the fear of infection overrode greed, and apart from a couple of drunks no one has disturbed the buried cattle."

"Did you ever speak to the gatekeeper who must have admitted them to the estate that night?"

"I couldn't. He died in his sleep a few days after the event."

"Was his successor or deputy of any use?"

"Only in a minor way. Burial at night is preferred so that the inhabitants would not be aware of the extent of the cattle infection, and secondly the story of outsiders could only partly be true. A condition on the use of the Medlowe pit was that the person dumping the cattle was a local property owner."

"Would your gatekeeper have a list of who dumped the cattle?"

"I followed that up. They had a list but it was not detailed. It did not list the time or day, just the week. The particular dumping in question could have been in the name of seven or eight people, many of whom are here at the moment."

That gave Luke an idea, but he had one final question. "Ranald, had there been any major robberies in the area just before this event?"

"Not that I have heard of. But on past experience a lot of wealthy people who have been robbed, never report it."

"If this event was not simply the dumping of infected cattle, have you any idea what might have been interred?"

"Yes, it is completely circumstantial. It occurred at the time the wealthiest republican landowner and magistrate disappeared. He would not have been able to take a lot of his assets with him in fleeing to the Dutch republic. Maybe he buried some of his wealth and possessions here. When times changed and he returned, they would be easily accessible."

"Why have you not dug up the pit to find out?"

"For the moment no one wants to dig up a pit full of infection. While nobody appears to have been infected by the cattle so far, there is widespread fear that too close a contact may be dangerous. After the lime, soil and time have done their work, I will be able to persuade the servants to dig."

Luke visited the gate house himself.

The new gatekeeper listened intently as Luke explained his needs.

"Yes, Colonel, I do have a record of everybody who deposited infected cattle into the Medlowe Abbey pit."

The gatekeeper found the relevant estate record book, and Luke quickly reached the pages that interested him. For the relevant week there were nine entries in the rather almost undecipherable hand of the late gatekeeper.

Luke turned to his successor.

"Were these entries made at the end of the week, or as they happened?"

"Does it matter?"

"There is a great difference between your predecessor noting at the end of the week those who had sent cattle to be interred, probably in random order. If he noted down the visitors as they came and went, I may be able to work out who came on the night that caused those rumors to spread through The Blue Dog. The problem interment took place at the end of the week."

Luke noted that many of the current guests were on the list—Orlando, Phineas, Job, Winston and Alexander. Also the late Julius Petty featured twice but by far the most common entry was simply *Medlowe*.

Luke asked for an explanation as to what this meant. "The Earl has many local properties in the area. These were cattle from those outlying farms that had been infected."

Luke perused the list and carefully noted the last few entries appeared to be Orlando, Job, Julius and two Medlowe references.

Luke's mind was racing. He could exclude Edwin and Piers from leading a group of alien horsemen on the fatal night as their names did not appear on the list. If the names were in chronological order he could also exclude Phineas, Winston and Alexander. It looked as if Orlando, Job or the late Julius may have been involved.

He discussed the situation that evening with Mark who suggested that while Ranald was not living at Medlowe Abbey at the time of the incident, he could have been living at one of the outlying properties which deposited infected cattle.

"I would not exclude Ranald from our list of suspects for whatever happened that night nor any of the others. The list is probably incomplete either through incompetence, or the gatekeeper turning a blind eye to those he feared, or to those who bribed him."

"If Ranald led the group, it would explain why the gatekeeper did not ask or note the unnecessarily large body of horsemen involved," said Luke.

"It's a pity that all this happened during the transition period from republic to monarchy. Those in authority at the time, the old republican magistrates and politicians may have some relevant evidence regarding marauding strangers, robberies and the details of the cattle infection."

"Unfortunately the man who would have known most has become central to the mystery—the missing Sir Septimus Ingle," remarked a frustrated Luke.

"There must be plenty of other republican figures we could question?" asked Mark.

"There is one. He commanded the local militia under the republic—a former officer in my cavalry regiment many years ago, Captain Wilfred Mills. He lives not far from here. I will visit him."

"But you can't Luke. You are still under quarantine."

"Then Miles can contact him, and we can meet in the gatehouse, a safe distant apart."

17

Two days later Luke, Miles and Mark met with Wilfred. Miles included his deputy in the quarantine garrison, Lieutenant Mutton Johnson, in the discussion. Luke outlined the situation.

Wilfred replied, "The time to which your refer was a couple of weeks of chaos. My militia was in the process of being stood down, and an illegal Royalist group had already emerged, which weeks later was finally sanctioned. It was ruthless in exacting revenge on many of our people."

"Who led this illegal Royalist squad?" asked Luke.

"Its commander wore a hood. I discovered subsequently that several people took turns as leader. When it was legalized the designated head was Job Elliott. One of the last acts of the Earl as restored Lord Lieutenant before he moved to London was to stand him down."

"Who did you suspect as interim commander of this group?"

"It could have been anybody, but among the locals only Edwin Symes had military experience."

"Interesting! Edwin returned here at about the right time," mused Luke.

"Were there many strangers traversing the county at the time?" asked Mark.

"There were reports of marauding bandits, and many of our people were attacked, but whether it was by strangers or disguised local Royalists I don't know. It was so bad that with the imminent return of the King I had trouble raising sufficient militia to defend the leading Cromwellians of the county. I was forced to ask the government to send troops from London to protect Sir Septimus Ingle. I had hoped for a company of dragoons but they sent a dozen musketeers. I attached these to Ingle's household, while my depleted mounted militia tried to cover the rest of the county."

"Did Ingle give you any hint he was about to flee to the Netherlands in anticipation of the King's return and the renewed dominance of the traditional Royalist families in the county?" asked Mark.

"Quite the opposite. When I insisted that he have protection, he argued that it was unnecessary, given his friendship with the Earl. He fully expected that with the Earl's influence, the King would retain him on the bench."

"Which he has done with existing magistrates in other counties," added Luke.

"Have you any evidence of his leaving for abroad?"

"No, and I do not believe that he did leave."

"Then what happened to him?"

"He has been abducted. He will be used as a pawn by someone to achieve their ends. Given rumors circulating at The Blue Dog about horsemen with West Country accents roaming the county, he could be a prisoner in Devon or Cornwall, or even in deepest Wales."

"Not logical! A former Cromwellian magistrate is not a likely bargaining point with the new Royalist government," Luke replied. "In addition what did the abductors do with his wife and twelve soldiers?"

"His wife may be still with him, and the soldiers were probably paid to disappear. Ingle was a very wealthy man. He rivals the Medlowes. His abduction is personal, not political. Expect a ransom note!" suggested Wilfred.

"How serious was the infection of local cattle, and how long did the crisis last?" asked Mark changing the topic.

"It has been going on for six or more months. In the beginning it was chaos. Nobody knew what to do. The local wise women who traditionally look after the health of cattle failed in everything they tried. They concluded that the cattle had been bewitched. For a short period I anticipated a renewed witch hunt. Luckily the Earl acted. He argued that as the infection seemed to spread through other cattle in a herd, the infected beasts had to be culled. There was some argument about whether the cattle should be burnt or buried. The Earl decided on burial, dug an enormous pit and required all local landowners to be rid of their infectious livestock."

"During the period when the populace was looking for a scapegoat as a witch did their search go beyond the village elderly?" asked Miles.

"Surprisingly yes. Two upper class women were named by some of the distraught villagers who had lost cattle. One of them, given her Catholic beliefs in these Protestant, if not Puritan parishes, was not unexpected. In this anti-Catholic hot house, Lady Ursula Hall was often accused of witchcraft whenever a scapegoat was needed. The only evidence produced by her current accusers was that a week after she returned from the continent from her period as a nun, the infection broke out."

"Who was the other woman?"

"That accusation astounded me. It was Veronica Petty."

"Why name her?" asked Luke.

"She was the most powerful Royalist woman in the county, and a strong influence on the Earl of Medlowe. The distraught peasants simply hit out at their betters."

"Or was the idea suggested to the credulous masses by her vindictive husband?" asked the astute Miles.

Luke presented Wilfred with a list of names. "These are the Royalist gentlemen currently at Medlowe Abbey. Did any of them come to your attention over the past few years?"

Wilfred whistled as he read. "Where do I start? Most were suspect at one time or another. The one that I had no dealings with as he was overseas was the now apparently unstable, Edwin, Lord Symes."

"I understand a woman he lived with died as the result of his violent temper, but he left the country before any prosecution could begin," Luke commented.

"It was much worse than that. He beat his mistress to death probably as a reaction to the news he gave her that he had abducted a 12 year heiress and married her. He immediately moved to the continent with his child bride who died in childbirth the following year. His lordship obtained from this marriage a large number of estates, which have been managed by his father during his absence abroad. If he had returned earlier there was a warrant for his arrest which has now lapsed. His desire to be a magistrate or member of parliament is driven by a desire to prevent any similar warrant being reissued. He probably hopes that he inherits his father's title before this happens and then the House of Lords will be the only body empowered to try him."

"Which other names strike you?" asked Miles.

"Alexander Kemp, a man distantly linked with the Symes."

"Kemp and Symes are connected?"

"The heiress that Symes abducted was a relation of the Kemps. When she married, most of her property went to her new husband, Edwin Symes, but a few estates devolved to the closest male heir. Alexander Kemp appeared from nowhere and staked a claim."

"By the tone of your voice, you doubted the claim?" queried Luke.

"Yes, the Kemps are Scots. Our Alexander does not have the slightest hint of a Scottish accent. He claims he came to England to fight for the King, but was captured before he could take up arms, and returned to a Scottish prison from where he was soon released. I had enquiries made in Scotland. Yes, an Alexander Kemp did spent time in prison, but his family thought he had died there. His family all speak with the broadest Scots accent."

"So Kemp is an imposter. What did you do?"

"I informed Sir Orlando of my doubts when Kemp began to court Elspeth. He seemed unconcerned, and then almost immediately, I was ordered by Ingle not to continue with my enquiries."

"Was Kemp the republican spy that Thurloe was so proud of?" asked Mark.

"That would certainly explain the lack of action on behalf of the then government," commented Luke.

"No, Kemp was not one of our key agents. He was and is a do-nothing ditherer who avoided Royalist activities. He was hardly accepted into their society, even after he married Elspeth—but he did have extensive business connections with Finch," replied Wilfred.

"Who then do you think was Thurloe's agent amongst the Royalists," asked Mark.

"It's all over now. We live in a new age. Nothing will be the same. The past is best put to rest. That seems to be what the King is attempting by reconciling the old Cromwellians like us, with his supporters."

"This issue is still relevant now. In fact a matter of life and death— possibly my mine," replied Luke.

"How?"

"Someone tried to blow me up a few days ago. One possible motive is that the bomber was Thurloe's agent who thinks that as I was in intelligence I might know of his or her past activities which in these changed circumstances he or she does not wish to be revealed."

"My guess is that the bomber is a Royalist who openly or covertly opposes the attitude of the dominant clique led by the Earl and Julius Petty, or secondly those whom the previous government suspected of causing trouble whom Ingle was inexplicably told not to investigate further."

"And who fits the first category?" asked Luke.

"My suspects fit both categories. Job Elliott was actively participating in Royalists plots, and conspiracies against the policy of the Earl and Petty. Septimus Ingle may have received orders not to prosecute him, but Septimus explained that he did not want to punish the Earl and Petty who had co-operated with the Cromwellian regime, just because of one bad egg. I was simply to monitor Job's activities, but not arrest him. Lord Ranald who during most of my period did not live at Medlowe Abbey was also known to consort with active Royalists, against his father's wishes. Again Septimus adopted a tolerant attitude."

"What about the women?" asked Miles.

"We gathered very little evidence against any of those on your list. Elspeth Kemp came under suspicion because her multitude of affairs were seen as unnatural by Septimus, who concluded it was a cover for Royalist plotting. He saw Elspeth as carrying vital information from one Royalist activist to the next. After investigation Elspeth's range of companions revealed no political or religious bias."

"Any other?" continued Miles.

"The two women who both think they are the dominant female powerbroker in the county, and whose rivalry may explain a lot of the issues you are currently confronting. Veronica Petty was increasingly disappointed with the Earl. Her previous influence was declining, and then with her growing estrangement from her husband, her dominance of the county scene had almost disappeared. She may have sought her revenge in spying for Thurloe, and obstructing the designs of her husband and the Earl. However my guess as our effective agent in the county would be Lady Caroline Medlowe. She has in a few short years wrested dominance within the county from Veronica, is the darling of her father-in-law, the Earl, and whose brother was one of Cromwell's most effective soldiers."

"But no evidence to support any of this?" asked Mark.

"None."

On that note the meeting closed.

N ext morning Luke, in the presence of Jane and Mark summarized the state of their mission. "Our assessment of the suitability of the local Royalists for positions of power in the county has been conveniently enhanced by our need to solve three diverse problems—who murdered Julius, if any one; who exploded the bombs that nearly killed us: and who was Thurloe's agent amongst these Royalists?"

"There are two other possible issues that might help us obtain an even clearer picture of this county community—what happened to Septimus Ingle and whether Alexander Kemp is an imposter?" added Mark.

"I once believed that when I was confronted with multiple murders it was good procedure to assume they were all committed by the same person."

"How did that help?" asked Jane.

"It made the first logical step in any investigation to seek the answer to a simple question. Who would want all the victims killed, in this case who would want Julius, Piers and ourselves out of the way?"

"Is it an effective approach?" probed a skeptical Jane.

Luke smiled as he confessed, "Not always! It is useless and a waste of time if there is more than one murderer."

"Which is most likely in this situation. Julius was a victim of a personal vendetta, whereas the bomb meant for us could only be political," added Mark.

"Let's concentrate on Julius! Lady Veronica has just lost her husband. Her son has not yet arrived. She seems to have been sidelined from any effective political influence, except that Ranald has made her his acting hostess – a decision itself worth pursuing. It is the time to come the heavy. I will try to intimidate Veronica with a combination of lies and threats, while she is most vulnerable," Luke brutally announced.

Jane was not convinced. "Before you do that, let me try a gentler approach as a woman who understands what Veronica is going through. To have a widowed marchioness on her side, may loosen her tongue. You go to The Blue Dog, and question the local riff-raff. Surely someone would have been out and about at the time Julius left the inn and made his way towards the Abbey?"

"You forget Jane that we are confined to the Abbey, until the quarantine is lifted," Mark retorted.

"That is ridiculous. I am responsible both as a magistrate and the King's special agent for the implementation and execution of the quarantine. You and I, Mark, are clearly not infected, so I am lifting the quarantine for both of us. While I'm at it, I will also release both Job and Phineas from the pest house. Job's servants must remain as the course of the infection does not seem to have run its course in their cases. I will also raise the morale of the other guests by hinting that the curfew will soon be lifted. Mark, you inform the people concerned of these changes! I will visit The Blue Dog."

Luke was well received there by Blackie. "I thought you were locked away in the Abbey for a few more weeks?" he remarked.

"The forty days was a bit of an over-reaction, but it is the law which I have authority to modify within the Abbey. I am here to continue my investigation into what happened to Sir Julius. I will spend the day here, and question as many of yours customers as I can, especially the poacher, Little Johnny."

"Your luck is in. Johnny is in the far drinking chamber."

Luke, carrying a couple of tankards of beer, approached Johnny. He introduced himself as the officer investigating Petty's death.

"You have spoken to one of my men regarding the assumed burial of treasure in the cattle pit at the Abbey. I know you are a poacher, but because of the value of the earlier information, whatever you tell me that incriminates you will not be acted on—information in return for non-prosecution of your alleged misdeeds."

"I told your man all I know about the night of the alien horsemen, so how can I help any further?"

"I am interested in the night that Sir Julius disappeared. You continued to poach in Medlowe Woods up to the time my troops surrounded the estate?"

'Yes, most nights."

"If you are such a regular poacher, how is it that the Earl's gamekeepers do not catch you?"

Johnny laughed, "A combination of family influence and bribery. Many of the gamekeepers are relatives of mine. They preferred the Earl's deer to keep my family alive, rather than having to assist a needy relative themselves. Others were bribed with a share of my kill, which they collected from Blackie, but for decades his lordship has turned a blind eye to my activities, like you are contemplating, in return for information."

"The night of Sir Julius's disappearance—anything unusual?"

"When was that?"

Luke answered.

Little Johnny sipped his beer and eventually replied. "It was that night or the one before or the one after that I was out of my routine. I heard that Sir Phineas and his family had gone to London. I knew that when the master was away his gamekeepers and warreners did not patrol the grounds but stayed in their quarters drinking and gambling. I thought a few of those fattened rabbits would make a change from lean venison. I reached the enclosed warren, let myself in and was about to snare a few creatures when I heard a commotion, and a group of gamekeepers descended on the warren. They had decided to take a few rabbits for themselves, but before doing so continued drinking from numerous flagons they had brought with them."

"So you were trapped. How long did you hide there?"

"Most of the night. The group only left the warren when they were informed that one of their number, who had obviously left earlier had either accidentally or deliberately let the dogs off their leashes. They needed to be rounded up. When they all left, I grabbed a couple of rabbits, but decided I also needed some venison to pay off my debts."

"So you went to Medlowe Abbey but much later than usual?"

"Yes, but I never entered the grounds."

"Why not?"

"Unexpected company—and the time. I never take the highway when moving about at night. The way not to be seen is to move along the inside of the hedge rows. As I moved along, hidden from the road, I heard raised voices on the road side of the hedge. Both men were on foot. This surprised me. By the way they spoke, they were gentlemen and gentlemen ride, and usually in daylight. The argument became louder and then I heard a thud which could have been one man striking the other, but the only words I could decipher were *You will regret that.*"

"Did you recognize the voices or catch a glimpse of the men?"

"I did not recognize the voices, but by their accents they were both local. When I emerged from behind the hedge I could see a figure approaching the gatehouse, and another going in the opposite direction back towards The Blue Dog. The fact that I could vaguely make two figures out, brought to my attention that day was breaking. It was too late. Daylight poaching is suicidal."

"There is nothing else that you noticed that would help my enquiry?"

"Your promise holds that I will not suffer punishment for what I did or did not do?"

"Yes."

"On my way home from near the gates of Medlowe Abbey I was confronted by three vicious dogs who had probably escaped from the Leigh estate. I fed them my two rabbits and escaped. An absolute disaster of the night. I finished with nothing."

"Sir Julius was attacked by dogs."

"Yes, that is why I did not reveal what had happened to me. It put me too close to whatever may have happened to Sir Julius."

"What do you think happened to him?"

"It depends on whether he was the man heading back to The Blue Dog, or was the one approaching the gatehouse of Medlowe Abbey. The man returning to The Blue Dog could easily have been attacked by the dogs that confronted me. Two rabbits would have hardly satisfied their hunger. The man about to enter the gatehouse would have been safe."

Luke thanked Johnny for his co-operation, and headed back to Medlowe Abbey more confused than ever.

He mused, "If the man attacked by dogs was Julius who may have turned back towards The Blue Dog, who was the man who approached the gatehouse? Conversely if Julius was the man approaching the gatehouse, he could not have been attacked by the dogs Johnny described. Perhaps the gatehouse keeper can enlighten me."

The gatekeeper was as usual completely unsatisfactory. Luke's instinct was that the man prevaricated, if not lied. He was another small person named inappropriately Samson. Samson claimed that he was asleep at the time in question, and that it was his assistant who was responsible for opening and closing the gate so early in the morning. Luke asked to speak with the assistant but was told that the person in question had left the Earl's service some weeks earlier.

At that moment the gatekeeper's wife, Bettina who had obviously been listening to the whole discussion burst into the room. "Don't risk everything for others, Sam! This man has a reputation as a ruthless soldier and magistrate. He won't have you arrested. You will simply disappear."

For once Luke was happy with his ill- deserved reputation, and he turned to the buxom wench that confronted him, "And what is it he should tell me?"

"We both rose early that morning because a meeting was to be held here between Sir Julius and the Earl or one of his family."

"But everybody must have known that the Earl was too sick to attend?"

"So we thought but assumed that Ranald or perhaps the steward would take his place. In the event despite the cooking I had done for the meeting, no one turned up. Later my husband received a note advising him to forget that such a meeting was ever planned."

"Was this note sent immediately after Sir Julius disappeared, or some days later, after his body had been found?"

"Almost immediately," replied Samson.

"Who sent it?"

"Any one of the Medlowes. It was on their special notepaper, and simply signed Medlowe. The obvious options are Lord Ranald and the Earl, even though he was supposedly in London on his death bed," he replied.

"What about Lady Caroline?"

"She's a woman. It would not be appropriate for her to interfere in men's business," replied Samson.

"I would not be so sure. She could have acted for the old Earl. Those two are very close. Too close, I suspect. The old man is having an affair with his daughter-in- law," uttered Bettina.

"Enough of that rubbish, my dear. The Colonel does not want his investigation complicated by silly women's talk."

Luke thanked the couple for their assistance. Bettina who seemed to have undone the top buttons of her bodice during the discussion was effusive. "Come again, anytime Colonel. It must be boring locked up in the big house with all those artificial women. I make the best mince tarts in the whole county."

While in the area, Luke decided to question the out servants and other workers who may have been in the vicinity at the time of Julius's demise. As it was summer they would have had to be on duty from an early sunrise. He questioned a dozen nor so men, who collectively added little useful information.

A hedger who began his work near the gatehouse had a vague recollection, as he had his back to the road most of the time, of a coach disappearing in the direction of London. Another worker who was taking fresh milk from the Abbey to The Blue Dog had to discharge his musket to frighten away three dogs that threated to attack his horse.

Another servant met an agitated Nathan Petty, who being told that neither his father or mother had yet arrived at the gatehouse galloped off in a frenzy. Several commented on the unusual sight of Ranald, Edwin and some of his other guests about so early in the morning—and so far from the house.

19

While Luke was at The Blue Dog, Jane struck up a conversation with Veronica. Jane started with what Luke would call a misleading comment, but which she, with a more refined moral compass, knew was a downright lie. "I thought I should warn you, Veronica, that Colonel Tremayne sees you as the prime suspect in the death of your husband."

"I don't know how you, and for that matter the King, can work with such a ruthless Cromwellian assassin?" was the bitter reply.

"Precisely because of this notorious reputation. The Colonel is absolutely devoted to the concept of the state. In previous times that was embodied in the person of the Lord Protector, Oliver Cromwell, now it is represented by the King. That is why Colonel Tremayne can make the transfer from his previous service to his current role without the moral turmoil that would confront most of us."

"Why does the Colonel think I had a part in my husband's death?"

"He is aware of your marital tensions, and the growing estrangement between you and Julius, climaxing in his attempt to have your child Nathan declared a bastard on the ground that he was not the father."

"I cannot understand how Julius came to such a ridiculous conclusion after decades of marriage. He knew of my previous relationship when we married."

"Surely a comparison of relevant dates would indicate whether you were pregnant well before your marriage, perhaps when you were betrothed to Job Elliott," suggested Jane.

"Yes, but if I had slept with Job just prior to being forced to marry Julius and slept with the latter before our marriage—who fathered the child would still be difficult to determine? Julius was no fool. Why did he not reject his family's plans, if he had doubts about me then. I repeat, why has he taken decades to act in this matter?"

"How would you answer those questions?"

"Simply an excuse to be rid of me."

"Why would he do that? Another woman?"

"Not for any romantic or sexual reasons. Julius was not of an affectionate nature, and after the first few years of marriage he has never bothered to claim his conjugal rights."

"Then why is he acting towards you as he is? Is it simply as he obviously sees it, revenge for tricking him over several decades? His honor has been damaged, and he must get his revenge? Or is there another reason?"

"Julius was a politician. Position and power was all that ever mattered to him. He found republican rule hard to take, and his every move was designed to ensure that sometime in the future, he would return to a position of influence. The political purpose of my forced marriage to him by my father who was his competitor for dominance in the county was completely nullified by the republican takeover. I was irrelevant to his political standing until the return of the King. That is why the timing of his attack on Nathan and myself is illogical. It is with the return of the King that he begins his attack."

Jane sensed a possible explanation that even surprised her.

"Do you think he gave up waiting, and decided to accept the Cromwellian regime, and he now fears that with the return of the King, you might remember some of his actions in that direction?"

Veronica's face lit up and she clapped her hands, "Jane, some of that intuitive brilliance that your Colonel is renowned for, must be rubbing off. Until you raised it then, I had never considered that Julius would betray the King. The Earl and he always argued that it was not the time for royalists to rise against Cromwell, but that eventually circumstances would change. Until that happens we were to accept the current regime and keep our powder dry. This was their constant mantra. If I accept your suggestion that he was about to jump ship, I can remember a number of incidents that might support such a hypothesis."

"And if Julius thought you knew about this proposed change of loyalty, he would not want you bringing it up when the King returned."

Veronica was silent for some time but finally responded. "Julius often met with Septimus Ingle, the dominant Cromwellian in the country, but I doubt that it involved changing sides. No, on reflection I have to reject your suggestion that Julius's attack on me is related to a treacherous change of sides. And if Julius wanted me to keep quiet about any politically suspect actions, he might have taken in recent years, accusing me of adultery and trying to illegitimize Nathan is not the way to do it. He would know how I would react to such claims. Rather than keep quiet, I would spread every iota of unfavorable information I had about the man."

Jane was warming to her investigative role. Another misleading statement followed. "Veronica, the Colonel is also inclined to believe that the man who acted on your behalf in killing Julius was not you original lover, Job, or your brother Phineas, but your son, Nathan."

"Absolutely ridiculous! Nathan was not here. In fact I have not been able contact him to tell him that his father had died. He lives on and manages one of our smaller properties in the south of the county. Since the growing tension between Julius and myself, and the shocking treatment by Julius of Nathan, the separation was a necessity."

"Not true! Nathan was here on the very night Julius died. He came to see you and was surprised that neither you nor his father were here. The Colonel thinks that a man on the road at the time Julius died, and who was reported to be arguing with him, was Nathan. Find your son before the Colonel has him arrested for patricide!"

Jane stopped. Perhaps she had gone too far. Luke had never mentioned such a development.

Veronica began to cry. "How can I? We are quarantined. The Colonel is absolutely wrong. Nathan is not the sort of person to resort to murder, especially of his own father. Job is a far more likely character, given his everlasting bitterness at how he was treated."

"If it was not Nathan, the Colonel considers Phineas a distinct possibility. It was his dogs that may have attacked Julius."

"Phineas was in London. And any dog attack on an open road could not have been controlled by their owners. It may have been a simple misadventure."

"There was a mysterious coach heading back to London. Your brother could have arranged to meet Julius at the gate house, killed him, let the roaming dogs devour most of his body, and returned to London."

"That does sound like one of your Colonel's wildest fantasies."

Jane was really getting into the mood to continue her investigation. She was now on a high. She changed the direction of her questioning."

"Another wild speculation of Colonel Tremayne is that Cromwell's secret agent within your royalist society may not have been the Ingle friendly Julius, but yourself."

"Why would I betray the King?"

"Because you were no longer the respected and powerful leading lady of the royalist families in the county with a direct link to the Earl of Medlowe."

"And what makes you say that? Who is the hostess of this gathering? I am."

"Only because your replacement and the dominant woman today, the future Countess of Medlowe, Lady Caroline, has a more important task—nursing the Earl during his last days."

"She has certainly made herself indispensable to Algernon. She is closer to him than his own son. It is true that because of her closeness to the Earl, she exerts considerable influence, but the majority of the county royalists still see me as the most reliable advocate of their interests. If power was important to me, then I would have kept closer to Julius who you may forget was the Earl's strongest supporter during the King's exile."

"I know you were asked this by the Colonel, but much has happened since that interview. If you or your friends or son were not responsible, who killed Julius? Who do you think then tried to kill the Colonel and others with the bombs? And whom would you suspect as the Cromwellian agent in your midst? If you can suggest someone else, and provide evidence, it will take suspicion away from you and your friends," Jane cleverly added.

"The traitor in our midst had to be either someone whose convictions had changed and began to think a Cromwellian monarchy was preferable to a Stuart, or someone who was so dispirited as a result of the royalist situation that he saw his future in being onside with the then government. In the first category many leading royalists including the Earl and Julius were seeing more and more virtue in the solid Cromwellian administration than that offered by the inexperienced and fun loving prince in exile. I am sure Ranald may have inclinations to go further in that direction than his father, and his marriage to a sister of a senior Cromwellian officer, in hindsight, may be telling."

"In a sense any royalist of influence who was changing his position could have been the agent? That does not help. What about simple vested interest?"

"I hate to admit it but the only person I can see as so embittered as to turn to the then government for support, is my old love, Job Elliott. He is a very bitter man and blames everybody else for the many misfortunes he has suffered. Losing me was only the beginning of his troubles. By sheer mismanagement, and stupid decisions, he lost a lot of property and money in supporting ridiculous schemes to get the King back. When no one else joined him in his stupidity, we were all blamed. I doubt if Job would nowadays murder Julius to protect my honor. I think love has turned to hate."

Jane felt that this assertion, if true could change Luke's perception of the situation. A Veronica-hating Job would have a very different perspective on proceedings, as a still besotted lover. Jane changed the direction of her questioning. "What about the bomber?"

"The Colonel was not the target. What would be the point? Kill the Colonel and the King would simply send a replacement. The Colonel has only known those here at Medlowe for a week or so. In that time he could not have created an enemy determined enough to kill him."

"The Colonel thought it could be related to the previous question. The Cromwellian spy in your midst may have thought that the Colonel having been in intelligence, may have been aware of his or her activity—that Luke may recognize the traitor and reveal his or her identity to the gathered fanatical Royalists."

"A distant possibility. Edwin and Ranald are far more likely suspects. Some of the old guard believe the young aristocrats are trying to alter the policies of their fathers. The more extreme younger gentry coming back from exile also do not want the aristocratic influence to prevail. In Edwin's case there would be many women, their husbands or fathers who might seek revenge for what he is alleged to have done. And I only heard today that young Kemp is a distant relation of the heiress that Edwin abducted.

His leaving just before the explosion is certainly suspicious. That note sent to Piers Carey supports my interpretation. The younger newcomers are out to destroy the aristocrats and the older leaders."

"The Colonel noted Kemp's fortuitous departure from the bowling alley. What about the killer of your husband?"

"There I have little to offer but I can see why the Colonel has focused on me," bemoaned Veronica.

"If you and your friends had nothing to do with Julius's death, whom else benefitted from his demise?"

"I cannot see anyone whom needed to get Julius out of way, except myself and family. Phineas and Julius had reconciled, and were to present an united front for the traditional ways against both the aristocrats and the newcomers. The issues were to be decided here over several weeks of discussion. Nothing has so far surfaced in the debates that would explain the murder and the bombings."

Jane suddenly had a flash of insight.

"Veronica, you earlier expressed surprise that Julius waited decades to suggest that Nathan was not his child. You found the timing did not make sense. What if Julius's attack was not directed at you, but solely at Nathan which was purely political? What if Julius discovered that his son and heir was conspiring with his political opponents to bring him down? You suggested political power was more important to Julius than family."

"Such a view puts suspicion back on Nathan. I must find him," concluded Veronica.

20

Luke and Jane pooled their information in front of Mark who was surprised at the amount of evidence that they had gathered.

"We certainly have a clearer picture of Julius's last hour. He almost reached Medlowe Abbey, but was either murdered just before the gates, and then eaten by the dogs, or the dogs acted alone—finding the chicken he carried insufficient to satiate their appetite," said Luke.

"And if he was murdered, it may have been the man on the road heard arguing with him, possibly Nathan, or more remotely someone who was to meet him, and then disappeared in a coach headed in the direction of London," added Jane.

"The priority in this investigation now is to find Nathan Petty. He seems to have disappeared, and according to his mother is not even aware of his father's death," Luke concluded.

"Or quite the opposite—having murdered his father, he has gone into hiding," suggested Mark.

Later that day Jane had an unexpected opportunity to reassess her interpretation of events.

Veronica knocked on the door of her apartment accompanied by a gentleman with short brown hair and a pointed beard of the same color. He was dressed more like a working farmer than a courtier.

Veronica introduced him, "This is my son Nathan. I told him that he was suspected of his father's murder, and that he should talk to you, before the Colonel arrested him."

"I am very pleased that you have come to see us. The Colonel was about to issue a warrant for your apprehension as a suspect. I will send a servant to fetch him."

Luke and Mark arrived. The former indicated with his eyes that Jane should ask the questions.

"Nathan, you have emerged as a suspect simply because someone that may have been you, was heard arguing with your father, and not much later you were at the gatehouse seeking to talk to your father or mother. The fact that you seemed surprised that neither were at Medlowe Abbey may stand you in better stead. Were you on the road approaching the gatehouse, just before dawn, arguing with your father?"

"Yes, I was on the road, and I did argue with father."

"How did you happen to be on the road at the same time?" continued Jane.

"I visited the family home, Petty Grange, the morning of the previous day to talk to my parents concerning their escalating conflict. The steward told me that both parents were away. He did not know where mother was, but knew that father intended to meet someone at The Blue Dog that evening, and then someone else at Medlowe Abbey early in the following morning, to bolster his influence in the forthcoming conference."

"Why didn't you see him at The Blue Dog?" Luke interjected.

"That was my intention, but he was never alone. The inn was completely full and rather than share a room with a group of possible ruffians I went to The Three Lions some miles away, prepared to rise before dawn to catch father on his way from The Blue Dog to Medlowe Abbey. This I did. To my surprise he was walking, having left his horse in the stables at The Blue Dog."

Jane resumed her questioning. "What did you argue about?"

"Father's treatment of mother. I offered to legally renounce my claim as heir to the Petty title and estate, if father withdrew the attempt to have me declared a bastard, and by implication declaring my mother a fornicator or adulterer."

Veronica squeezed Nathan's hand as a tear ran down her face.

"And how did he react?" asked Jane.

"An outburst of vicious abuse and continual insults."

"What form did this take?"

"Two areas of insult—that mother was a whore and that I was a traitor."

Jane picked up on this and eagerly asked, "Were you about to join your father's political opponents?"

"I had made no decision in this matter, but I had been talking to uncle Phineas on several issues. I did not realize that father had become so embittered. I returned the abuse suggesting that I hoped I was not his son, given his poisonous personality. I turned my horse and galloped back towards The Blue Dog."

"So your father was alive and well at that point? Did you hear or see any dogs at that time?" said Luke.

"Yes, to both questions. Father continued striding towards the Abbey, and I heard, but did not see a pack of dogs."

"Then why did you come back to the Abbey?" Luke continued.

"I arrived at The Blue Dog to have something to eat, and Blackie told me that father had left his horse behind, which he recognized as a favorite from my younger days. I thought about the situation. I would take the horse to the Abbey and leave it with my family's servants, who would have accompanied my parents, and seek to have another talk with both father and mother."

"On your second trip towards the Abbey, did you see your father?" asked Mark.

"At the time I did not think so, but I soon began to think the worst."

"Why?"

"As I approached the Abbey, I saw a torn and blood stained piece of green fabric on the verge, and dogs chewing away on some meat. I could hear others on the other side of the hedge. I continued on to the gatehouse, and was amazed that neither father nor mother had arrived. I decided to continue on to London to talk to some members of Parliament that I know, to block father's proposed legislation. I have been at Westminster, canvassing as many members as I could over the last few days."

"The fact that your father, who was so close to the gatehouse never made it to the Abbey, clearly concerned you?"

"Yes, and on reflection the green fabric—father was wearing a dark green cape. At the beginning I thought he may have been attacked by the dogs, and in protecting himself he had given them the roast chicken he was carrying and probably thrown the cloak over them to obstruct any attack. Then yesterday I heard at Westminster that father had been killed by dogs, so I came here immediately to comfort mother."

"You probably returned to the area not long after your father was killed. After a brief stop at the gatehouse to enquire of your parents you headed for London. A coach also left the area at about the same time. Did a coach pass you, or you pass a coach on the London road, reasonably close to Medlowe Abbey?"

Yes. I was surprised as the coach bore the arms of the Medlowes. Given that the Abbey was to be the gathering place of the county's elite that morning, I wondered who was leaving the Abbey at that critical time. Which of the Medlowes was escaping the gathering?"

"You did not see who was in the coach?" continued Luke.

"No the windows were curtained."

Luke turned to Veronica, "The marchioness has already made you aware that you too, are a major suspect in this case. Where were you on the day before your husband died, and on the morning of his death. You did not arrive here until mid-morning."

"I too was in London for the same purpose. I was to meet my brother Phineas who was there to obtain recognition for a friend of our father and his astronomical discoveries. After my brother had met with the scientists, he was to accompany me to meet some of his parliamentary friends to help scuttle Julius's plans."

"And did that come to fruition?" asked Luke.

"No, Phineas entered a plague ridden area and was confined there. I was with his wife Alice who needed comforting as she was convinced that Phineas would die. While in London I decided to visit the Earl at his town house. I was shocked that his servants whom I had known for years refused me entry. I went back to Alice, quite distraught. The Earl and I went through a lot together over the last two decades. I was not going to give up. I demanded that I see whoever was in charge of the Earl's convalescence. I waited in a small entrance hall and eventually Caroline appeared."

"Was your conversation cordial?" Jane asked.

"A mixture—on some issues Caroline was quite informative, almost friendly. She needed to talk to someone about her problems. On the other hand she refused point blank to allow me to see Algernon, or discuss his situation with me."

"On what grounds did Caroline refuse you, a longtime family friend, access to the Earl?" asked Luke, appearing surprisingly sympathetic.

"She claimed that the Earl was demented, that his mind had gone, that he recognized nobody and that it would only be distressing if I saw him."

"So what then did you talk about?"

"Without revealing too many details, I gathered she was having trouble with Ranald. It has been clear for some time that Caroline dominates the household, and probably influences Ranald in most of his decisions. She suggested that Ranald was not himself, and had to be watched carefully in case he made silly mistakes. She said that she told Ranald that given her absence from Medlowe Abbey during the meeting of the leading families, that I should act as hostess for the gathering."

"Did you get any hint of what was troubling Ranald?" Mark interjected.

"Another woman?" added Jane.

"Ranald continued his predatory courtier attitudes on his return to England, and after his marriage. He has slept with several of the women here, but tries to conceal unsuccessfully any such activity from Caroline. She claimed that Ranald was in debt to some unscrupulous money lender. Algernon never trusted Ranald with money, nor does Caroline."

"Who is he indebted to?"

"One of those wealthy newcomers, Carey, Finch or even Kemp."

Then out of the blue Nathan made an unexpected comment. "According to gossip Ranald is interested in an unhealthy way in men. This could explain attitudes to him, and his towards others."

"Well, I don't know if that sort of activity has continued. I know the Earl was appalled when he heard such rumors emanating in the early days of the King's exile," explained Veronica. "He thought Ranald's marriage would put an end to such unnatural behavior."

"Is Edwin his partner?" asked Luke undiplomatically. "Is that why Caroline wants to break up Ranald's friendship with Edwin?"

"No! Edwin, despite his years as a professional soldier has not strayed into that area. In fact during his military career he was known to have beaten suspected queans. Edwin had enough problems with women," was Nathan's second surprising contribution.

"Is Caroline more concerned about Ranald's erratic political attitudes and would-be alliances rather than his personal life?" asked Luke.

"As I told Jane, Caroline has views very different to Ranald's. Perhaps she is using the Earl's last days to influence him towards her position, rather than that of Ranald."

"And what would those views be?"

"To put it bluntly, I would not be surprised if she was a Cromwellian supporter, and perhaps that special agent his government had within our circle," replied Veronica.

Before Luke could continue, a servant entered the room and gave him a letter. While the rest of the group chatted, Luke moved to a corner of the room and read its contents.

He then addressed the group. "This is a letter from the King and he refers to matters that we have just been discussing. Given a report from his own doctor that the Earl was not improving, the King has had him removed to Whitehall, where he will be cared for by His Majesty's own people. As Caroline is no longer needed she will return to Medlowe Abbey within the next few days—that is if she wishes to enter a quarantine area."

"Did the King find something peculiar in the treatment of the Earl that has forced him to take this decision?" asked an intrigued Veronica.

"Yes, he reached a strange conclusion. He could find nothing seriously wrong with the Earl except some mild poisoning that had clearly occurred over a long period. There was no indication of acute poisoning since he had arrived at the town house, although he did not rule out a long term attempt to fatally poison the old man. Despite no acute changes in recent weeks the Earl suddenly believed he was dying. The doctor's only similar experience was with people who had been bewitched," recounted Luke.

"The Earl must have been bewitched! That would explain his behavior over recent months, but I do not know anybody with such powers who has been near him," replied Veronica.

"I will question Caroline on all of this, if she arrives."

Veronica and Nathan departed. Luke turned to Jane and Mark. "Let us see if anybody in the area who has had contact with the Earl is a witch, and who was in the coach which left here on the fateful morning."

21

Next morning while Mark attended the meeting of the assembled landowners Luke sought out the coachmen. He found two of them in the coach house. He commented, "I have been here several weeks, and have not seen the coach out and about during that time."

"That is correct, sir. In recent times the coach is only used by the Earl and Lady Caroline. With both of them away, the coach lies idle. We spend our time caring for the four coach horses. I am Lionel, the head coachman, and this is my assistant Bryan."

"When was the last time the coach was used?"

"The morning this current gathering of gentlemen began," replied Lionel.

"Who was in it then?"

"Nobody. It had to have one of its wheels repaired so we drove it to a wheelwright a few miles up the London road. After the repair I drove it home. While we waited, I delivered the Earl's daily meal of mushrooms to the Medlowe town house, riding one of the coach horses.

Luke was disappointed. He had hoped to find that a leading member of the household had been on the road at the time, and therefore in the vicinity of where Julius had died.

"I have another question to you that might appear strange. But as you have driven the Earl around the countryside for years before his illness you might have heard or noticed something. Has the Earl been in contact in recent months with a witch?"

"There are dozens of wise women among his tenants and workers who are often accused by disgruntled neighbors of being witches, but they work at a level below that of the Earl, and I have not heard of anything disastrous in recent years. The soldiers of the late Lord Protector made sure that you accused people witchcraft at your own peril," said Bryan.

"It was different ten years ago when the Parliament ran the country, and the Presbyterians the church," added Lionel.

"What happened then?" asked Luke.

"At that time the Earl was very close to an alleged witch and helped protect her. It was the wife of his best friend," Lionel replied.

"A gentlewoman? That is unusual," Luke commented.

"It was Lady Ursula. She is both a Papist and Welsh. She is proficient in the use of herbs, and unlike most gentry women takes a leading role as midwife, and herbalist to the women on her estate. Years ago there was an earlier serious outbreak of a cattle disease which spread rapidly and with deadly effect. A travelling preacher convinced a vulnerable community that it was due to the fact that the community tolerated a Papist in their midst—Lady Ursula. The popular frenzy was so bad and Lady Ursula so affected by it, that she would not only eventually move to the continent, but became a nun. Sir Orlando provided a considerable dowry for her to enter the convent," continued Lionel.

"Has the Earl seen Lady Ursula since her return?" Luke probed.

"Not that I know of. She is not one of the ladies here at the moment, although Lord Ranald has had her in to look at his prize cattle from time to time. She was still abroad when the Earl first moved to London."

Bryan interrupted, "But she might be here. Only a day ago I saw her outside the gate house talking to the woman she brought up, who is now married to that Kemp fellow—Mistress Elspeth."

Luke whistled, "That is very interesting. Perhaps I should ask you two a lot more questions. I did not realize coachmen knew so much."

"Only because we see most of the Earl's servants during the day, and indulge in the current gossip," Bryan explained.

"I am looking into three issues—who killed Sir Julius, who tried to kill me and others in the explosion, and who among the gentlemen and their ladies gathered here, was a Cromwellian spy over the last five years?"

"There is no one among the gentlemen here, apart from Lord Edwin, who has had any military experience. The rest of them were too old or fled overseas to avoid fighting for the late King. No wonder we lost. He never had effective forces in this area—and Parliament's London militia was too strong and too close in any case," answered Lionel with a touch of bitterness.

"You fought yourself?" asked Luke.

"I was a musketeer for the King, but I was wounded at Edgehill."

"We probably fought each other. I was a young captain of cavalry for Parliament having just returned from the Dutch Republic. Lord Edwin may have been a soldier, but does he know anything about explosives?"

"He certainly does. That was his specialty in the French army— digging under Spanish defenses in the Netherlands, and exploding bombs that would destroy their walls and buildings," replied Lionel with some authority.

"How do you know this?"

"A few months ago as the republican government collapsed, and various groups of the army began fighting each other, the Earl called a muster of tenants and workers. Lord Edwin who acts as a deputy lord lieutenant took us all to the estate's armory and explained the types of weapons and forms of ammunition. He discussed in detail modifying mortars to make the sort of bomb that nearly killed you. He showed us how to covert mortar bombs and grenades into explosives that could be detonated by a burning fuse."

"Valuable information, but it doesn't solve my problem. Edwin was one of those along with myself who could have been blown up, " replied a frustrated Luke.

"All is not lost, Colonel. There is no doubt that Edwin prepared those bombs. They were probably the ones he demonstrated to us at the muster. He could have also placed them in the cellars, perhaps at the behest of Lord Ranald in case the manor was attacked by renegade soldiers or religious fanatics," said Bryan.

"And somebody who knew of this simply had to light the fuse," added Lionel.

"A possibility! It alters my whole outlook on the scene. A woman could light a fuse or two—and women were seen in the area," said an impressed Luke.

"In that case you were not the object of the attack Colonel. If it was a woman she would be out to kill Lord Edwin. Some think he is a serial killer, who murdered more than one woman in his life—and up to now has got away with it."

Luke sensed that both men were uncomfortable discussing the alleged misogynistic and possibly murderous activities of their neighboring aristocrat, but he had one last question on the matter.

What does the Earl think of Lord Edwin?"

"A bad influence on Lord Ranald. Lord Edwin is only here because the Earl and Edwin's father are close. The Viscount hopes that the Earl and Ranald might be a good influence on his wayward son," answered Lionel.

"What is the popular view of Julius's death ?"

"There were a lot of us about at that time on a summer morning and we all claim Julius never made it to the Abbey, although he was seen by a couple of laborers walking towards the gatehouse. Julius was not the person who created enemies, so I could not see why anyone would murder him. Although recent rumors suggest all was not well within his family. If any of them had killed him they must have had little time to achieve their end and get away. No, most of us think it was an accident, " said Lionel.

"And it was probably not the dogs that had escaped from the Leighs. Some people saw a large pack of feral dogs, quite separate from the three or four Leigh estate dogs. I heard that the Leigh dogs had already been fed by several passers-by as an act of self-preservation. What the other dogs did to Julius, suggest these attackers were still ravenous," added Bryan.

"So the general opinion around the estate is that Julius was attacked by dogs? What about my last question? Who among those within the royalist hierarchy of this county spied for Cromwell according to the Earl's workers?"

"Are you serious about that enquiry? People know you were one of Cromwell's top intelligence agents. Surely you knew who acted for you here?" probed Bryan.

"I was in military intelligence, and had no knowledge of the spymaster-general, John Thurloe's agent. Even he did not know the true identity of this spy. He or she was known as Exodus."

"This was during the last five years of the republican government?" continued Bryan.

"Yes"

"The only event that occurred five years ago that disrupted the local community was the return of Lord Ranald followed very quickly by his arranged marriage to Lady Caroline and what amounted to their expulsion from Medlowe Abbey to a smaller manor house several miles away," answered Lionel.

"Are you suggesting that Ranald or his wife was the agent?"

"Not necessarily, but their arrival could have upset someone so much that they turned to the republican government to exact revenge," replied Lionel.

"I don't think their arrival upset anybody. It was a different matter when they moved into Medlowe Abbey on the illness of the Earl. Lady Caroline very quickly became a popular figure to the chagrin of some of the previously dominant ladies," said Bryan.

"And the arrival of her cousin, Reginald, Lord Vaughan certainly put many noses out of joint. He was a bumptious north country peer who came to stay with his cousin, until the King had set up apartments for him as one of the Gentlemen of the Bedchamber. In a short time he usurped many of Lord Ranald's activities," said Lionel.

"Including satisfying his wife," added Bryan cheekily.

"He was sleeping with his cousin?" asked a dubious Luke.

"They certainly did not behave like cousins. They appeared very close and did not seem to care who noticed their intimacy," answered Lionel.

"Ranald must have been furious?"

"He seemed more concerned that Lord Vaughan was interfering in the one area in which Lord Ranald excels—his understanding and treatment of cattle. Lord Vaughan believed that we southerners could learn a lot from the north and did not hesitate to make those views known throughout the estate," explained Bryan.

"Surely Lord Ranald could have asked Vaughan to move on?"

"Vaughan was to become a courtier of the King, and his lordship did not wish to upset the King, at the very time he himself is attempting to gain influence or preferment," was Lionel's considered response.

"Back to my question, who was the Cromwellian spy?"

Lionel, the head coachman remained quiet for some time and then said, "I have absolutely no direct evidence, but my guess is Sir Job."

"But he has been described to me as the most aggressive Royalist in the county during the King's exile."

"Precisely, what Elliott did from time to time constantly put all of us at risk. Many a time we have driven the Earl to Elliott's so that the master could reprimand him. No one could have been so silly to do what he did at the time he attempted it—yet apart from being brought into line by the Earl, Elliott suffered no punishment, let alone investigation by government officials. Maybe because he was one of them," suggested Lionel.

"I heard he was not punished because of the good relations between the Earl and the government's top man in the county, Sir Septimus Ingle."

"That would have made a convenient cover for protecting Elliott's identity, and continued freedom to act overtly against the government, and covertly for it," concluded Bryan.

Three days later, Luke received a message from Lionel. While drinking at The Blue Dog, a shepherd from an estate some miles to the west had mentioned to him that two days earlier they shot a pack of eight feral dogs that had been living on the waste lands, and conducting fatal forays on the sheep. They had also attacked a number of shepherds and herdsmen.

Luke informed Jane and Mark of this and together they decided to end the investigation into the death of Sir Julius Petty. He had died of misadventure being fatally savaged by a pack of feral dogs.

22

Luke would now concentrate on the bombing, and seek further details from Edwin. He accosted the aristocrat as they both left the rectory after an early afternoon meal. They sat down again at one of the empty tables and Luke commented, "You were a military engineer in the Netherlands, an expert on creating the very explosives that nearly killed both of us?"

"Yes, and I created the very ones that exploded. I converted several mortar bombs during a demonstration for the last muster."

"And placed them conveniently in the coal cellar?"

Edwin hesitated and then confessed. "Yes. I did place them there."

"Why?"

"During the early part of the civil wars the Earl had explosives laid throughout the lowest floors so that should the Abbey be attacked by Parliamentary forces, he had the option of destroying it rather than allow it to fall into enemy hands. They remain in place today but with much reduced potency as the Earl now wishes simply to discourage intruders not demolish his house. As the ninepin alley was a new creation Ranald thought the coal cellar was a good place to place the new bombs I had created from the muster."

"Did you attach fuses to them?"

"No, whoever exploded them provided their own fuses."

"So, a woman could have attached the fuses and lit them?"

"A child could do it."

"If it was a woman, the general opinion is that the bomber was out to kill your lordship."

"I will not incriminate myself, so I will not discuss any allegations concerning my treatment of women. The Protector had a warrant out for my arrest which prevented me returning to England until it lapsed."

"I have no wish to infringe your legal rights, but are there any women currently at the Abbey who might want to kill you?"

"No, if there were women out to have me killed, none of them are here. And they would have done it years ago."

"Let me go through the list of the women who are here. How do you react to them to them."

"Veronica Petty."

"Since returning to England I have not met her until this gathering. I was well aware that she was opposed to what Ranald and I were hoping to achieve here, but I cannot see such a conservative and traditional gentlewoman trying to murder anybody."

"Elspeth Kemp."

"A very sensuous woman, who has not rejected my advances."

"Lucy Finch."

"My sister, she hates me, but in the end our blood relationship would calm any murderous impulses."

"Charity Elliott."

"Never met her before this gathering. She stayed here for the course of the war, and I was on the continent."

"The Ramsden sisters."

"They were part of the King's and Ranald's early group of courtiers. I was never part of that group having joined the French army. Of all the women you named, I have not had the opportunity to provoke any of them to murder."

"What about two women who are not here at the moment, but have a close association with the Abbey—Ursula Hall and Caroline Medlowe?"

"I had never met Ursula Hall until a fortnight ago, when Ranald asked her to look at his cattle. Caroline and I detest each other. She thinks I am a poor influence on her husband and has turned the old Earl against me."

"Why is she so opposed to you?"

"At first I thought it was my lifestyle which she did not want her husband to emulate. Now I think it is the reverse. She is not the faithful, modest wife that one would expect from the future countess. I have been warning Ranald that the big noting Lord Vaughan who left here just before you arrived is not her cousin, but her lover. But I do not believe she would go as far as to try to blow up her husband, even if it did have the additional bonus of getting rid of me, and of her unwelcome interrogator, yourself."

"Then who would try to get rid of Ranald?"

"If Ranald was the target there is one obvious suspect, Elspeth Kemp. Ranald is quite rightly challenging her claim to be his illegitimate sister, and even if he concedes that, in rejecting her right to any part of the Earl's inheritance. We aristocrats, unlike the monarch, cannot and must not recognize our bastards."

At that moment a servant entered the refectory to clear away the dishes. As he came near the table at which the two gentlemen were seating Edwin picked up a wooden platter, hurled it at the servant. He followed up with a torrent of meaningless abuse.

Luke was momentarily surprised, and then concerned. Edwin was having what appeared to be a mild fit. Then after a few minutes he appeared semi-conscious and Luke had to jump to his feet to prevent Edwin falling backwards off the bench. Luke grabbed a jug of strong spirits from one of the tables and poured Edwin a small glass and made sure he drank it. For some time Edwin remained confused and babbled on incoherently. Luke helped him to his feet and guided him to his apartment. The door was opened by his valet who asked "His lordship has had another turn? That is the second this week." Luke helped the valet half carry half drag Edwin to his bedchamber.

After Edwin was in his bed and asleep Luke asked the valet, "What form does his lordship's turns usually take?"

"Irrational behavior, unconsciousness, incoherent speech and then a deep sleep. And then there is the almost invisible turn, often difficult to detect when his lordship becomes a different personality, and behaves in ways that one would not expect."

As Luke made his way back to his lodgings he recalled Lady Caroline's comments regarding Edwin. Did Edwin recall what this other personality did? Perhaps it was Edwin who had been bewitched?"

Luke was more than ever convinced that the bomb was meant for Ranald, Edwin, Piers or Alexander. Edwin had made a good case that if the bomber was a woman, none of the current residents at Medlowe Abbey had a grievance against him, except his sister. In Ranald's case Elspeth stood out as the most likely possibility, and as for Alexander, Luke thought his leaving just before the explosion suggested he was more likely in league with the bomber than a target. The late attempt to trap Piers did suggest that Winston might be the culprit, yet he was trying desperately to join the establishment, not destroy it. Or was he?

Given the rumors circulating of perhaps illegal deposits of valuable objects in the Medlowe Abbey infectious cattle pit and the burst of fine weather, Luke ordered a unit of the troops to dig a series of small pits in the four corners and the center of the larger pit.

Luke and Mark supervised the operation, preventing any of the inhabitants or employees of the Abbey from coming anywhere near the activities. Almost immediately the barely decomposed body of an animal was unearthed. It was not cattle. It was a horse. It had been a magnificent animal with quite distinct markings.

Luke left the site and walked quickly to the coach house. He found Lionel and asked if he was aware of any horses with the markings he described. "I am not quite sure what you are describing Colonel. If I saw them in the flesh I might have a better idea."

The coachman accompanied Luke back to the digging site and immediately inspected the unearthed horse. There was an immediate sigh of concern. Lionel turned to Luke. "I would recognize this horse anywhere. Most people in the county would know it. It was the favorite steed of the Cromwellian magistrate who ran the county, but was nevertheless a friend and constant visitor to the Earl. This is Loyalty, a horse of the missing Sir Septimus Ingle."

Luke immediately reorganized the dig. The whole of the top layers of the pit would be removed. His men would now start at one end, in a line that stretched across the width of the pit, and slowly work their way along its length. There was a temporary delay as they waited for wooden planks on which they would stand to avoid sinking into the quagmire of rotting flesh.

Luke sent an urgent message to Wilfred Mills to join him immediately as they had evidence regarding Sir Septimus Ingle. Wilfred arrived within the hour and verified that the horse that had been unearthed was indeed that of Sir Septimus. Another hour of painstaking digging revealed nothing but the decomposing bodies of infected cattle. Luke's men were becoming restless. They all knew terrible diseases were transmitted through foul air. Thoughts of a possible mutiny were suddenly sidetracked at least momentarily when there was a shout from one of the diggers.

"The first of bodies I expected," mused Wilfred.

He was wrong. The officers were dismayed as the men slowly unearthed and carried to the edge of the pit three large chests. Luke prized them open and announced, "They contain no treasure and no bodies. The first is crammed with muskets, the second chest with gunpowder and the third with shot."

"Who would hide arms and ammunition in this pit? It makes no sense," said Wilfred.

"What happened to the Republic's arsenal for the county?" asked Luke.

"That was located at Ingle's, and I personally supervised its transfer to the arsenal here," answered Wilfred.

"We have a problem. The new government's arsenal is here at the Abbey, but someone has hidden a large cache of weapons and ammunition in the pit. Who is currently awaiting the opportunity to rise against the government of the King?"

"Only the religious fanatics—Quakers, and Fifth Monarchy Men," said Mark.

"And the Papists. Some of them may have believed the falsehoods that all the Stuarts had converted to Roman Catholicism, and now that they see that this is not true, they are unhappy," added Wilfred.

"It must have been intended as a short term burial. Even in the chests the arsenal would deteriorate very quickly."

"It may have been intended for use over the last months before the King could establish his control firmly on the county. Maybe the quarantine and the resultant guards around the perimeter prevented it being recovered when it was needed."

The digging was resumed. After another half hour another cry went up.

Very carefully the diggers unearthed body after body. Males dressed in their underwear, all shot countless times in the chest. Decomposition varied, but Wilfred identified them as Sir Septimus' body guard.

"None of these corpses are Septimus himself? asked Luke.

"No, Septimus was a big man. None of these bodies are above average height. We may yet find him."

They didn't.

No more bodies were found but at the far edge of the pit just below the surface the diggers discovered several canvas bags stacked with silver plate and candle sticks.

"Looks as if one of the servants has purloined some of the Earl's silver and has been unable to get it out of the Abbey because of the quarantine."

Luke, Mark and Wilfred mulled over the result of the day's dig.

"The horse and the bodies of the London militia bodyguard were obviously buried by that group of masked horsemen who clearly kidnapped or killed Septimus, and was led possibly by Job Elliott or one of our aristocrats. But the buried arsenal does not seem to fit their profile. Where did that stockpile come from and what was its intended use? The royalist gentry already have access to all the weapons and ammunition they needed in the Abbey's arsenal," Luke concluded.

"It may belong to a gang of brigands and have nothing to do with the gentry of this county," added Mark.

"Maybe it belongs to gunrunners ready to sell to the highest bidder. They may be waiting for customers, before they recover the arms and ammunition," suggested Wilfred.

Luke changed the topic and asked, "Does Sir Septimus Ingle still live? He may be safer in the hands of brigands, than a prisoner of political opponents. The fact that we have not received any ransom demands is however worrying,"

uke was feeling good. Julius's death was a misadventure created by
feral dogs. The bomber, probably Elspeth was after Ranald, and
the Cromwellian spy was either Caroline or Job. Ingle have been
kidnapped by out of county horsemen led by a local, which could have
been Job, Ranald or Edwin.

The inhabitants of the pest houses had been freed, apart from Elliott's
servants whose condition had worsened. No one else appeared infected.
The King continued to supervise the nursing and care of the Earl of
Medlowe at Whitehall.

Overall in investigating these and associated matters, Luke had
obtained an excellent insight into the local royalist gentry and aristocrats—
the subject of his imminent report to the King.

The behavior of three women immediately shattered Luke's good
humor.

The first entered his consciousness subliminally, and he was slow to
register its import. He was taking an early morning walk up to the gatehouse
when he noticed an unusually large herd of cattle in the adjacent field. Several
cowherds were spread out across the field while a well-dressed gentlewoman
held the head of one of beasts and appeared to be whispering in its ear.

Luke approached one of the cowherds seeking an explanation. "Sir
there was a minor stampede and the herd was so agitated that some of them
crashed through the hedge. The stock master summoned a well-known
wise woman who had cured and calmed many local cattle over the decades.
She whispers to them, and they calm down. As you can see now the herd
is quite settled."

"Who is this effective wise woman ?" asked Luke.

"Lady Ursula. She is Welsh," stated the cowherd as if her Celtic ethnicity explained everything.

Luke was annoyed. He was not aware that Lady Ursula Hall was on the premises. She certainly did not come with her husband.

Luke immediately asked Ranald, if he knew of her attendance.

"Some of our guests, when they realized they were confined here for forty days were worried about the pregnancy of their wives. Many had used the services of Lady Ursula in the past. Others thought Ursula should be given a chance to talk to some of the gathered elite, to counter what they considered the untrue claims of her husband. Father was very fond of her, and I have used her since she returned from the continent to check on my cattle. She works wonders on them. She arrived here two days ago and is staying with Nathan Petty, but has kept a low profile."

As Luke left Ranald, two thoughts dominated his thinking. Where was Ursula the morning that Julius was attacked? And if an animal whisperer could calm animals down, could they also incite them? Maybe after all the feral dogs that attacked Julius had human encouragement.

The second female intervention was even more dramatic. Luke had only just entered his apartment when a servant announced that Lady Lucy Finch wished to speak to him urgently. "To what do I owe this pleasure, my lady?" asked Luke as he directed Lucy to a large comfortable chair.

"I know who led the band of West country horsemen that probably killed Ingle and buried his horse and soldiers in the infectious animal pit," she announced.

A cautious Luke asked, "Do you really know, or do you just have your suspicions?"

Lucy blushed. "Judge for yourself colonel! That villain was my brother Edwin. My father sent servants to Plymouth to meet Edwin and escort him home. He landed there with a number of his own troops, Englishmen who had fought under him in the French army, and all of them West Country men. While the servants left for Symes Hall with most of his possessions Edwin indicated that he and his unit had one last mission to complete before they disbanded. The timing fits. The group of horsemen who were only temporarily in this county had West Country accents."

Lucy hated her brother, and Luke found it difficult to separate sisterly antagonism from objective discourse. "Why would Edwin who had been away from this county for almost a decade have suddenly ridden here and carried out what may have been a series of murders?"

A truculent Lucy replied, "Ask him!"

Luke did.

He found Edwin half asleep on one of the many garden benches. He was direct. "My lord, I have just been told that you led the posse of hooded horsemen that terrorized this area some weeks ago, and buried some of your victims in the Earl's animal pit."

"The little witch. I did not think she would have the courage to tell you. Perhaps it was part of her seduction technique?"

"You don't deny it?"

"Of course not. What I did was legal, and under the authority of the Lord Lieutenant, The Earl of Medlowe."

"Let me hear your defense—in what sense was it legal?"

"While I was still on the continent, awaiting a ship home I received an urgent letter from the Earl appointing me a deputy lord lieutenant and appealing to me to hasten home as he feared that chaos would overtake the local area between the collapse of the republican government, and the creation of that of the restored King. As the only local landowner with military experience, I was to raise a body of men to maintain law and order here until the new regime had been established. Fortuitously several men I served with in the French army were on the same ship, and I suggested one last mission together."

"And what did your band of marauding horsemen accomplish?"

"Very little, and I almost immediately resigned my role which was then taken up by Job Elliott with a group of locally raised militia."

"So you and your men are innocent of the Ingle massacre?"

"There was no massacre, and Ingle is probably still alive."

"Explain!"

"When I arrived in the county there was no chaos. Law send order had been well maintained by Ingle. Imagine my surprise when one morning we came across Ingle, his wife and a bodyguard of a dozen men leaving the county. I ordered them to stop, assessing that Ingle was escaping the oncoming retribution of the new royalist government. He ignored my command, and a skirmish began during which Ingle and his wife disappeared. The conflict was no massacre. Both sides consisted of experienced soldiers, and the fatality rate was high."

"Surely not one hundred per cent?"

Edwin smiled. "Some men were so badly wounded that it was more humane, to put them out of their pain. Rather than leave evidence of the battle for the county folk to see, we took the bodies away and buried them in the Earl's animal pit. There were considerable casualties among my own men with the dead and wounded taken back by their comrades to the West Country. That is why the unit disappeared so quickly and without trace."

"Your men did not abduct Ingle?"

"No, since that skirmish I have tried to find Ingle, but without success. He too has simply disappeared."

As one soldier to another, Luke found Edwin's explanation convincing, but he was interested in Edwin's assumption regarding the source of his information. "Who did you assume gave me gave this information? Lady Ursula?"

Edwin seemed appalled. "How would Lady Ursula have any such knowledge? I did not know she was anywhere in the area until a few weeks ago when I saw her whispering to some cattle. No, it was the strumpet Bettina, the gatehouse keeper's wife."

Luke ended his discussion with Edwin, and walked straight to the gatehouse to confront Bettina. The scantily dressed woman, all flounce and bounce made clear her desires. "How can I help my colonel?" she purred.

"It has come to my attention that you can prove that Edwin, Lord Symes was the leader of the band of horsemen that buried their victims in the Earl's animal pit."

"I can prove nothing without some incentive," she purred as she revealed her ample breasts.

"My dear Bettina, it is difficult to resist your charms, but I am sure that several pieces of silver is a better reward for your assistance to the King's government, than momentary pleasure. I am intrigued to know how you could recognize the leader of that band of horsemen, when no one else could."

"Simple! On the night concerned, I entertained the leader while his men buried the victims."

"Surely he remained hooded during his time with you?"

"Yes, he did."

"Then how did you recognize him?"

She giggled, "I didn't at the time. It was only during the last few weeks that I knew who he was."

"How?"

"Many of the gentlefolk here, with or without their wives, appear to need regular sexual activity. I have readily offered my services. A few weeks ago Lord Edwin sought my companionship and I immediately recognized his approach to love-making as identical with that of my hooded horseman."

"Did you broach the subject of recognition with his Lordship?"

"Yes, I thought I might receive a regular payment to keep my secret, but Lord Edwin told me to do my worst. Whatever he had done, he claimed he had acted legally."

"You took a big risk Bettina. In similar circumstances I have known threatened males, not only refuse to pay, but take steps to eliminate the would-be blackmailer. While I'm here, and for another silver coin, is there anything else of interest concerning the ladies and gentlemen gathered here, that might help my many investigations?"

"Only it has not been as profitable for me in the last few weeks as in the first fortnight as several of the gentlewomen are making themselves available to persons other than their husbands. They have seriously reduced my income."

"Names?"

"I can't help. I know the names of the males, but not their illicit partners."

"Liar! I should take back my silver coins. You know precisely which women are involved, but whereas it is futile and dangerous to blackmail the males in any of these affairs, the women could easily fall victim to your demands. If I find you murdered over the next week or so I will not have to look far for a motive."

"A poor woman has to make up for lost earnings. Extracting a fee from these superior women who have contributed to my penury is not an immoral act."

"I would have thought the patronage of the elite troops that surround the Abbey would have made up for any losses on the gentlemen within the perimeter of the estate."

"As you would know Colonel, soldiers do not pay as well as gentlemen."

24

Luke had for several weeks avoided the political discussions that occupied most mornings and afternoons. His presence might have inhibited a free and open debate as the rival claimants to various county positions jockeyed for support. After heavy negotiations, horse trading, and apparently perceived double dealing and betrayals, decision time had arrived.

As Luke passed the reception hall in which the meetings were held, he heard a cacophony of catcalls, booing, and rhythmic clapping unusual from the previously staid assembly. He climbed the stairs and made his way into the musicians gallery to observe the commotion.

Ranald had just proposed a list of candidates which he presented as the accepted wish of the county and sought endorsement to forward it to the King for possible appointments, and for the group to proceed with nominations to the various parliamentary seats. As the names were read out a variety of reactions occurred, although negative responses appeared to outnumber the positive.

What was clear to Luke was that the names reflected the interests of the aristocrats and some of the old guard. The younger generation were ignored. As the final name was read the hall broke into uproar. Led by Winston Finch and Alexander Kemp, both of whom rose to their feet, stamped the floor in unison, and jeered derisively, half of the assembled gentry stormed out of the building, declaring proceedings a joke.

Ranald had failed to reach a consensus. But had he even tried? To Luke it appeared that Ranald was determined that the Medlowe interests should continue to dominate—with no concessions to potential rivals.

Finch refused to submit to this attempt by the pre-war ruling group to resurrect their power in a new age, in which new ideas embodied in him and his supporters, were needed. Expanding London should be utilized to the benefit of local landowners, and old alliances with parliamentary and republican neighbors put to an end. Finch led his group into the chapel where they continued their opposition meeting.

Luke heard later that the chapel meeting rebels had produced a rival list.

Luke's attempt to stay above the factional disputes ended early in the afternoon when Sir Winston Finch sought an audience with him. "Colonel, I understand that you are aware that our weeks of meetings have ended in deadlock with roughly half of the group supporting one list of candidates and the other half a rival list."

"Yes, but it is not in my remit to take sides in this dispute."

"I realize that, but how will the King react to this division?"

"I cannot answer for His Majesty, but in many ways two separate lists might lead to more balanced final nominations. The King might choose candidates from both lists, rather than place the future governance of the county in the hands of one faction or another. And for the parliamentary seats a contest between candidates drawn from each list would give the county and borough electors a choice. To be cynical, you are giving the government what they often have to work hard to achieve—a divide and rule situation. Your division would suit any central government," replied a pragmatic Luke.

"I doubt if our division matters. In the end your recommendations will be more important than either of the lists."

"But my recommendations will concern an individual's ability and character rather than his political views, factional allegiance or close associates. And that recommendation will be for the King's eyes only."

"Sir Luke, I trust you have not been swayed by the noise of the county, which in many cases is wrong, prejudiced, and created by vicious villains out to destroy upright men," pleaded Finch.

"This noise of the county was simply described in the old ecclesiastical courts as ill fame, and by most common people as gossip. I will base my assessment on verifiable evidence," declaimed Luke with a tinge of pomposity.

"Since returning from the continent, Lucy and I have been subjected to the most foul of rumors all put about by our host, simply to maintain what he sees as his family's rightful place as the most powerful group in the county," explained Finch.

"Don't worry Sir Winston, I will give you an opportunity to confront these unfavorable rumors before this gathering ends."

Luke had no sooner returned to his apartment when he received a summons from a clearly irritated Ranald. "You have been talking to that knave, Winston Finch?"

"Yes, he consulted me regarding how the King would react to what is happening here. I told him that I could not anticipate the King's reaction, and he warned me that in making my report to His Majesty, I should ignore the lies that have been put out about him."

Luke decided undiplomatically to provoke Ranald into a reaction which may be helpful to his various enquiries. "I am surprised my lord that Finch was able to gain support of almost half the attendees. Of the eight gentlemen who took a lead in the discussion and subsequent negotiations, you only won the support of yourself, Lord Edwin, Nathan and Job. I was surprised that Piers and Phineas were in the rival group."

"Colonel, ignore the quantity of support for each group, look at the quality. My list offers the county elite—the two aristocratic families and the leading traditional gentry leadership of the Pettys. On the other hand Leigh has traditionally opposed the county majority for decades while Finch, Kemp and Piers are relative newcomers with no established roots in the county. Let Finch play his games! They will do him more harm than good."

"Why is Orlando missing from both lists?"

"He refused to pledge his support to either faction."

"It is an omission that the King will need to be briefed on. I will talk to Orlando."

"Don't waste your time! The man is aging fast, and seems to have lost his grasp on the situation. He is obsessed with Roman Catholicism and the behavior of his wife."

Luke left Ranald determined to find out why the key gentlemen engaged in what was developing into a month long talkfest, had committed to one side or the other, and why Orlando appeared on neither list. He would talk to Orlando, Phineas and Piers as soon as possible.

He discussed the issues with Mark and Miles in the gatehouse later that evening. Mark commented, " As you know Luke, I attended most of the sessions over the last few weeks, and nothing that occurred openly in those debates, would have led me to predict the results that emerged today with the rival lists ."

"What surprised you most? "asked Luke.

"That Piers and Phineas appeared on Finch's list and Orlando on neither."

"Any explanation occur to you?"

"Piers' position was determined by his courtship of Charity Elliott, and Job's negative reaction to it. If Ranald stuck with Job, I could see why Piers changed sides. As he is clearly a favorite of the King, his defection is a loss of face for our aristocratic host. Siding with Job over Piers is another example of Ranald's complete lack of political acumen. Phineas' support for the Finch ticket was in political terms at the county level even more serious. Phineas has led the county opposition to the Medlowe interests for decades. He has many lesser gentry associated with him and their support in the parliamentary elections could prove critical."

"And why did Orlando miss out?" asked Miles.

"Did he miss out, or did he refuse to align himself with either party?" answered Mark.

"This must make your task easier," Miles said to Mark and Luke. "You can now probe more deeply into the political views of these gentlemen and assess their loyalty to the King and their ability to serve him at the county level."

"That won't be easy. The two groupings reflect personal rather than political issues. There are supporters and opponents of an expanding London on both lists, as there are hardliners concerning the treatment of former republican officials. And there does not appear to be a consistent religious position in either camp," replied Mark.

"This nevertheless is our chance to probe the potential loyalty and efficiency of the current inhabitants of Medlowe Abbey for royal service. I will start with Orlando," concluded Luke.

Next morning Luke visited him. "Is your absence from either list your choice, or have you been rejected by both factions?"

"I was unacceptable to the young aristocrats. In the first place I wanted Ranald to guarantee some part of an inheritance for his half-sister Elspeth, and secondly I made clear that if elected to Parliament I would want all Roman Catholic peers ejected from the House of Lords. Their lordships claimed this would be an unconstitutional interference by the House of Commons in the affairs of the Lords. As for Finch., the man's reputation for corruption made it impossible for me to become his associate, while some of his group particularly Phineas are too tolerant of Catholics and Nonconformists. If you speak to the King, tell him that I alone of all the gentlemen gathered here, demand a purified Church of England, as was in the days of his blessed father and Archbishop Laud. My demand that all dissenters be immediately expelled from any livings was also not well received."

"Did any of the decisions of the meetings surprise you?"

"Yes, I do not know why Lord Ranald retained on his list that embarrassment, Job Elliott. Elliott acted stupidly during the King's exile, and there is no sign he has altered his ways. And Alexander Kemp—he is an imposter that has no right to the inheritance on which his rise to influence in this county is based."

"Do you have any evidence for this, other than that he has a Scots name yet speaks with a local accent?" asked Luke.

"Talk to my adopted daughter, his wife, Elspeth!"

"Any other surprises?"

"The ease in which Phineas outmaneuvered Ranald yesterday, and is now in the process of replacing Finch as leader of the anti-Medlowe faction."

"Phineas rather than Finch is the real leader of this anti-Medlowe coup?"

"Yes. As we speak Finch will realize he was simply a front man for the shrewd old politician. Phineas gave him initial support to embarrass Ranald and the Medlowe interest."

"How did he achieve it? He was in the pest house for much of his time here?"

"In the absence of Petty, he had most of the lower gentry who stayed in England during the exile in his camp and managed to split those who went into exile cleverly between the arrogant aristocrats and the corrupt and trimming newcomers. It was all helped by lots of London money. He did not go to London before this meeting to discuss comets with the astronomers. He went to raise money for his political campaign. It may have been originally intended to be in alliance with Petty, which may have been ruptured by Julius's attack on his wife, Phineas's sister."

"Surely Finch will not sit back and allow a group he had carefully put together, be taken over by another?"

"And Phineas is not someone who would show his hand, unless he was absolutely certain of his position. The silent majority of the gentry are not impressed by aristocratic machinations on the one hand, nor the corruption of people like Finch on the other. And unfortunately most have put self-interest above the interests of our true English church and those of the returning King."

25

Next morning Luke was surprised to hear a cornet blast from the vicinity of the gatehouse. The veteran soldier recognized it as a summons to be battle ready. He ran to the gatehouse and confronted Miles, "Why the alarm?"

"Look up the road, Colonel."

A group of some thirty horsemen appeared on the horizon heading in the direction of Medlowe Abbey. "I did not expect this display of force by either side. Maybe it's an attempt to break the deadlock. I will assume command of our defenses."

As the group came nearer it appeared to be a motley collection of farmers and laborers rather than an experienced military force. Luke dismounted from his horse and walked along the road to greet the group obstructing their advance. "I am Colonel Tremayne, commander of a unit of the King's dragoons. What is your intention?"

The leading horseman answered, "We are tenants and workers on the estates of Sir Nathan Petty. We received a summons last night that our master and his mother Lady Veronica were in danger. We have come to ensure their safety."

"My good man, your master and his mother are in no danger. Law and order is maintained on this estate by the King's own dragoons, and secondly this is a plague designated area. The King has ordered that no one should enter or leave the Abbey estate until the quarantine period expires, which has about seven to ten days left. Return home! I will inform Sir Nathan that you answered his request."

"No colonel, we stay until Sir Nathan personally rescinds his request."

Luke replied with a mixture of forcefulness and diplomacy. "My good man, I understand your loyalty to your new young master and his mother. To be blunt your group are solid farmers and laborers. There is hardly a man of military bearing among you. My men are battle tried veterans who, if I raise my hand and bring it down suddenly, would wipe you out . Nevertheless I will send for Sir Nathan. Meanwhile move your men into the field on the left of the road and dismount."

The group followed Luke's instructions while he returned to his men and addressed Miles. "Send someone to fetch Sir Nathan, and a fast courier to Whitehall, to request a company of cavalry. If you look to the hills on the east there is another group of horsemen headed this way. Tell Ashcroft that we need them to prevent a forcible breach of quarantine, and a major outbreak of civil unrest."

As the second group hove into sight, Luke became alarmed. It consisted of a number of well-armed men who had the bearing of experienced soldiers. To Luke's dismay he recognized its leader. It was the former republican commander of the militia, and Luke's recent adviser, Sir Wilfred Mills."

Luke rode out alone to meet the second contingent some distance from the gatehouse. "What's this about Captain Mills?" he asked formally.

"We are the tenants and retainers of Sir Phineas Leigh and his many supporters. There are more of us headed this way."

"And what exactly do you hope to achieve?"

"Sir Phineas has been very successful at the meeting, but there is a possibility that malcontents will not accept the decisions made in his favor. We are here to ensure that the free decision of gentlemen gathered at Medlowe Abbey, are not overturned by force."

"My dragoons are sufficient to maintain law and order, especially with the imminent arrival of a detachment of royal cavalry. How is it that the former commander of the Cromwellian militia in the county is leading this group of royalists?" asked Miles.

"Sir Phineas has a moderate attitude to former republican and Cromwellian tenants and neighbors. There are several of us here, mostly former soldiers in Parliament's New Model army. I had the senior rank."

"I cannot allow your group into the Abbey. I have confined a rival collection of Petty supporters into a neighboring field. Do you intend to stay and do you wish to talk to Sir Phineas?"

"We are staying—but I do not need to see Sir Phineas. My instructions are to camp near the Abbey and be ready if needed. Treat us as an auxiliary company should you need support in subduing the Petty group or any other armed force that might emerge. We could take over the external defense of the Abbey from your men, who could withdraw into the Abbey to personally protect all the participants. The King would not want his dragoons involved in any battle against local gentry and their supporters," Mills concluded undiplomatically.

"I, also, would prefer the local gentry to fight it out amongst themselves, rather than involve the King's men, yet to maintain the King's peace we may have to get involved. Get your men to camp in the field to my right. Meet me in the gatehouse around noon! By then your rivals may have disbanded."

Luke returned to the gatehouse just as Nathan arrived. He was irritated by being summoned on the orders of the former Cromwellian officer. "What is the meaning of this, Colonel?"

"That is the very question I was about to ask you. You have summoned your associates and retainers to invade the Abbey by force to impose the will of Ranald and yourself on the rest of us. That is a clear breach of the common peace, and I will have you in The Tower unless you come up with an acceptable explanation."

Nathan looked confused. Luke pointed out some thirty horsemen whose leader turned out to be Sir Nathan's steward who approached to talk to his master.

Nathan, either to defend himself, or from genuine surprise asked, "Why are you here, Bancroft?"

"A young lad brought a message to me last night that you and the Lady Veronica were in great danger, and added protection was urgently required as a group of malcontents at the Abbey were about to resort to violence to get their way."

Luke intervened, "That so called group of malcontents is now led by your uncle and Lady Veronica's brother, Sir Phineas. He is unlikely to use force against such close relatives."

Nathan stunned both his steward and Luke. "I did not send any boy with any message. You have been summoned here by persons unknown, who wish to embarrass me, and destroy my credibility."

"Do you have any suspects?"

"That nefarious knave, Finch."

"What would be his motive? You are openly in different camps. What would he have to gain? Order your steward to return your men to their homes, and my soon to be reinforced troops will monitor your uncle's larger and better trained group of supporters that have encamped apparently for the duration of the meeting in one of the fields. Any conflict between the two groups would lead to the massacre of your men, Sir Nathan."

"Perhaps that is what Finch hoped would happen," he replied.

Nathan left after ordering his steward and his men to return to their homes.

Miles stood his men down.

Luke next received Wilfred Mills.

"I see you have dispersed the Petty contingent," he commented.

"Quite strange. Nathan claims he never sent a message requiring armed assistance."

"Who does he think did so?"

"He claims Finch did it to discredit him."

"It is more likely that Petty's allies did it to give themselves some support, without leaving themselves open to a breach of the peace. I suspect one of the aristocrats."

"Interesting speculation. I am about to chat to Phineas, is there any message you wish me to convey?"

"No Luke, other than to inform him that we are encamped outside the manor, awaiting any instructions he might have."

Luke was well received by Phineas who commented only half in jest, "I trust the military are not interfering in the give and take of county politics?"

"Only so far as to prevent any breach of the peace which looked likely an hour ago."

"My men will not create a breach of the peace. I sent for them to provide you with assistance should my defeated rivals try by violence to undo the victory I have almost achieved. Whose retainers did you send packing as my men arrived?"

"Those of your sister and nephew."

"I did not think the boy had it in him."

"He probably didn't. He denies calling on them to ride here this morning."

"Then it was most likely my sister. It was she who kept the Petty interests allied with the Medlowes at the top of the tree for decades."

"There have been suggestions that it may have been one of your group trying to discredit him, or one of the Medlowe team who thought they needed help, but did not want to be seen in what could be construed as a breach of the peace."

"Both possibilities. Why in particular have you called on me at this crucial time?"

"To congratulate you. After decades of taking second place in the county you seem to have emerged as the most powerful figure as a result of this meeting."

"A little premature Colonel! There is still much to be done to consolidate my position. That is why the less involved the army becomes, the better for my progress."

"What still needs to be done?"

"I am not going to reveal my hand until I am more certain of the situation."

"If I am to keep my investigations and the army out of your way, I need to know the areas you suggest I avoid over the next few days."

"Suffice to say I am working on winning over some members of the Medlowe group, and removing a name or two from my list."

"How did you emerge triumphant not only against the Medlowes, but seizing leadership of the opposition from Finch?"

"Finch did not realize that the bulk of his initial support came from my supporters. I simply let him lead the attack on the Medlowes."

The discussion halted at the sound of the cornet once again emanating from near the gatehouse.

"I trust your men, Phineas, have not done something silly?"

"Captain Mills is well aware of what he can or cannot do without provoking your men."

Luke and Phineas strode to the gatehouse where Miles informed them of a couple of groups of horsemen on the eastern horizon, who appeared to confronting each other, and another larger group coming up the London Road.

Luke was jubilant. "Stand down your men, Miles! The group coming up the London Road are the royal cavalry I sent for. I will immediately send them to break up the potential conflict to the east. Any trouble from Mills and the Phineas cohort?"

"No, I have invited the officers to dine with me in the gatehouse. Would you like to join us?"

"No, Sir Winston Finch deserves my immediate attention."

26

Luke's plan to question Finch was put on hold. He had no sooner returned to his apartment when Jane burst in.

"Luke, you have a major problem. A battered and disoriented Elspeth was found in her room by one of the servants. She is passing in and out of consciousness, but was able to say that her husband Alex had to be stopped. He was about to kill someone."

"Did Alex catch his wife with someone, justly punished her and now seeks to deal with her lover?—all matters of honor that does not require my intervention," commented Luke.

"You do not know that. Alex may have embarked on an unprovoked bout of violence. Hitting his innocent wife, and now seeking to punish a possible innocent companion. Rumors spread rapidly in this environment. You cannot stand by and allow what might be a cold blooded murder to occur. Or for that matter a series of murders—Alex could be out to kill all those who may or may not have slept with his wife—and there are so many," pleaded Jane.

"Return to Elspeth, and let me know as soon as she can be questioned! I will catch Mark before he goes off to the meeting and ask him to inform the assembly that one of their number has gone berserk, and is about to kill one or more of them. That should add a bit of spice to proceedings," said Luke.

"What else will you do?"

"I will have Miles send most of his men into the Abbey to protect the guests individually. The newly arrived cavalry can take over the defense of the perimeter. Ranald's steward can organize a search of the estate for the elusive Mr. Kemp. I'll meet you in Elspeth's rooms in about half an hour."

Luke was soon in the office of Medlowe Abbey's elderly but efficient and almost invisible steward, Dr Hector Gregory. He was a lawyer and a schoolboy friend of Algernon, Earl of Medlowe. It was Hector rather than Ranald that kept the complex estate, and the additional burden of a major and prolonged meeting running smoothly.

Hector was appalled at the assault on Elspeth but implied that her lifestyle may have provoked it. "I do not know why the Earl allowed that girl to marry an almost unknown stranger. She was very willful. Orlando never stood up to her. She is very spoilt by the men in her life."

"I have heard Kemp is an imposter, is that true? That could be relevant."

"The Earl was about to investigate that just before he was taken ill."

"What exactly do you know about Kemp?"

"I'll answer your question in a few minutes. Let me organize a search of the estate for Kemp. My bailiff will co-ordinate his efforts with your military commander Captain Oxenbridge."

Luke agreed to return in half an hour. In the interim he would question the Kemp servants.

Alexander's valet, had also been assaulted. He had large lump on the back of his head and was still being attended to by Jane. Elspeth's lady's maid sat traumatized in a large chair, while Elspeth herself was still abed receiving herbal medication from Ursula.

Luke asked Ursula for an update on Elspeth's condition.

"As far as I can tell she has received several blows to various parts of her body and I have applied ointment to the developing bruises. I have not been able to speak to her to ascertain where she is suffering pain, or to discover what exactly happened. As you can see she is barely conscious."

Luke turned to the valet, "What happened here? Your master has fled, your mistress remains unconscious, and your fellow servant is traumatized."

"Colonel, I can only recall part of what happened as I was out to it for some time. About two hours ago master and mistress were abed when there was a knock on the door and a woman's voice sought entry. The door burst open and two men and woman all wearing masks entered. I tried to stop them but was punched in the face by one intruder, and as I spun around the other hit me from behind. When I came to, I feigned unconsciousness, as one of the men harangued the mistress. She and her husband were ordered to leave the manor immediately. They were undesirables that brought disgrace upon the respectable members of the community. Mistress was defiant and asked what would happen if they didn't. The woman who concealed her features and clothing beneath a large cape signaled to one of her men who responded by punching Mistress Elspeth in the face. This was too much for the master who threw himself at the assailant. I rose to my feet and threw myself at the other intruder. The lady signaled her brutal companions and all three left as quietly and as quickly as they had arrived. Mr Alex asked me to fetch Lady Jane as Mistress Elspeth did not appear to be breathing."

"Did Mr. Alex threaten to kill someone?"

"Not exactly. He said he knew what it was about, and he would get his revenge. He left instructions for looking after Elspeth, and said he would disappear for a while."

"Was he armed?" interrupted the anxious Jane.

"Yes, he had two pistols in addition to his sword and a Scottish dirk."

"Did you recognize the intruders?"

"No, the men were obviously rough retainers, but the woman was by her bearing and clothing a gentlewoman."

"That is what I find intriguing. Why would a gentle woman with a grievance against Mistress Elspeth risk being recognized? She could have simply hired those ruffians to beat up the Kemps, and be well away from the assault. It suggests a very personal motivation."

Luke returned to Hector Gregory who listened intently as he was informed of what the Colonel had just heard. Luke asked, "You have been steward here for decades and have known Elspeth all her life, and Alex since he came into the county. What do you think is behind this vicious attempt at intimidation?"

"I am afraid any investigation could open a Pandora's Box. Most households have deeply hidden secrets."

"Where do you suggest I start?"

"Who have the couple upset? In the first place Elspeth's determination to obtain part of the Medlowe inheritance has infuriated young master Ranald, but he would only have to wait until the death of his father, and he could legally put an end to her claim. I cannot see him using such physical tactics, which if the Earl was informed might lead to increased generosity towards Elspeth. I discussed this very issue with Ranald. Elspeth as a bastard has no legal claims whatever. The old Earl should give her a gift now and settle the matter."

"And Alex upset the Symes family?"

"Yes, when Lord Edwin married his child bride, she brought to the family an immense dowry of estates. On her death, to the Symes's surprise, a considerable portion of those lands did not remain with the husband, but devolved to the nearest male relative of her mother. After a time Alex Kemp emerged to claim them but immediately the Symes's denounced him as an imposter. Unfortunately the key participants in the transactions were killed in the civil war as were most of the Kemp relatives. The Symes have continually tried to undermine Alexander's standing in the county, although he has done little to help himself. A third possibility is simply a rival gentleman who does not approve of Kemp's apparent rise to some influence—and who has been jolted into action by Kemp's appearance on the Leigh ticket. He has alienated many people over the past few years. And finally given the involvement of a woman, it may be a cuckolded gentlewoman, whose husband has been seduced by the over generous Elspeth. You, Colonel are the renowned sleuth, but this will not be easy to unravel."

"We must find Alex. He does not appear to have threatened any named individual as the first reports suggested. He simply stated he thought he knew what was behind the attack and has gone into hiding. Whether this was to save himself from further attack, or simply to give himself time to plan his revenge is impossible to ascertain."

"Don't take any risks. He may be better armed than you think. I just received a report that the arsenal had been broken into and a musket and ammunition stolen. With a musket he could pick off his target from a number of sheltered positions," explained the methodical Hector.

"Is the manor full of secret tunnels that lead to positions in the forest or any of the outhouses?" asked an increasingly anxious Luke.

"Yes, there are several, but Alex would not be aware of them. Neither he nor Elspeth have spent any time here until this meeting."

A servant interrupted the discussion to inform the steward that a unit of soldiers had located Alex's tracks in Medlowe Woods and were following him. They required further instructions.

Luke acted. "I will take over the unit—and bring Alex in."

The soldiers were relieved that the colonel had taken control. Their corporal confessed that he were not sure that their quarry was indeed Alexander Kemp. "Our only evidence is that one of the regular poachers told me that a gentleman from the manor armed with a musket had entered the woods. I picked up a trail of broken branches and crushed grass by someone avoiding the designated pathways through the forest."

"Well done! I learnt to track from the American Indians a decade ago, but you have done very well."

"By the damage that he is doing, I suspect he does not know where he is going. He is looking for a place to hide," suggested the corporal.

"I know the poacher whom you have mentioned—Little Johnny. Have one of your men inform Captain Oxenbridge of developments and have him bring Johnny here as soon as possible. He should know every possible hiding place on the estate. For the moment make a lot of noise. This might lead our quarry to take temporary precautions and stay put until he is sure we are on our way."

Luke's plan seemed to be working as Alex appeared to be moving slowly in a circle and not progressing far—or fast.

Little Johnny arrived and explained that there were only two small caves and two woodcutter's hovels within the wood that would offer a fugitive any comfort. He suggested that if he was the quarry he would avoid all of these places and when evening fell should simply cover himself with bracken.

Luke dismissed his troops apart from their corporal. They were to make a big noise as they left the woods, hoping to lull Alex into a false sense of security. Meanwhile Luke, the poacher and the corporal would stake out each of the possible hiding places.

Led by Johnny the two soldiers moved silently through the woods and eventually heard someone blustering their way through the undergrowth. The poacher observed, "He has seen one of the shacks. He won't be able to resist it."

Luke sent Johnny and the corporal to the back of the shack while he strode out into the clearing in front of the ramshackle building and gently asked, "Alex, this is Luke Tremayne! Your hiding place is surrounded. Please come out and lay your musket on the ground. We are not here to arrest you, but to put you into protective custody, until we can get to the bottom of the assault on you and your wife."

There was absolute silence and then in what surprised Luke a strained voice in a broad Scottish accent shouted, "I am coming out."

Alex emerged, placed his musket on the ground and revealed both his hands to Luke indicating that his pistols were not in play. Luke moved forward and gave Alex a hug and commented, "You are a Scot who has trained himself to lose the accent, except when under stress."

Suddenly the silence of the woods was shattered by a burst of concentrated fire. Luke and Alex both fell to the ground—apparently dead. The corporal sent Johnny off to raise the alarm and get assistance, as he stood guard over the two bodies.

The news spread quickly. The King's representative Colonel Tremayne had been shot dead trying to apprehend Alexander Kemp.

Mark took charge, and had both bodies taken to what had been the pest house occupied earlier by Phineas and Job. He sent to Whitehall for two army surgeons, placed a cordon of troops around the cottage, and permitted only one visitor Jane, Marchioness of Nith.

Jane was greatly relieved and pleasantly surprised to find Luke sitting up in bed issuing orders, and anxious to discuss the developing situation with his officers. "The whole Abbey thinks you are dead," she murmured.

"Yes, when shots were fired at us, I fell to the ground pulling Kemp with me. I whispered to him to pretend to be dead. Subsequent shots missed us both, although initially both of us were hit several times—minor flesh wound for me on the arm, and a more serious but not fatal upper leg wound for Kemp."

"The rumor circulating is that Kemp shot you dead when you attempted to apprehend him."

"Complete rubbish! Who started such a rumor?"

"Were you the target?"

"I do not think so. I am sure Kemp was the intended victim. Consequently I am about to have Mark spread a rumor of our own. Firstly that I am still alive but just, and have been taken to Whitehall, and that Kemp is also alive and recuperating in this cottage. The coach that brings the army surgeons to examine us will return to Whitehall with Kemp who will be kept in protective custody. I will remain here hoping that the would-be killer will make another attempt on Kemp, if he believes he is still here. As I have presumably been taken to Whitehall, Mark will withdraw the guards."

"Not all of them, I trust?" asked Jane.

"No, there will be a couple of visible guards that are there to protect every individual in the Abbey. There will be an additional three soldiers in addition to myself concealed within the cottage."

"What am I to tell Elspeth?"

"The army surgeons will visit her after they look at us here. She will disappear to Whitehall with her husband. If she has recovered sufficiently I will question her before she leaves, and then ascertain the views of several people on what has just happened."

As Jane approached the main building an agitated Ranald appeared, "Are both men dead?" Jane explained that Luke was being taken to Whitehall to recover, while Alexander Kemp would stay in the old pest house cottage until he was able to be moved.

"Thank God for that! Will they both recover?"

"I don't know. Sir Mark who has taken over command of the King's men in Luke's forced absence, has sent for army surgeons who have yet to examine both men."

Jane was learning from Luke, and decided to put pressure on Ranald. "It certainly won't endear you to the King if his representative dies. You may need to find the potential killer. It would certainly help redeem your political position, which can't afford anymore setbacks."

"Why? Do the soldiers suspect I had something to do with the initial attack on the Kemps, and then the shooting of Tremayne and Kemp?"

Jane, in the Tremayne tradition lied. "Yes, I did hear some of the soldiers talking. Apparently almost immediately after the shooting the woods were surrounded by troops, but no suspects were found. The shooter had simply disappeared within the woods."

"How does that reflect negatively on me?"

"It is rumored that there are several tunnels that lead from the Medlowe Woods back into the house. Only someone familiar with those tunnels could have used them to escape. How many people outside your family would know of them? That may be the way Mark is thinking."

"I, for one, don't. You would have to ask Hector. He might have such knowledge."

"I repeat. To prevent yourself being seen as a possible suspect have the whole estate looking for the shooter—and for that matter the bomber as well."

Jane smiled to herself as she walked away. She sensed that Ranald was rattled. Luke would have been proud of her. Women, she began to think were probably better sleuths and interrogators than men.

She entered Elspeth apartment, where the victim was sitting up in a chair and being looked after by Ursula.

The latter looked up and commented to Jane, "Elspeth is much improved and appears only left with some heavy bruises. She claims a few aches, but apart from that, she is not seriously harmed."

Elspeth commented, "I appeared much worse than I was, because I was simply in a state of shock. I could hardly comprehend that people had broken into our apartment, and assaulted Alex and myself. How is Alex? One of the servants heard that he was dead, and another that he had killed Colonel Tremayne. Ursula said they were only rumors."

"Ursula is right. It is false news. Neither men are dead, and your husband did not shoot Tremayne."

Jane lowered her voice and whispered,"There is even better news, but the Colonel needs to maintain secrecy, and I am not sure that Ursula is discreet."

Elspeth staggered to her feet, walked hesitantly across the room, grabbed Ursula and paraded her before Jane, "Ursula and I also have a secret, which guarantees she will not act in any way to endanger me."

Ursula was beaming, "Lady Jane for your ears alone, and maybe that of the Colonel, I am Elspeth's mother."

Jane was stopped in her tracks.

"Whom else knows?"

"Nobody other than the Earl."

"Did the Earl seduce his best friend Orlando's wife?"

"No, I met Algernon long before I met Orlando. I became pregnant and of course as an impoverished Welsh gentlewoman, was not a fit partner for the then future Earl of Medlowe. I was sent back to Wales and delivered of a child that was immediately taken from me. Months later I was called back to Medlowe Abbey to be a companion to the Earl's new wife. There I met Orlando who was a constant visitor here, and we were eventually married. After we were unable to have children of our own the Earl asked if we would become guardians for an illegitimate child of one of his tenants."

"When did you discover that this child was in fact your own, and the Earl's?"

"We all knew that the Earl was the father since Elspeth was a little girl but I never knew she was my child until my return recently from the nunnery. Algernon was unhappy with Elspeth's lifestyle and asked me for help."

"Could someone else have been made aware of this and was provoked to attack her, and demand that she leave the county?" probed Jane.

"I don't know," answered Ursula.

Jane turned to Elspeth, "You will join Alex almost immediately. Colonel Tremayne is sending you both to Whitehall for your own protection. When the army surgeons arrive to have a look at you, you will be smuggled out in their coach, and taken to London."

"Ursula, the Colonel wants all this kept secret in hope that the assailants will make another attempt on Alex whom they will be led to believe is in the pest house. You and I will stay here, and pretend Elspeth is still with us. The Colonel will send more of his men to stay with us, while he with a few others will hide in the pest house awaiting the return of the assailants."

Jane turned to Elspeth, "Why do you think you were attacked?"

"To frighten us into leaving the county."

"If it was only to frighten you, why did someone then try to kill Alex?"

"But were they after Alex or the Colonel?" she asked.

"According to the Colonel, he just got in the way of a fusillade directed at Alex. Who is behind this and why?"

"It could have been Ranald determined that I should not harass him over the inheritance, but the presence of a woman suggested to me that it was more likely an alienated woman whose husband I might have slept with, or even a group of wives who have come together to get me out of the area. With Ursula's latest revelation it may be related to someone discovering the real details of my birth and Ursula's role which they want to keep concealed. If Ursula receives a similar threat we have found a motive."

"Could it be Lord Edwin anxious to force back some of Alex's land into his family's hands?"

"Not Edwin. He and I have a steady relationship, and he has expressed the view that if circumstances change I could become his next spouse. Neither of us are really serious, but it does lead to a fulfilling time together. Edwin is sorely misunderstood by most women. I doubt if he would want me to leave the area."

"If it is a jealous wife who would be your prime suspect?"

"That's the problem! I can hardly think of a single relationship in which my intrusion has had a negative effect. I have remained friends with most of the wives who have found that my intervention has improved their lot. To most of the gentlemen involved a relationship with me is not a big deal."

"What about Lucy Finch? Have you not most recently toyed with her husband?"

"Yes, but that has been quite open. Winston is well on the way to achieving an annulment of his marriage, which Lucy is not contesting, and he has clearly made overtures to me regarding a future together."

"Would he act to get your current spouse out of the way? That's a motive if he is serious about his relationship with you," added Ursula.

"He would not have been involved in the initial assault. He would not hurt me and the last thing Winston wants is for me to leave the country. There is only one person at present at the Abbey that could be behind the initial assault on me—and that is a mother, not a wife."

"And who would that be?" asked Luke.

"Veronica Petty! Since he arrived at the Abbey I have slept with her beloved son Nathan several times. He mentioned his mother had warned him off any relationship with the twins or myself until his political position was established. Nathan infuriated her by saying he was simply imitating the King, and any affairs would be a political positive."

A coach arrived and one of the surgeons, having ascertained that Elspeth was fit to travel, bundled a heavily disguised woman into their vehicle. The other surgeon with Jane and Ursula went to the old pest house.

The surgeon examined Luke and deemed him fit. Alex was dressed in female garb and accompanied Ursula back to the coach.

Jane stayed behind and reported her discussion with Ranald.

Luke was delighted and asked, "Visit Hector and find out who among those currently at the Abbey has knowledge of the tunnels that lead from the woods into the house."

28

Meanwhile Ranald, Edwin, Job, Caroline and Veronica met in a council of war. Veronica was fired up, determined to inspire the others. "Ranald you cannot allow your family interest and that of the Symes and Pettys to be overcome by my opportunistic brother, who seems to have gathered a disparate group, whose only common denominator is opposition to us."

"What do I do?" asked Ranald. "The assault on the Kemps has not helped our image. The Colonel thinks I am involved—driven by impending defeat to remove our opponents by force."

"Fortunately the Colonel is out of action for some time. If we act quickly we can regain lost ground. Win back Orlando and Piers. With their support and that of their associates, you would regain the majority," continued the aggressive Veronica.

Caroline intervened, "I have already advised Ranald how to act. Orlando wants to ensure that Elspeth receives some inheritance from this estate, and wants support in taking measures against Roman Catholics and wives. Offer Orlando a considerable sum to gift immediately to Elspeth. She will not be satisfied, but he will be. Pretend that the money has come straight from the Earl himself. On the anti-Catholic issue, an anti-Papist position won't do any harm in the short term. We can always change our stance, when the situation warrants it."

"What about Piers?" asked Edwin. He is the King's favorite and was your number one choice. What went wrong?"

Ranald looked embarrassed and with his eyes appealed to Veronica for assistance. She obliged and turned to Job. She spoke softly as if re-igniting their love match of decades before.

"Dear Job, Piers refuses to join us because he believes that you are preventing your niece from marrying. I am sure it is all a misunderstanding. You should be delighted that Charity has found her future husband among the King's favorites. This must be to your long term advantage. You do not know where such a powerful connection might lead."

"It is not that simple my dear. On her marriage I lose half the properties I have had over the last two decades. I lost much during the wars, and the King has done little to recompense those who gave all for him and his father. To lose such a large proportion of my income on top of all my other disasters has to be resisted, or I will not survive. I need to retain Charity's properties as long as I can, to recoup my losses."

"In that case at least welcome Piers into your family and agree to a wedding date. Piers is so wealthy in his own right he may as a peace gesture allow you to retain some of the disputed properties as a long term tenant. Unlike previous suitors for Charity he does need any additional land. To bring Piers back into our camp is vital. You can also begin to negotiate a bride price that given Pier's immense wealth would go a long way to recoup your losses," added an irritated Edwin.

"And that is not all," said Veronica directing her attention back to Ranald. "You must undermine several of Phineas' team. Kemp looks as if he is out anyway, and Finch would not need much more well placed gossip to completely destroy his reputation. With carefully aimed targets you can reduce my brother's support to the minority level it has been at for decades. By the way, where is Nathan?"

Ranald had a strange look on his face and mumbled, "He was invited and I received no reply that he could not come."

After Veronica and Caroline left the room. Ranald confessed to Edwin, "I have been approached by one of our opponents to join us."

"And what is his price?" asked a cynical Edwin.

"The agreed nomination to a parliamentary borough."

"Who is it?"

"You brother-in-law, Finch."

"Are you mad? He will decrease our credibility and support even further. What can he do for us in return for the nomination?"

"He claims he has the ability to persuade a significant number of the lesser gentry to support us rather than Leigh."

"His only weapon of persuasion is blackmail. He has no other leverage."

"Not true. He is a much wealthier man than we all thought, and he seems willing to spend a fortune to gain support. His money would be a great help as father does not see the need to provide incentives to a large number of lesser gentry, and I have few resources of my own."

"Ignore him. Veronica would be beside herself if you show any support for Finch. Thank goodness, my sister will soon be rid of him."

"The reason I need to consider Winston's help is that a decision that will really upset Veronica is about to be made public. Her dearest son is about to join his uncle. I lied to her ladyship. Nathan informed me he would not be attending, and was about to announce his removal from our list and his support of his uncle."

"Good God, we need to rethink of our position. Immediately approach not only Piers and Orlando but Phineas himself. Turn the last named into our leading candidate. Offer him all that he wants," suggested the increasingly pragmatic Edwin.

"I hate to admit it, but despite his archaic views I need father to return and put everyone in their place," admitted a desperate Ranald.

"Is your father recovering?" asked Edwin.

"I don't know. Since the King has undertaken to care for him, and Caroline has come back here, I have had no contact."

"Ask the army to find out! Sir Mark, unlike the Colonel, was a long time courtier."

Later that day as Luke debated with himself the wisdom of hiding in the former pest house hoping someone would try to attack Alexander Kemp whom the potential murderer had been led to believe was still there recovering. His boredom was interrupted by an almost inaudible knock, and the gentle voice of Jane, seeking admission.

The guards withdrew into a neighboring room assuming that this was a lover's tryst. Luke was vaguely interested, but Jane was highly agitated and perspiring freely.

"Forget this charade! You are needed immediately. I was approached by Winston Finch who appeared to me to be on the edge of a breakdown. He has to see you or Mark now, before it is too late."

"Where is he? In his room, yours or mine?"

"Neither, he wants to meet you in the chapel now."

"Did he indicate what was so urgent?"

"Only that he believed that like Kemp, an attempt would be made to assassinate him."

"He does exaggerate his own importance. He means simply that someone is out to kill him," replied Luke acidly.

Luke sent a message to Miles to send an officer or senior sergeant to man the potential trap to catch Kemp's shooter, while he accompanied by Jane hurried to the chapel of Medlowe Abbey. The chapel was dark, illuminated by two large candles on the altar and a taper burning beside the entrance door.

At first Luke and Jane thought they had arrived before Finch as there appeared to be no one in any of the pews or seats.

Luke tensed. Lying prone in front of the altar was a body. Finch was not the religious type.

He asked Jane to fetch Ursula while he moved towards the altar.

The body was Finch.

He was dead—the victim of five deliberately placed dagger wounds in the shape of a cross.

The alarm was sounded and troops surrounded the chapel, but nobody had seen anyone approaching the place of worship, and nobody left. However the chaplain pointed out the chapel could be accessed by a number of secret passages.

Ursula examined the body and concurred with Luke. Five dagger thrusts had been responsible for Winston's death. She suggested, "Colonel, the murderer has relied on the sharpness of the dagger, and not the strength of the thrust. The murderer may have been a woman."

"This murder was well planned and the weapon carefully selected. Finding it would be a good beginning."

Luke, Jane and Ursula moved to the Finch apartment to inform Lucy of her husband's death. A servant blocked their admittance claiming that Lady Lucy had been sleeping most of the afternoon. Luke sensed a problem. He forced his way past the servant and went straight into Lucy's bedchamber.

By the color of Lucy's face, a strange tinge of blue, and the contorted look on her face the trio initially believed she was also dead. On closer examination Luke detected a faint breath, and Ursula immediately ordered the servant to provide any emetics she could find. Depending on how long ago Lucy had swallowed the toxic material, an emetic could save the day. If too long delayed, it would be useless. The women stayed with Lucy while Luke went to inform Ranald about Finch's murder, and Edwin concerning the plight of his sister.

Edwin was irrational. "That knave has killed my sister before doing himself in." Luke saw it was not the time to explain that Finch had been murdered, and had not killed himself.

If Edwin's reaction surprised the balanced Luke, Ranald's response completely perplexed him.

As Luke recounted the circumstances of Finch's death, Ranald's mouth fell open, and he began to hit his head with his hands.

"You say that the wounds were in the shape of a cross?"

"Yes," repeated Luke.

"The curse of the Medlowes!"

"What's this 'curse of the Medlowes'?"

"A hundred and twenty odd years ago when King Henry gave Medlowe Abbey to my ancestor, the deposed Abbot cursed the family and predicted that through the ages several of us would die by the sign of the cross."

"And how many Medlowes have died as an apparent result of this curse?"

"Only one, my grandfather. He was found decades ago in the chapel in the very spot you say Finch was found, and with identical dagger wounds. But Finch is not related to the Medlowes. I do not think a curse exists. This is someone who has knowledge of the family history perhaps sending us a message. Kemp, Finch and now maybe a Medlowe is next?"

"Was your grandfather's death straightforward, or did it have any other elements of the curse than the stab wounds in the form of a cross?"

"The murderer was a Catholic priest who openly declared he was carrying out the predictions of the last Abbot."

"The only open Catholic roaming Medlowe Abbey at the moment is Ursula," commented Luke, largely to himself. Where was Ursula before she joined Jane and himself?

Ranald continued, "Father has never believed that interpretation of what happened to his father. He believes his father was murdered on orders of a highly placed rival for King James's favor, and the accusing of a Catholic priest was designed to discredit the Catholic peers who had supported grandfather in his battle for influence. Our enemies at that time got rid of the Earl and a number of supporting catholic aristocrats by this one act. It was a political masterstroke that utilized the anti-Papist feeling following the Gunpowder Plot."

"Were these anti-Medlow families known at the time or since?"

"Nothing has changed much in over fifty years. The Leighs were the most prominent then with strong support from the London merchants."

"You're not suggesting that Phineas is involved, and has chosen a method that might cast suspicion on both Medlowes and Catholics?"

"You cannot ignore the possibility."

Luke returned to Lucy's quarters and was pleased by the positive report delivered by Ursula. "She has vomited several times, and has probably removed much of the toxic material. She is breathing normally, and I have giving her a herbal drink to encourage sleep."

"Has she spoken?"

"No, and we have not told her of her husband's death," added Jane.

Luke turned suddenly to Ursula, "Where were you when Jane found you and brought you to the chapel?"

"With Veronica."

"I did not think you had much in common?"

"We don't, but Veronica is desperate. Her power is dwindling at a great rate, and she feels that if I can persuade certain persons to join Ranald against her brother she could help me in my relationship with Orlando. Unfortunately I told her I couldn't help, because everything she wanted depended on winning over Orlando. My relationship with him is toxic. He would simply do the opposite to whatever I asked. She was not happy."

29

Luke visited Lucy the next day. She had recovered from the attempted poisoning and had time to reflect on the murder of her husband. Luke asked, "Why was an attempt made to kill both of you?"

"I can only be collateral damage in an attempt to destroy whatever Winston knew or had. It had to be people who believed that Winston confided in me. Personally I have no secrets and no enemies."

"You think that the person who killed Winston is the same person who tried to kill you?"

"It would be a very great co-incidence if two separate people were involved. It must be the same person."

"Are you sure that you have no secrets stemming from your early days at the young King's court-in-exile in Paris. The identity of your rapist is perhaps a secret that someone does not want to be revealed."

"Why wait a decade or more to hush me up? I didn't know who it was then, and I don't know now."

"But does the would-be murderer know that? Circumstances have changed in the last few months. Winston and you were proceeding to an annulment. Someone might have believed that Winston knew who the rapist was and was now ready to name him. Piers may have told you who it was, or even your brother may have come across evidence damning someone who was there at the time. From all of these sources you might have picked up a minute clue that would have led you to identity the villain. Nothing that any of these people said to you in recent months helped your memory?"

"No, over the years I have at one time or another suspected one of five or six of my fellow young courtiers, but was never sure that it was any of them."

"Could it have been the King or his brother?"

"That is treason sir! Those Stuart boys were openly predatory but all of us girls were throwing ourselves at them. They had no need for disguise or force."

"Could the attack on your life have nothing to do with your past or even present. Could it be to prevent you following a particular path in the future?"

"Like what?"

"After you and Winston separate if you are planning to remarry again fairly quickly, this may have alienated a woman, or relatives of a woman who has designs on the same man as yourself?"

Lucy beamed.

"Colonel, you deserve your awesome reputation. You appear to have stumbled on my current secret that no one other than the man concerned and myself know. I have yet to inform my father or brother, but they will be delighted. The man and I have had little time together as Winston and I are still married, and the man's relatives are proposing a range of possible wives that do not include me."

"A distinct motive! Who is the lucky man?"

"No, Colonel. If you are right and this could account for my poisoning, the less anybody, including you, know the better."

"Why was Winston murdered?"

"The real question is why was Winston not murdered years ago. He was into every corrupt deal imaginable. The illegal import of Irish cattle, the illegal export of wool, the illegal activities of several London companies, the activities of criminal gangs, the blackmail of our friends and neighbors, the unauthorized draining of water lands and the damming of rivers. The list goes on."

"As you said, it is a wonder he lasted this long."

"It was no accident that Winston lasted as long as he did. He kept a record of every transaction he was involved in, and made sure that his accomplices were well aware that a record had been kept. If anything happened to Winston, all would be revealed, and others would go down with him."

"Have you got those records?" asked Luke suddenly seeing a new line of enquiry.

"No, but they exist. Most evenings during our married life, Winston entered a record of his days activities into a diary. The most recent is bound in green Moroccan leather."

"And you do not know where it is?"

"No, I asked Ursula and Jane to search these rooms for it this morning. They found nothing."

"When did you last see Winston?"

"About an hour before he died."

"Did he say what he was about to do?"

"Yes, he was very excited. He said he was about to pull off a political coup that he had only dreamt about in the past."

"Which was?"

"To become Medlowe's leading man in the county."

Luke could not hold back a laugh. "Come Lucy! Winston could not have been serious. Was he going to blackmail the whole county?"

"Now you are being silly Colonel. Winston was corrupt, but he was no fool, and everybody underestimated his political acumen. He was about to make Lord Ranald an offer his lordship could not refuse."

"Do you know what that offer was?"

"Yes, Winston was very proud of it. In return for being the Medlowe front man in the county and a member of Parliament for one of the boroughs, Winston would deliver Ranald enough lesser gentry to enable him to swamp the Leigh interest in any contest."

"Ridiculous! Winston has no credibility among the lesser gentry. They would not act at Winston's say so, unless it was blackmail which is not a good guarantee of continuing loyalty."

"Winston was well aware of how the county gentry viewed him. If the Republic had continued much longer the Presbyterian leaders of the county would have had him imprisoned for corruption and his commercial and criminal empire dismantled."

"How then was he going to win over these reluctant gentry?"

"Very simple—bribery. Winston was much wealthier than he pretended. Much of his illegally gained fortune remains hidden. In the last few weeks a substantial amount of gold and silver was smuggled into

Medlowe Abbey for distribution to the needy gentry. Many of these had lost much during the King's exile and their expectation of generous relief on the King's return had been dashed. Many of the King's most loyal followers are destitute. Winston was their lifesaver, and all the recipients had to do for this semi-fortune was to support the Medlowe interest over that of the Leighs—and not reveal any connection to the notorious Winston Finch."

"Had these plans progressed far?"

"Winston had told Ranald of his plans, and Winston went off to finalize the details with him just before his death."

"Where was the meeting to be held?"

Lucy hesitated. "Until everything was finalized, neither party wanted to be seen together. Ranald had told Winston that the last person to know of any agreement must be Veronica. They were to meet in the chapel."

Luke nearly choked, "Do you know what you just said? Winston was to meet Ranald in the place where at around the designated time, he was murdered?"

"Yes, but Jane said that you thought the murderer was a woman. A man would not have used such delicate dagger thrusts."

"An ex-courtier might," mused Luke. "Your evidence has been most enlightening Lucy. In essence Winston has left two things which his murderer and others, might wish to get their hands on—his diary and his readily disposable gold and silver. Both of these could completely revolutionize the politics of this county at least in the short term. Are you sure you do not know where either is?"

"Only two small clues. He had the diary with him when he set out to see Ranald, and he has spent considerable time in recent days in the vicinity of the armory. Given what happened to Kemp I initially assumed that he was seeking arms to defend us. Now I think he may have been hiding his gold and silver there."

"Thanks Lucy. Now how did you come to be poisoned? Has Ursula isolated the poison, and means by which you came to ingest it?"

"Yes, and on reflection it may not have been meant for me. As Winston left he shouted out that the mid-morning trolley of sweetmeats from the kitchen had arrived and it was stacked with one of his favorites, almond cakes.

I usually do not indulge but in this instance I ate one. It was so delicious that I had several more. According to Ursula they were all infused with arsenic."

"So your poisoning may have been accidental. The intended target was Winston. It fits. When it was seen that the poisoning had not worked and Winston was about to speak to Ranald, desperate measures had to adopted."

Luke left Lucy and sought out Ranald. "My lord, I have just received information that you were the last person to see Winston alive—and that was in the chapel."

"Not quite accurate, Colonel!"

"Correct me!"

"I was to meet Winston there and finalize one of the greatest political comebacks of all time. With Winston's fortune I would gain support from the impoverished Royalist gentry who had become disappointed in the King. We agreed that such assistance could be depicted as a pro-Royalist measure designed to stabilize the county in support of His Majesty."

"What happened when you met?"

"We never did. I was delayed when Veronica came to harangue me about Nathan leaving our faction and joining his uncle. I was to stop it at all costs. By the time I disentangled myself from a very distraught mother I was confronted by Jane leaving the chapel and informing me that Winston was dead."

"You did not kill him?"

"No, although in the past there have been a many occasions when I could have. Now it was the opposite. Finch was saving my political life and in doing so the family name. Examine Leigh and his allies!"

Luke ignored the advice and asked permission to search the armory.

"What do you hope to find? The daggers that killed Finch are more likely to found in a gentlewoman's cabinet than in a military armory."

"Finch has been spending time in the armory in recent days. He may have hidden some valuable evidence there."

"Such as his diary?"

Luke was taken aback. "You are aware that he kept a very incriminating diary?"

"Yes, when Finch first approached me about changing sides he had intended to blackmail others into joining me. Both of us realized that this was not a viable option. It was then that Finch confessed to a fortune almost as great as ours, and a willingness to use it to buy support."

Luke and a cohort of his men searched the armory from top to bottom for the rest of the day. Finally they found one calico bag that should have contained gunpowder. It was full of gold coins. A large number of bags were missing. Had Finch done this before his death to bribe his comrades, or had his murderer stolen the fortune for his own use?

Those gentlemen who had received Finch's gold were now in a perfect position. Unless Finch's diary was found their identity would remain a secret. They could pocket the money and continue to support Leigh, and the world would be ignorant of their association with the perfidious Sir Winston Finch.

30

Fear spread through Medlowe Abbey. The murder of Winston and the attempts on the life of Lucy, Elspeth and Alexander had panicked many of the guests. Would they be next?

Luke discussed the situation with Mark, Miles and Jane and they agreed that such fear did not exist in a vacuum. The most affrighted probably had something to hide. They disagreed as to whether they were facing one or more killers and whether the attacks on the Kemps and Finches were part of the same murderous campaign.

Luke as was his usual approach argued for the one killer, and the immediate task to discover which person had strong feelings against both the Finches and the Kemps. Mark pointed out that the attack on both families was vastly different. The Kemps experienced minor violence, and were simply advised to leave. Finch was murdered.

Jane suggested that the timing of both attacks seriously upended any obvious explanation. "If this happened a week ago, it could be seen as an attempt of the Medlowe faction to discredit the two weak links in the Leigh faction, however Finch was murdered just when he changed sides."

Miles was pragmatic. "Let's concentrate on what we can achieve. If we find Finch's diary and money, and thoroughly examine the secret tunnels that run into the woods we may be able to achieve a result."

Throughout the Abbey, the atmosphere of fear worked in Luke's favor. Several people decided that confession to the King's representative might improve their situation. The first to have such thoughts was surprisingly Lucy Finch. She asked to see Jane and Luke.

Luke opened the discussion with an optimistic question. "Lucy, you have found Winston's diary?"

Lucy smiled, "No, but I can solve one of your mysteries for you."

"Why the change of heart?" asked Jane.

"Winston is dead, so that anything I now say can do him no harm—it might even help his memory in some quarters."

"What can you clear up for me?" Luke responded gently.

"Until the recent assaults and murder, your major interest was in who was behind the bombing that could have killed you, Ranald, my brother Edwin and Alex Kemp. The bomber was Winston."

Luke was genuinely surprised and mumbled, "Who was he after?"

Lucy smiled, "You. You humiliated him in front of everybody. He was seething. Winston was a hot head who had a liking for pranks but he was surprisingly sensitive, and any affront to him was taken deeply. It had to be avenged."

"Surely my reprimand of Winston was not sufficient to provoke him into killing the King's representative?"

"He did not intend to kill anyone, but by time the plan was executed, he could see advantages in frightening the other three potential victims— especially to warn Kemp to keep in line. At the last minute he got a message to Kemp to leave just to underline what might have happened to him without Winston's support."

"Surely to play a prank against the two aristocrats who eventually you wanted to impress was stupid. You must have thought of warning your brother?"

"No, because Winston said the worst that could happen would be for the victims to be cut by flying glass."

"But it was a lot more serious than that. If any one of us three had been nearer the center of the room we would have been killed."

"Yes, Winston was a little concerned at what actually happened. He was never a soldier."

"Then how did he come to set off the bombs?"

"He was present here when my brother Edwin gave a talk to the would-be militia captains, and spent some time on the issue of bombs. Edwin later in private conversation mentioned that much of the Abbey was protected by bombs. If the Parliamentary troops had invaded the

Abbey during the Republic they would have been impeded by a series of explosions which would have destroyed the house. The key message that Winston received from Edwin was that the bombs were now not designed to demolish the house, but to create concern to any intruder. As a layman Winston assumed that should he ignite the bombs under the skittle alley, there might be mild injury but not death. Clearly the bombs were more powerful than Winston understood."

"So I was the intended victim of the bombing?"

"Initially yes, but before it happened Winston could see advantages to himself in putting some pressure on Ranald, Edwin and Alexander as well."

"Did you help him light the fuses?"

"No, he paid one of the female kitchen hands a small fortune to slip out of the kitchen with a burning taper to light the fuse and then disappear up the stairs before there was any explosion. Winston himself was nowhere near it."

"Winston was a much more effective operator than I realized."

"Money not murder was his main weapon. Although his enemies called it corruption, Winston's well placed use of money was always very effective throughout his commercial and political career."

"Nothing else to reveal?" asked Luke gently.

"Regarding the diary. When he went off to meet Ranald he had it with him, but mentioned that before he went to the chapel, he had to go to the gatehouse."

"The gatehouse is occupied by my troops. Did he have a contact among the soldiers?"

Lucy giggled. "You are such an innocent at times, Colonel. Winston's only contact at the gatehouse was that slut Bettina."

"Well, there is a chance that Winston left his diary accidentally, or on purpose at the gatehouse. I will go straight there."

Bettina was momentarily delighted when it became obvious that Luke was anxious to talk to her. "This is a pleasant surprise, Colonel but you are not here unless you want my help."

Luke was in two minds. To succumb to Bettina's charm might increase her chances of talking. On the other hand the direct offer of silver or even a gold coin might be sufficient. He compromised. A little bit of cuddling and earthy conversation might put Bettina in a talkative mood.

He had completely misread the situation.

"Don't pretend, Colonel ! You are here to collect Winnie's green book."

Luke was almost rendered speechless. He lied. "Sir Winston was anxious that should anything happen to him his green book should be given to me."

"He came here just before he was killed and asked me to mind his book."

"Which you would not have done for nothing?"

"Winnie paid me a fortune to look after a book for what has amounted to a day and a bit. A good deal!"

"But he took a risk. You could have sold the book to someone else for more than Winston gave you."

"Who would buy a book written in a foreign tongue?"

Luke was surprised. "What exactly did Winston say about disposing of the book if he died?"

"That I should give the book to you, which you might be able to use to find his killer. He said you would pay generously for it."

"I will. If it had been written in English, you would not have handed it over so readily?"

"True, and if I had not been told that Winnie had told you that I had his green book, I would not have contacted you."

"But you didn't, I came to you."

"What is so important about this book?"

Luke lied again, "I don't know. Finch may have written a history of himself in which he names those who did not like him, or have threatened him. At least that is what I hope I will find, if I can translate it."

Bettina disappeared and returned carrying a smaller bound volume than Luke had expected. He opened it, and was gravely disappointed. "Damnation! This is not in a foreign language. It is in some sort of code. On second thoughts Finch was not a fool. To put too much down on paper that would be easily readable would be self-defeating."

Luke took the book to Hector Gregory. As steward he may be familiar with various codes that merchants and financiers might use to conceal their business dealings.

Hector was most enlightening. "Nothing too mysterious about this, Luke. It is simply an account book. The only thing missing are the names of those involved. The names of the participants in every transaction have been converted to numerals. One of your government's code breakers could probably easily unravel the mystery."

"That takes time. And every day I fail to solve the Finch murder makes it more likely that I won't. Did you have any dealings with him in recent months?"

"I doubt it. But I will get the book keeper to check our transactions. If we have, you might be able to tell from the amount involved which was ours and what numerals are used to describe us. That could help in the decoding."

Later that day a servant brought a note to Luke from Hector. *"Two months ago we bought some Irish cattle from Finch at the cost of five pounds twelve shillings. I hope this helps."*

Luke quickly found an entry that agreed in date and price to that outlined by Hector. The numerals that identified the buyer were 1426915124 (6) He called in Mark and Jane to consider the code. Jane did not mince works, "I never thought Winston was too bright, low cunning yes, but not a great intellect. He would keep it simple—and what is the simplest numerical code equating A with one, B with 2, C with three and so on."

Luke did some calculations on a sheet of paper and eventually announced "ADBFIEABD tells us nothing."

Mark commented, Did you apply the six in brackets to your calculations?"

"In what way?"

"I think it indicates the number of letters involved. Reorganize the numbers into six sets!"

The three of them set about the task assuming that no numbers exceeded twenty six. Surprisingly they came up with only two options 14,26, 9,15,12, and 4; or 14,26,9,15,1, and 24. Neither were helpful- NZIOLD or NZIOAX.

Mark continued to scribble away. There must be more possible combinations than those two. Jane who had also continued her calculations began clapping. "I'm a genius," she joked. "Well gentlemen, cease your efforts. I have an answer. Finch was almost as stupid as I thought. He simply reversed the simplest code A was equivalent to 26 and B to 25. If you translate the first set it spells out clearly MEDLOWE."

"Great Jane, that should give the answers we need."

"Leave the book with me, I will transcribe it for you," offered Jane.

31

Luke's great hope of utilizing the Finch accounts to solve his murder did not eventuate. Jane's translation of his last few months of activity simply provided a list of transactions several of which including the Medlowe purchase of Irish cattle were illegal. Illegalities and price gouging which revealed Winston's overall sharp practices, did little to narrow down Luke's field of prospective killers. Anyone of a hundred deals could have contributed to his murder.

Luke immediately discarded the accounts as a useful source.

Jane was not so pessimistic. If the accounts gave Luke no assistance in finding Winston's murder, why was he so determined that they finish up in Luke's hands? They must have missed something.

Meanwhile the fear that pervaded Medlowe Abbey brought more anxious women out into the open. Luke's next visitors opened up a completely new line of enquiry that may or may not have been related to any previous issues.

The Ramsden sisters asked Luke to visit them. As he approached their apartment he was surprised to see double the number of his men on guard duty. He asked one of the soldiers why Captain Oxenbridge had doubled the guard. "The ladies, Cassandra and Hyacinth reported seeing a face at their window, and as Mr. Carey was spending most of his time elsewhere, they became very anxious."

"Have you any evidence that this has occurred?"

"None of us soldiers have seen anything unusual but like some of the women, a couple of us have felt that we are being watched from the shadows. Quite a few of the serving girls in adjacent apartments have made similar claims."

"What actual claims have they made?"

"Some explicable, some weird! The two most common are a face at the window, and a sense of being followed. The strange one is that they report a knock on the door and when answered there is no one there."

"Similar to the schoolboy prank—knock on the door and then run away?"

"Yes, but to what end?"

"That is anyone's guess. It could simply be a prank by one of the younger guests, or it could be a serious predator hoping to create an opportunity for more serious aggression. Or even some unbalanced individual anxious to increase the atmosphere of fear."

Luke thanked his trooper, and sought admission to the twins' apartment. He explained that he was aware of a general feeling of insecurity in the area in terms of a face at the window.

Hyacinth was effusive. "Colonel, we are not silly young girls. There has been a face at one of our outside windows many nights since we have been here, but we did not complain before, as many of the gentlemen gathered here have made inappropriate suggestions in our direction. We interpreted it as part of their warped minds. With Piers living here, neither of us saw it as a serious problem, but now with his almost continual absences with his beloved Charity, and the attacks on the Kemps and the Finches, we are scared. Captain Oxenbridge helpfully has doubled the guard on our chambers."

"When he was here, did Piers ever see this face?"

"Piers saw many of the earlier faces and his recognition of them largely put an end to their games. He has never seen the current face, which has only appeared to Cassandra and myself, and apparently some of the serving girls."

"It has been the same face all the time?"

"Yes."

"That suggests that you would recognize it?"

Cassandra spoke for the first time. "That is what is strange. The face reminded me of someone. Maybe someone from our past but whoever it is, he is heavily disguised."

"Describe the face!" demanded Luke.

Luke's spirits sank as Cassandra described the face as having long red hair and a ginger moustache.

"It is a disguise. He is wearing a wig and a false moustache. That face is too easily identifiable to be genuine. Does he go out of his way to be seen, or do you just catch a glimpse of him watching you?"

"He goes out of his way to attract our attention," answered Hyacinth.

"And does someone knock on your door and run away?"

"Not since your men have been guarding us. One night Piers answered the knock and saw a figure disappearing down the corridor," continued Hyacinth.

"Did Piers have any comments?"

"Only that the disappearing figure appeared to be a small young woman," said Cassandra.

"So the villain could be a small woman wearing a red wig and a false moustache?"

"Maybe," was the reply.

Luke thanked the women for their information. "Ladies, I do not think you should be too worried. I am sure that the attempts on the Kemps and Finches was very much concerned with the current political struggle in the county. You, especially since your separation from Piers, are in no way involved in such a struggle. This voyeur may be harmless, but I will still maintain the increased guard until he is caught."

"It is not that simple, Colonel. The attack on the Finches may be related to events years ago in the early days of the King's court-in-exile. We were there, and played a major part in its activities. The Finches could have been attacked by the person who raped Lucy. He is now frightened that since many of us are together again, that the truth will come out. If Winston was killed because he knew who raped Lucy, then the murderer may believe we also know. We may be his next victims. We have to be killed to prevent us telling you or anybody else, who he is."

"But you told me before that you have no idea who the rapist was."

Luke now hoped they might be more forthcoming. He was disappointed.

"Very true, but does the would-be murderer know that?" said Hyacinth.

"Or maybe he doesn't care. Maybe his revenge on what happened to Lucy, is to kill everybody involved in our group at the time," added Cassandra pessimistically.

"That is a stupid thing to say, Cassie. If that were true then the King and the Duke of York would be in danger—and you would hardly try to kill the victim Lucy, if you were avenging her rape," declaimed the more pragmatic Hyacinth.

Cassandra then astounded Hyacinth and Luke. "What if there was no rape? What if for decades Winston had saved Lucy from nothing?"

"You are really being silly. What could possibly have been the motive for such a vast conspiracy?" replied Hyacinth.

"Piers and Ranald were always playing jokes. Lucy was a lovelorn teenager who may have lusted after Winston. She was aware that her parents would not approve of the match in normal circumstances, so she and her friends concocted this tale."

"Did Piers tell you this?" asked an astounded Hyacinth.

"No, but as you know he was always very cagey about his role in bringing Winston and Lucy together."

Luke intervened in the sisterly discussion. "While it is a possibility I cannot see the daughter of a viscount destroy her reputation, and to the outside world be forced into an unsuitable marriage in return for her family accepting Winston as her husband."

"In those days Lucy was wild," added Cassandra.

"I will ask Lucy," commented Luke who had to admit that the idea advanced by Cassandra could alter his whole understanding of the situation. Who had lost and who had gained by the apparent forced marriage between Winston and Lucy?

The news spread quickly that Medlowe Abbey was overrun by predatory males who delighted in peering through the windows of attractive females. Several other women reported a similar looking red headed and ginger-moustached male slinking around the corridors of the Abbey after dark.

On hearing the news Hector took steps to protect his own staff, and wondered whether he should mention a specific concern to Luke.

He decided against it.

Later that night Jane visited Luke. She was highly excited. As Luke poured her some sweet mulled red wine he asked gently, You must have something very important to tell me. I have rarely seen you so elated."

She gave Luke a big hug and passionate kiss. "Luke, I have solved all your problems."

"I am beginning to appreciate your sleuthing abilities and logical reasoning, but what exactly have you solved?"

"I have not really solved them. Finch did that. I have simply found his evidence."

"What do you mean?"

"I could never understand why he wanted you to have his green book when we discovered it contained nothing that really helped you in your investigation. I went over those accounts from front to back several times without any further enlightenment. Then the book accidently fell to the floor and landed in a manner that bent back its cover. Then I saw it. A piece of paper had been concealed beneath the front cover. I extracted it."

"And what does it reveal?"

"He names Lucy's rapist. Who might murder him. And who was the Cromwellian spy in Medlowe Abbey. It is the same person."

Luke read the note and laughed. "We cannot believe a word of it. It is very dubious evidence as it covers the three issues that Finch knew concerned me. He gives me the answers to all three on a plate. The man hated me. This is his final revenge from the grave—make a fool of me."

"At least consider whom he has named," pleaded a deflated Jane.

Luke remained unimpressed. "The issues he raises are too focused on what he knew I was investigating. He provides no evidence just a name. While he may have information regarding Lucy's rapist, and some wild idea of who might murder him, how would he know anything regarding Cromwell's man or woman in Medlowe Abbey? During most of the time he was either abroad or in London."

"You do not give his note any credence at all?" asked a deflated Jane.

"Quite the opposite. It was designed to confuse me and two of his claims can be immediately disproved. The person named as his would-be murderer was the one person to lose heavily by his death, and the Cromwellian spy was active in the Abbey long before Finch arrived. The name offered as Lucy's rapist is however more believable."

"As you have read, he offers the same name for all three activities. What would be his motive? You surely can't believe he would go to all this trouble, and as one of his last acts seek to communicate with you simply as a prank?"

"To put the best interpretation on it, one might say he wants me to focus my attention on the individual he names, our host Lord Ranald Medlowe.

Mid-morning the next day Luke heard a cacophony of cornets. He started for the gatehouse and saw that the fanfare was not a call to arms, but an act of homage for the royal coach that was coming down the drive, flanked by two of the King's Household cavalry.

Luke wondered who the visitor might be. The first figure to disembark from the coach was someone he immediately recognized. It was Captain Matthew Hatch, a member of his special unit, and also his brother-in-law who had remained at Whitehall, while Mark, Miles and himself had been sent to Medlowe Abbey. Matthew assisted an elderly figure from the coach. Although stooped, the sprightly figure almost bounded up the entrance steps to be greeted by Ranald, Hector and an army of servants.

It was Algernon, Earl of Medlowe returning from his convalescence in London, and latterly in the Palace of Whitehall. Luke was surprised that he was followed out of the coach by one of Luke's junior officers currently based in the gatehouse. As the Earl and his entourage entered the Abbey, Luke made his way towards Matthew, "Well this is a surprise!"

"I am killing two birds with the one stone—an appropriate escort to the returning Earl, and as a personal messenger with urgent news from the King."

32

"The unexpected return of the Earl will certainly upset the political solution that was emerging, and undoubtedly affect my investigations. Do I have new written instructions?"

"Come Luke, you know by now that Charles does not put sensitive matters onto paper. I have come personally, and apart from the King, and Ashcroft, you and I are the only persons to know what I am about to reveal."

"In that case, let us walk through the orchards to avoid any accidental or deliberate eaves dropping!"

"The King is learning from you Luke. He persuaded the Earl to return, simply to upset the developing balance that was emerging in the hope that the changed situation may bring more of his enemies, and your various suspects out into the open. An essential fact that you need to be aware of is that someone has been poisoning the Earl over several months. It started here and continued at the Medlowe town house. The King was not happy with the report of the first physician who examined the Earl. Further tests and examinations led to a revised diagnosis. The combined assessment of physicians, surgeons and wise women put the source down to the fresh mushrooms sent from here every morning by Ranald."

"But I received a report that after Algernon left his town house and Ranald continued to send his daily meal of mushrooms no toxic element was found."

"Apparently because all those learned gentlemen were looking for an added toxic element. Clearly none of them were country boys with a knowledge of mushrooms. A wise woman who looked at the last lot of mushrooms sent to the town house was appalled that among a range of edible fungi was a particularly poisonous variety. As a result the King suspects Ranald was slowly killing his father?"

"No, not necessarily. Someone else might have added the poisonous variety to the initial Ranald supply."

"The only other suspect at the town house would be Lady Caroline, but she and the Earl are very close?" commented Matthew.

"A closeness that might have hidden darker motives," suggested Luke.

"I can see His Majesty's thinking. Throw the Medlowe family into turmoil with the return of the Earl and see how Ranald and Caroline react."

"There is another aspect to increase the tension. Did you see one of our junior officers leave the coach with the Earl and myself?"

"Yes, that badly disfigured young Johnson. He had almost half his face blown away. He is based at the gatehouse, and has been deputy to Miles in enforcing the quarantine.

"Well, Mutton Johnson may not be his name. He now claims to be James Medlowe the rightful heir to the earldom."

"Does the Earl accept his claim?

"The Earl does not yet know about the claim."

"What do we know about Johnson?"

"A couple of years ago he approached Ashcroft who was in charge of security at the court-in-exile seeking a position. He claimed as Mutton Johnson to have been in service in the navy of the Ottoman Empire and had suffered his hideous disfigurement due to an explosion on one of the Sultan's galleys."

"So when did his claim to be James Medlowe surface?"

"Only since the King has been at Whitehall. Johnson spoke to Ashcroft when he heard that a detachment of the King's troops was being stationed at Medlowe Abbey, and that the Earl of Medlowe was critically ill, and being cared for at Whitehall. He asked to be moved here. The King agreed subject to the clear understanding that he must not approach members of his family with his claim without the express approval of His Majesty."

"What excuse have you given to the Earl for placing such a disfigured individual in his household?"

"None, because he is not attached to the Earl's household. He is being relocated from Miles's gatehouse detachment, and attached to you personally as valet and equerry."

"To what end?" asked Luke.

"You will make him aware that you know of his claim and that he has been attached to you in order to discover ways in which he might be able to prove his real identity. You are free to use him in any way to put pressure on the Medlowes."

"Has the King turned against the Medlowes?"

"Not against the Earl, who now that he has recovered will be reappointed as Lord Lieutenant of the county, and in command of any militia forces raised within it. His membership of the House of Lords will put him in a commanding position in determining who will be the candidates for the various boroughs in the county—a position and influence that Ranald has squandered."

"So much so that it will not be an easy task to recover any Medlowe influence at all. Sir Phineas Leigh who led the opposition to the Medlowes for decades now has overwhelming support."

A servant approached the two men. Colonel Tremayne was asked to meet with the Earl at noon.

"Your new adventures are about to begin. You only have a week left before the quarantine is officially lifted, and your various suspects allowed to disperse. There is also another major surprise which the Earl will explain," teased Matthew.

Luke was ushered into the Earl's library. "The King has no doubt informed you that I was being slowly poisoned, probably by members of my own family," commented the Earl.

"Not necessarily your family. Many people could have added toxic mushrooms to those that Ranald supplied, but this is clearly another problem I will investigate."

"In any case the poisoning was only adding to a more serious problem which none of the physicians, surgeons or wise women could explain. At times and without warning I found it difficult to breathe. To cover their ignorance they suggested that I was bewitched."

"Yes, I did hear a report regarding bewitching."

"Enough of that rubbish. Down to business. I have received reports from Hector and from Ranald as to what has happened here since I left. Frankly they hardly agree on any major issue. Ranald believes he has been undermined by almost everybody in his futile effort to maintain the Medlowe dominance in the area. He is very pessimistic. Hector on the other hand considers Ranald's lack of political acumen in his dealings with the county gentry has caused a mere temporary problem, and that a few word from me is all that is needed to restore our dominance. I need the truth."

Luke was blunt, "Your long-time rival Sir Phineas Leigh has majority support amongst the county gentry. Ranald's lack of political experience did contribute to this result, but it will require a lot more than words from you to regain your influence."

The Earl sat silently for some time and then changed the subject. "I am appalled at the number of murders or attempted murders that have occurred here in my absence. Have you solved any of them?"

"Some. Your old companion Sir Julius died from misadventure—a pack of feral dogs. The attempt to blow up the lords Ranald, Edwin and myself was a vindictive prank devised by Sir Winston Finch. Regarding the attacks on the Finch and Kemp families, I have as yet no clear suspects," lied Luke.

"Finch's death does not surprise me. He was probably the target of a disgruntled business associate. Since his return from the continent Finch has wormed his way into a key role in many of the major enterprises, legal and illegal in the county. He always drove a hard bargain," suggested the Earl.

"The one thing that suggests the motive may have been different from what you suggest, is the way that he was murdered."

"How so? I heard he had been stabbed multiple times."

"He was, but in a way linked to your own family tradition. The stab wounds formed the outline of a cross just as your own father was murdered—and in the same chapel before the altar. Hector told me of the Medlowes being cursed by a deposed Abbot."

"That was a complete concoction! My father was murdered by a conspiracy of ultra-Protestant opponents to destroy his power, and that of a few Papist neighbors. They had father killed in a way that cast suspicion on Papists to fulfil the terms of the curse."

"Why kill Finch in that way? He is not a Medlowe."

"The murderer was trying to underline that we Medlowes are tarred with the same corrupt brush as Finch. Treat Finch as a Medlowe, and the county will get the message. Medlowes are no better than the Finches. Was Finch stabbed by an extremely long but very narrow weapon?"

"Yes, why do you ask?"

"The Medlowe family's treasure house contains gold, silver, jewelry and other precious items. Since Cromwell sold off much of the Stuart possessions our treasury rivals that of the King. One of the most valuable items in that collection is a dagger such as you describe. It was the dagger that killed father. Come with me to the treasure house which is hidden deep within the armory to see if that dagger is still in place."

The Earl's face fell. The dagger was missing.

Luke asked, "Access to the treasure house is possible only with the key you inserted?"

"Yes, And while I was away it was hidden in my library. Not even Hector knew about it. Who used the library in my absence, Ranald?"

Luke was impressed by the Earl's practical approach. He would certainly prove a stronger opponent to Phineas and his supporters than his son Ranald.

While the two men were alone in the isolation of the treasure house the Earl made a revealing confession. "Colonel, when I was moved to my town house in London, I did not allow any visitors. There was a reason, and as I became more ill, my daughter-in- law continued that approach. You found the bodies of some Cromwellian troopers and the favorite horse of the dominant Cromwellian magistrate, Sir Septimus Ingle in my infectious cattle pit."

"Yes, initially I was told that Ingle had fled the county to avoid the returning Royalists, later it became clear that he and his wife may have been murdered or kidnapped, although the lack of any ransom note weakened the case for the latter. I was left with the thought that extreme Royalists may have sold him and his wife into servitude in the Americas as that was his normal punishment for young Royalists who came before him."

"Let us return to the library!"

The Earl and Luke entered the library to find an awaiting couple. The Earl announced with a broad grin, "Colonel Tremayne, may I introduce Sir Septimus and Lady Ingle."

Lady Ingle spoke, "Colonel, we have met before. Some ten years ago we entertained the commander in chief of the Parliamentary army, General Cromwell. You commanded his bodyguard."

After introductions were completed Luke turned to the Earl. "My lord, I am sure you have a story to tell me regarding the disappearance and now re-emergence of Sir Septimus and his wife.

"A group of out-of- county Royalist militia, technically acting in my name set upon Septimus and his men. While his men fought valiantly against overwhelming odds, Septimus and Maud, abandoned their horses and possessions and sought shelter here."

"Why come here?"

"We were close. Although we were enemies in terms of the King or the Parliament, we remained good friends. Septimus treated most Royalists with total fairness. I realized that Medlowe Abbey would receive a visit by this unofficial Royalist militia. I immediately ordered my coach, and accompanied by two persons disguised as my servants, left for London within a quarter hour of them arriving here."

Luke turned to Septimus. "And where were you during the Earl's severe illness?"

"We left the Medlowe town house when Algernon was moved to Whitehall and stayed with merchant friends in London. I received a note a few days ago from the King asking me to return home with the guarantee of protection, and a question to which he wanted an answer. You must have gone through the same dilemma. The King wishes to know should it be offered, would I be willing to serve on the bench. He seemed to imply that the meeting here was not highlighting many possible nominees in which he could have great faith."

"Septimus, I would keep that observation to yourself. The atmosphere is very tense. There is a murderer running loose, and not all Royalists are as tolerant as the King and Earl to ex-Cromwellians like ourselves. Unfortunately, although the rules are broken constantly, having entered a quarantined area, you are obliged to stay here for a week."

33

Luke decided to risk good manners. To have both the local leading Cromwellian and leading Royalist in the same room, he had to ask, "Gentlemen, one of the other responsibilities thrust on me by the King is to uncover the identity of Exodus, a Cromwellian spy closely associated with Medlowe Abbey. Thurloe never knew who it was, and nobody is sure whether Exodus was a genuine Cromwellian supporter or a double agent really serving the King. Were either of you aware at the time that such an agent existed? And even more useful to me—who it was?"

Algernon answered, "I was well aware that many things discussed confidentially by the Royalists was known to the government. Septimus on many occasions quietly suggested we not proceed along certain lines because Thurloe was already able to thwart it, and would punish any perpetrators."

"Did you have any idea who it was?"

"There were a limited number of possibilities. At first I put it down to indiscreet pillow talk by males in the company of Elspeth Kemp, who passed it on to Thurloe and his agents. That idea was negated by the realization that Thurloe knew what was happening here years before Elspeth was an active companion of many county gentry. Next someone tried to sow discord within the family by suggesting that the obvious Cromwellian spy was my then new daughter-in-law Caroline, who came from a strong parliamentary family in the North. There was a similar weakness in that case. Caroline and Ranald did not move into Medlowe Abbey until years after Exodus began informing. I was left with everybody's scapegoat—Sir Job Elliott," confessed Algernon.

"Yes, I have heard that suggestion. He created so many extreme Royalist incidents that seriously embarrassed yourself and the Royalist leadership, yet he was never punished by the Cromwellian authorities," commented Luke.

"If it was Job, it was a double-edged weapon. In the first place he informed the government as to our plans, and in the second his behavior nearly got many of us arrested or possibly executed," added Algernon.

He turned to Septimus. The Earl was blunt, "Septimus, you were the local face of the government in this period. Did you receive orders not to prosecute Job Elliott in this period?"

"Yes, on many occasions, but it was not because Job was Exodus. As long as Job continued on his stupid and counter-productive way, we always had an excuse to come down heavily on the local Royalists. It was because he gave us a reasonable case to act against other supporters of the King, that he was allowed to continue. I never knew who Exodus was, but I did receive the information she or he had forwarded to Mr. Thurloe."

The Earl asked a servant to take the Ingles to their rooms and indicated that he wanted further discussion with Luke. "Despite your encouraging comments earlier about my family not necessarily being involved in my attempted murder, I want you to leave no stone unturned in investigating Ranald's behavior. If he has not attempted patricide, he has at least revealed a total incompetence to succeed me as Earl of Medlowe. Who did he listen to during my absence? Who manipulated him into his largely impolitic decisions?"

"I was not present when most decisions were made. I am not here to take sides, but simply to give the King an assessment of who might advance his cause, and were worthy of a position. Two people only had your son's ear—Edwin and Veronica."

"I feared as much. Edwin has always been trouble. He caused the incidents that forced both Viscount Symes and myself to send Ranald and Edwin to the continent at the end of the forties."

"I was aware that Edwin's problem with women caused his exile to the continent, but did not know Ranald's departure was also forced."

"Not as serious as Edwin's but it still involved inappropriate behavior with women. Ranald from childhood was a prankster. His schoolmasters wanted me to take him away from his school because of the harm his so-called pranks had caused to other students. I had to create a school of my own to contain the trouble that Edwin and Ranald were creating. Whenever he was at the Abbey in those early days, he tried to frighten both gentlewomen and female servants by appearing at their windows or confronting them when alone in the most ridiculous disguises."

Luke smiled inwardly. Another nail dropped into place. Was it being imbedded in Ranald's coffin?

"How did you know the prankster was Ranald?" he asked.

"One evening he confronted Ursula as she was returning from checking on a sick animal for me. Instead of being frozen in terror Ursula lunged forward and pulled his mask off."

"Has Hector informed you of a similar outbreak occurring now?"

"Yes, that is why I raise it with you. But there is even more potentially damaging information which I only received last week. The King remains vitally concerned with Lucy Finch formerly Lucy Symes. He still feels immense guilt that she was raped at his court-in- exile so many years ago. Given his companions at the time he believes the rapist had to be Ranald, Piers or less likely Winston. If the King holds these suspicions, and Ranald succeeds me as the Earl of Medlowe, his influence at court will be minimal. I want these issues cleared up because although I have recovered a little, my days remain numbered."

"My lord, this gives me the opportunity to raise a sensitive issue with you. Ranald is not your eldest, and I believe he has been canvassing the gentlemen gathered here to put an act through Parliament declaring his older brother James, deceased—and himself as heir to the earldom. What happened to James, and would knowledge of him assist in my various investigations?"

"It is so long ago and I have forgotten some of the detail. Meet me here tomorrow morning and I will have Hector with me! At the time and since he has maintained a keen interest in James, and in unveiling the many attempts over the years by imposters claiming to be him."

Next day Luke met with Algernon and Hector. He asked, "Have you had many imposters in the two decades since James disappeared?"

Hector answered, "One every two or three years."

"How could you be sure that one of them was not James?"

"Not difficult Colonel. James not long before he left suffered a riding accident in which a horse kicked out and blinded him in one eye, and made a major indentation in his skull. Only close family knew of this mishap, so any claimant with sight in both eyes, and a perfectly shaped skull is not James," answered Hector.

The Earl intervened, "James and Ranald could not have been more different. James was an excellent horseman and swordsman. He was popular with tenants and servants, and was anxious to learn from them. Although he spent many leisure hours with Ranald and Edwin who lived here for weeks on end, he also saw a lot of Ursula and the young Elspeth. He was very interested in Ursula's knowledge of herbs, and how they could be used to improve the condition of our cattle."

"Did James get on well with Ranald and Edwin?"

Hector looked at Algernon as if seeking permission to speak. The Earl was blunt. "Tell the Colonel what you have believed for years!"

"It was James's frustration with Ranald and Edwin that led him to leave. If his future involved having to live a life like that which Ranald and Edwin seemed to have contemplated for themselves, it was not for him."

"What in particular annoyed James?"

"Ranald and Edwin could think of nothing better to do than play pranks on the more unfortunate of the tenants and servants. James believed they should be improving their talents in a range of activities. He was particularly anxious that both Ranald and Edwin should become efficient hunters and swordsmen. The younger aristocrats greatly resented James's lecturing approach. They wanted a good time, not waste it on developing skills they may never need. James expressed his frustration to me many a time. He jokingly wondered if Ursula could create a soup that would make Ranald and Edwin conform to the model aristocrat that James wanted."

"What were the exact circumstances of James's disappearance?"

"Weeks before he disappeared James dropped hints that he would leave. He was convinced that Algernon had decades of life ahead of him, and he had no desire to settle down to the restricted life of an heir apparent. He wanted to see the world, and experience life outside of England. He had always been interested in the Turk. He told some of the servants that it would be marvelous to serve in the Ottoman navy," said Hector.

"The afternoon on which he left, James had been hunting in the woods with Ranald and Edwin who when questioned at supper claimed he was staying in the woods during the night to observe a badger that had aroused his interest. When he did not appear the next morning, I went to his room. His bed had not been slept in but on a small table was a sealed letter addressed to me.

It was a very short missive. *Forgive me father. I told the boys to lie for me. By the time you read this I will be sailing down the Thames, heading for the Mediterranean.*" Algernon explained.

"Did you receive subsequent letters from him?"

"Only during the first two or three years," said Algernon.

"And I was suspicious of them. Probably forged. I also believe that Ranald and Edwin know more about James's disappearance than they admit. They both left here a few weeks after James," added Hector.

Luke turned to the Earl. "Did Ranald resent the decision to send him to the continent, and eventually the opportunity to join the exiled young King's court?"

"No, he was as anxious as James to leave Medlowe Abbey."

"Why don't you have James declared dead and Ranald your heir?"

"It is not that I think James is still alive, but I have doubts about Ranald as heir," replied Algernon.

"If you by-passed Ranald who is next in line?"

"That's the problem. I have no other male heirs. I have contemplated asking the King to do for me what he has done for himself—legitimize my many bastards."

"My understanding is that they are all female whose marriage will automatically transfer all your estates and titles to their husbands."

Algernon smiled, "Well at least there is something you do not know. Not all my bastards are women."

Hector interrupted, "The King is not likely to accede to such a request. Now that Algernon is back on his feet, he should marry again and sire a new male heir as soon as possible."

Algernon slapped Hector on the back, "That seems a much better idea old friend than the lottery of a daughter's husband."

By the satisfied look on Algernon's face, Luke wondered if such a plan was already well advanced.

34

Luke would clarify one issue immediately. He summoned Mutton Johnson. The soldier may have lost the front part of his face, but the skull was clearly intact with no major dent. He was not James Medlowe.

"Lieutenant, you are not James Medlowe. You lack a vital characteristic. You may return to your duties with Captain Oxenbridge and the matter will not be raised again. If you wish to continue your false claim, I will have you arrested."

"I am happy to withdraw such a claim. It was not my idea. I was approached by a gentlewoman who was clearly impressed by my deformed face. She paid me a large sum to make my claim."

"Has this women approached you since you have been on guard duty here?"

"No, she contacted me on one of my previous assignments."

"Where was that?"

"When I was seconded to the Medlowe town house to escort the Earl and some of his possessions to Whitehall."

"Did you recognize the woman?"

"Not then, but since I have been here I realized it was the lady who is generous with her favors. The woman that was beaten up, and since been moved to Whitehall with her husband."

"Was her beating in any way related to your claim?"

"It may have been. The lady emphasized that her purpose was to provoke someone into doing something stupid, that would lead to his apprehension."

"Did she say who your claim was meant to provoke?"

"Well, it could only be the current heir, Lord Ranald. If he thought I was going to replace him, he might do something rash."

"But only if he knew of your existence. You made your claim to Lord Ashcroft who sent you here in case I could use you for the ends that the woman I know to be Elspeth Kemp, had intended. Unless Ashcroft or the King informed the Medlowes, none of them are aware that you exist. Did you and Mistress Elspeth speak to each other since you have been here?"

"No."

"So she might assume that you had taken her money, and not made any move to implement her plan?"

"Possibly."

"Mutton, if I were a suspicious person I could interpret what you have told me in a very different way. Having taken Elspeth's money you decided that to go ahead with her scheme was very difficult. To hide that you were being paid to make these false claims, it may have been you who gave Elspeth a beating, and then shot at her husband and myself."

"Why would I? She promised she would reward me further when I made my claim more public. Unfortunately, neither of us were aware that there was an aspect of me that would make it impossible for the family to accept me as James."

Luke left Medlowe Abbey and rode to Whitehall to speak to Elspeth. She was delighted to see him and asked that he allow Alex and herself to return to Medlowe Abbey.

"Surely the murder of Finch would lead you to the opposite desire—to remain in the safety of the Royal court."

"If I was allowed to enjoy the freedom of the Royal court I would never want to leave. Your lackey, Captain Hatch, keeps us away from everybody. We are prisoners. I would rather risk life at the Abbey. Have you come to organize our return?"

"No, but I will consider it. All the guests are so well guarded by my men that if they obey instructions, they are safe. There is less than a week to go until they can all disperse."

"Are you taking a break from your duties at Medlowe Abbey and seeking consolation in my company? I had heard that unlike many of the

Cromwellian troops you were a well-known womanizer, but I saw or heard nothing of the kind while you were at the Abbey."

"I am now a happily married man, and I am sure my friend the Marchioness would ensure that I did not stray. No, I am here to question you on an aspect of your past that you have kept secret."

"And what could that possibly be?"

"James Medlowe."

"Why the sudden interest in James? Does it have any bearing on your other investigations?"

"The precarious health of the Earl means that it is a constant and pressing issue. The appearance of an imposter claiming to be James has brought the issue to the fore—an imposter, paid by you to make false claims."

Elspeth showed a moment of annoyance that her activities had been uncovered and argued, "But it could be James. How do you know he is an imposter?"

"Very simply. James as a result of the horse riding accident had more deformities than the loss of an eye. Despite the hideous damage an exploding shell had done to the imposter's face, it did not create an additional deformity that James experienced. I am surprised you were not aware of it, as I understand he was quite close to you and Ursula."

"We were very close. Luckily he disappeared when he did. As a young girl I was besotted with him. At the time I was unaware that I was his half-sister. I imagine Lady Ursula would have told me before matters got out of hand. He was so different to his devious brother, and equally obnoxious friend Edwin Symes. What was this other deformity, the lack of which caught out my imposter?"

"That will remain a secret until the Medlowe succession is settled. What did you hope to achieve by your little scheme? And why do it now?"

"Since we all came to Medlowe Abbey I have spent some time with Edwin. On one occasion when he was extremely drunk, and he was incapable of performing the task for which we had met, he became very garrulous. He also seemed somewhat depressed, so to encourage him I said at least he would one day be Viscount Symes, and unlike Ranald there was no doubt about his succession. He responded by saying there was no doubt that Ranald was the heir, because James would never return."

"Was it a considered statement, or a slip of the tongue?"

"He probably does not remember having ever said it. It seemed to be a long held unmovable belief. The only absolute guarantee that James would never return was that he was dead. A horrible thought struck me. One certain way of knowing someone was dead was to have killed him. Could Edwin and Ranald have killed James on the day he disappeared?"

"You acted on such thin evidence?"

"Thinner than you think. You cannot be sure that anything that Edwin says has a basis in reality. He is quite a sick man who could die at any minute."

"I knew he had fits and a change of personality from time to time, but I did not know that his problem could lead to an early death," admitted Luke.

"Given years of exploding bombs under Spanish fortifications, he received several shrapnel wounds to the head. The surgeons over the years removed most of them, but a few are inoperable. Their movement at any time could kill him."

"So despite this knowledge, you thought you would stir the situation by creating a returning James?"

"If they were guilty of murder, Ranald in an effort to prove the person claiming to be James was an imposter, might find it imperative to prove his brother was dead, and reveal some incriminating facts—or even reveal where the body was buried."

"James disappeared years ago. At the time was there any hint that he may have been killed by anybody, let alone his brother?"

"Not even a whisper. James had made it clear to all that he was about to embark on a great adventure. As he was someone not keen on emotional events such as farewells his leaving without saying goodbye was considered normal. Maybe the adults at the time had doubts, but I certainly didn't, until Edwin's recent comment made me think. My first step was to visit the Earl and raise these doubts with him. I went to his town house but was turned away by his servants. However while there I noticed one of the soldiers had a badly deformed face. That's when I got the idea of substituting him as an imposter."

A servant entered the room, and whispered to Luke. He looked distressed. He took Elspeth by the hand. "Dear lady, I have just been asked to inform you that your husband has died."

Elspeth hugged Luke, but did not shed a tear. "Colonel, you are well aware of my relationship with Alexander. He was a good provider, but we were more like brother and sister. Since leaving Medlowe Abbey his superficial wound became toxic and the King's surgeon thought they might have to amputate a leg, but a herbalist that Captain Hatch brought in believed it was too late. The news is not a surprise."

"You may wish to take Alex back to his manor to be buried with his relatives and neighbors. Captain Hatch will provide you with an escort, as the source of your beating and now Alexander's death has not been identified, let alone caught."

"I will certainly accompany Alex back to our manor where the staff can prepare him for burial, but I would feel much safer at Medlowe Abbey. I will stay with my mother, Ursula."

Luke agreed and organized the escorts needed.

Another part of the message Luke had received from the servant was that he was to report to King before returning to Medlowe Abbey.

The King was anxious to hear Luke's report on the latest developments at Medlowe Abbey, and appeared delighted that the Earl had effectively resumed control, and that Sir Septimus Ingle's arrival had not led to any dangerous reaction from the more extreme Royalists.

Luke took advantage of his chat with the King to focus on the fate of James Medlowe. "Your Majesty, I know it was ten years ago when the young aristocrat, Ranald Medlowe joined your fledgling court and became a close companion of yourself and your brother. Did he ever mention the fate of his brother James at the time? There have been suggestions lately that he may have played a role in James's disappearance."

"No, the impression I got was that he was extremely jealous of James's world adventure, and that my humble little court was a very poor second prize for a young lad anxious to escape the routine of estate management and an England controlled by the Parliament and the army. The biggest upheaval at the time was that Viscount Symes had spent a lot of time and money having me agree to take his son Edwin and daughter Lucy into my court. Little Lucy arrived, but Edwin absolutely refused his father's orders and joined the French army."

"Any other relevant comments?"

"Edwin's refusal did not worry me, but Ranald was furious. His best friend of yesteryear refused to join him. His only comments about his older brother was an anti-Turkish rant. For someone who then and since has shown little regard for the Christian faith, Ranald was almost apoplectic that his brother hoped to join the navy of the Ottoman Turk. If he has, he may have fought many a battle against your victorious Cromwellian admirals, maybe yourself?"

"My only naval battle when I commanded a man of war was against the Papist Knights of Malta in defense of an Ottoman outpost. The Protector was then anxious for an alliance with the Ottoman against all Catholics."

"Unfortunately maintaining a powerful navy to be an acceptable ally of anybody is proving very costly. That is my problem. Back to yours—you have less than a week to uncover the Finch and Kemp murderer."

35

On his return to Medlowe Abbey Luke reported to the Earl who took the initiative. "Colonel, while you were away I inspected the woods as Hector had informed me that the deer needed to be culled, and the timber harvested. I met my old friend, that salt of the earth countryman, Little Johnny."

"I was surprised that he has freedom to poach on your estate, with all the authorities turning a blind eye."

"Years ago I offered him the position of head gamekeeper which he declined. However he has for years been my eyes and ears regarding what goes on in the woods, and generally what happens on my estate at night."

"And did Johnny have anything of interest to tell you?"

"He certainly did. That is why I asked you here."

"Just before my return Johnny had to go into hiding. Ranald had ignored all agreements and reported him to the parish constable as a poacher, and demanded that he be brought before a magistrate."

"Why would Ranald reverse what he must have known was your long term policy?"

"He wants rid of Johnny."

"Why?"

"Several times since the gentry of the county have been staying here Johnny has come across Ranald in the woods. The fact that Ranald appears and disappears very quickly suggested to Johnny that he was using some of the secret tunnels. I have only told Ranald of one of the many secret passages around the Abbey."

"Interesting, but does it bear on any of my investigations?"

198

"The night you and Kemp were shot at, Johnny met Ranald on the edge of the wood. Ranald asked him why he was there. He explained that you had called him in to help find Kemp. The key point, according to Johnny, was that Ranald said that the Colonel was in the woods."

"I can see where this is heading."

"The evidence is much stronger than you could think, and it does not look good for my son. Later in the evening Johnny happened to be near the exit of one of the tunnels—the only tunnel about which Ranald has knowledge. A small figure emerged with a primed musket and carbine, pushed some bushes aside, and fired both weapons. Johnny saw Kemp and yourself fall to the ground. The shooter disappeared back up the tunnel."

"Can you believe Johnny? It could be a disgruntled employee getting his own back on a master who sought his arrest."

"Maybe, some of the locals can be vindictive, but Johnny has never disappointed me over decades of co-operation. You may be able to find some concrete evidence to identify the shooter. Search the area around the tunnel exit, and make your way back up the tunnel! The shooter may have left some evidence of his or her identity."

"Was Johnny absolutely certain it was Ranald?"

"No. It was getting dark and he only had a fleeting glimpse of an over-dressed figure."

"It could have equally have been Edwin Piers, Winston Finch or a woman?"

"Yes, but as far as I know none of them are aware of that tunnel."

Later that afternoon Luke, Mark and four of their men searched the area of woodland around the tunnel exit. Luke recreated the circumstances of the shooting, standing where he and Kemp had been shot, while Mark crept carefully from the tunnel exit to a position where he had a clear view of Luke. The soldiers thoroughly searched every inch of the relevant terrain. Luke was not optimistic, given the time that had elapsed and the several unseasonal downpours.

As they raked through the rotting leaves numerous animal bones were uncovered. There was a shout of delight when a small piece of fabric was discovered near were the shooter would have fired. Luke jokingly called out, " I suppose it is an embroidered handkerchief with then initials R M?"

Mark examined the small piece of cloth. "Alas Luke it is the run of mill piece of fabric used to clean a musket. It is imbedded with gunpowder—so common that there is no way of determining ownership."

"Damn, let's light the tapers and explore the tunnel!" said a dispirited Luke.

The bramble bush that obscured a small trap door was pushed back and the soldiers began to climb down into the tunnel. Luke drew Mark's attention to the damp soil around the edge of the bramble. "There are several identical footprints. It is reasonable to assume they belong to the shooter."

Mark was impressed, "It is a strange print. It is very light and indicates a solid heel which is circular in shape."

"Well it is a start. If we can get access to Ranald's shoes, we may have the evidence we need." Working their way up the tunnel the soldiers achieved nothing other than to confirm the prints. On the dusty floor there was evidence that the last person to use the tunnel wore shoes with the unusual heel.

Later that day Septimus called on Luke. "Colonel, I seek your advice. Should I accept the King's offer, and continue to serve on the bench, but now as the loyal servant of King Charles II?"

"Yes. My justification for doing so was twofold. There was no alternative as our Republic and Protectorate had torn itself apart, and to preserve law and order, and the security of the nation the government of whatever hue now needed support. Since I have served the King over the last few months I see my decision is helping the King unite the nation. He has appointed as many former republicans and Cromwellians to his administration, as he has those who served him in exile. The loyal Royalists who stayed in England seem to have missed out, except perhaps our host the Earl of Medlowe."

"Thank you Luke, that was the way I was thinking. The Earl and I worked well together under the previous regimes. He pleaded with me last night to accept the King's offer, as he told me your investigations had discovered problems with most of the Royalist newcomers."

"While you are here, I need to question you regarding events when you were the government's senior magistrate."

"Well now that we are both back on the same side, I can be a little more forthcoming than I was the other day."

"I am still focused on identifying Exodus, and on why Kemp and Finch were murdered. My gut feeling is that the latter had more to do with the distant past than the present."

"Both Kemp and Finch spent most of the interregnum in London or in this county. Finch spent a couple of years on the edges of the King's court-in-exile a decade or more ago, but returned to here for his marriage to Lucy Symes."

"So either of them could have been Exodus?"

"Or both."

"What do you mean?"

"Sometime during the last five years, Exodus became the cover for two separate agents."

"How do you know that?"

"I was regularly briefed by John Thurloe. On one occasion he confided in me that he was worried about the information he was receiving from my county as its cost had just doubled. Exodus on his or her own initiative had recruited another agent on the grounds that much more information could be obtained."

"And was it?"

"Yes, the new recruit had obviously access into the inner circles of the Royalists."

"Finch or Kemp could have been the original Exodus and someone closer to the Medlowes, the new recruit. This puts a new slant to my investigation. It is quite possible that Finch or Kemp if the original Exodus, was killed by the new recruit to conceal his or her activity."

"Finch was the more likely original source. He had no firm loyalties, and was most likely protecting his future should the Protectorate last. The level of the intelligence that Thurloe recovered in the early days was the type that money would have bought from servants or disgruntled tenants. Finch was never close to the Medlowes nor to his in-laws, the Symes. But Ranald and Job Elliott, my suspects, were."

"Don't forget the women! Lucy Finch, Elspeth Kemp, Veronica Petty or Caroline Medlowe could have been that agent."

"I'd rule Lucy out. Winston kept her almost in isolation during those years. She rarely appeared at social events, let alone family get togethers. She would know nothing in her own right, only what Winston chose to tell her. Elspeth, on the other hand, given her generous approach to men, could have picked up a lot of sensitive information that she may or may not have passed on. Veronica and Caroline are both ambitious and able women. If we ever allow women to be politicians, those two would serve us well. Veronica was a thorn in my side, while more recently Caroline has been a go-between between the Earl and myself."

"The gatekeeper's wife is spreading a sordid rumor that the Earl and his daughter-in-law are inappropriately close."

"Possibly. Algernon has little time for Ranald, and in the months leading up to his illness and during the early part of his recovery, he relied completely on Caroline. She ran the estate from the Medlowe town house through Hector. Has she assumed overt control since her return?"

"Not that I noticed, but she is one of the residents I have not thoroughly probed. My only information is that she detests Edwin, and is working actively to break his influence over her husband, and weaken any similar influence over Ranald that Veronica Petty may continue to wield."

"I can understand the latter. The Earl used to rely on Veronica, but now she has been replaced by Caroline. There is only room for one of them at the top of the Royalist social ladder."

"Is there anything else I should know that might help in my investigations?"

"During the Republic and Protectorate the most troublesome person for the government amongst the senior Royalists currently here at Medlowe was Lady Ursula Hall. Fortunately she was absent for the last three years in a continental nunnery. Her recent return could have upset a lot of people."

"Did she actually cause trouble, or was she the victim of the county's prejudices. She is Welsh—not the most popular of races in this county. She is also a Papist, and openly so. And she is a midwife, herbalist and white witch."

"She has been a convenient scapegoat over many years. In times of trouble, many locals blamed their problems on Ursula whom they accused of being a diabolic witch. In the end she was saved because her herbal ointments and remedies saved many a farmer his livestock. During the years she was away in a continental nunnery, animal infections increased greatly. That is why since her recent return she has received surprising support, despite Orlando's attempt to be rid of her—and the lingering popular fear that she is a dangerous witch."

"And I was recently informed that she is the birth mother of the Earl's illegitimate girl Elspeth."

"Often rumored, but never acknowledged until very recently."

"Would Ursula have reasons to have Finch and Kemp killed?"

"As a midwife, she would know the secrets of many a gentry family, and maybe of any unwanted pregnancies caused by Finch and or Kemp. But given her expertise, poison would have been her weapon—not a dagger or a musket."

"Is she putting together an alliance of pro-Papist gentry as Algernon's father had done just before his murder? Finch's death in the same manner and place must have some significance."

"The timing is wrong. During the Puritan Protectorate there were many high church Anglican gentry who probably preferred an alliance with Papist comrades rather than the Presbyterian and Independent Puritans such as ourselves. But now with a Catholic Queen Mother and suspicions about the Duke of York, or even the King himself, there appears to be no point. If Ursula is active in opposing certain gentry and aristocrats, it is personal rather than political or religious."

"A personal question—when you were set upon by the out-of-county militia that we now know was led by Edwin, and your men slaughtered, were you trying to leave the county?"

Septimus smiled. "Yes, I was leaving the county, but not the country. Given the failure of the London generals to maintain law and order and the security of the state, and distrusting the several times turncoat, George Monk, I was trying to join up with John Lambert, who I saw as the only savior of the republic."

"At one point Lambert offered me command of his cavalry, but I was persuaded by Fairfax that Monk, and the return of King offered the most security. Let's hope I was not wrong."

36

Luke would question Caroline. Given her far from warm reception on previous occasions he diplomatically made his approach through the Earl who arranged that they meet in his library mid-morning. Caroline was no more sympathetic, opening the conversation with a hardly veiled attack on Luke's continued presence at the Abbey. "Colonel, you should be gone from here within a week."

"Not likely my lady. I have to solve the murder of Finch and Kemp and the King would like me to look into three cold cases—what happened to James Medlowe, who raped Lucy Symes, and who was the Cromwellian agent Exodus?"

"Have you progressed very far on any of them?" she asked sneeringly.

Luke lied. "The murder of Kemp, and the attempt on my life is all but solved. The shooter left behind so many clues that I expect to make an arrest at any moment."

Caroline showed intense interest which surprised Luke. "What type of clues gave this varlet away?" Luke mixed truth with fiction. "Footprints, handkerchiefs, pieces of fabric, spilt gunpowder, dropped musket shots. The shooter was very careless. Who do you think killed Kemp?"

Caroline's expression changed. She was beginning to enjoy the discussion. "Colonel, the intended target would not be Kemp. It was you. You have irritated countless people with your enquiries. And your continued use of military power, even though it is the King's name is unacceptable. Kemp was a nothing. He avoided annoying or pleasing everybody. Nobody would have wasted any ammunition on him."

"If I was the target, I would be surprised. I am simply carrying out the orders of the King. Should I be killed he would simply replace me with another agent. I agree that Kemp was not the person to provoke someone to the point of killing him, but what if the murderer thought that his wife Elspeth in her various adventures, had passed on to him very sensitive information?"

"Yes, maybe you were wise in sending the Kemps away. Elspeth is a danger to a number of people."

"Including your husband?"

"Ranald has misunderstood what his father has in mind for Elspeth. As a traditional aristocrat, he would not in any way alter the accepted patterns of succession. However he believes that his daughter should not be left without a secure income particularly now that her husband has been killed. He has decided only yesterday to give her a fortune in gold, silver and jewels that should calm Ranald down. As we speak Algernon is showing Elspeth through the treasure house to select the items she wants."

"Those jewels would have been passed down to you as the future Countess of Medlowe. How do you feel about them being given to Elspeth?"

"A petty gentry approach, Colonel! You have seen the family treasury. The Medlowe family jewels are so extensive that whatever Elspeth takes, will hardly be missed. Algernon will give her enough to see her through several years and with Alexander dead, Elspeth can make a lucrative second marriage. Ranald has nothing to fear from his half-sister."

"I was sent here to observe the tussle between the various Royalist families and groups for control of the King's county administration, and membership of the House of Commons. What has surprised me is the power and influence of two women—Veronica and yourself. Where have you positioned yourself in Ranald's unsuccessful attempt to maintain Medlowe dominance against Phineas Leigh?"

"That description of the situation is now obsolete. With the return of Algernon, Medlowe dominance is restored."

"In that case who is the real power within the Medlowe camp?"

"Algernon, with advice from his son and daughter-in-law. The only two issues we now face involve the Leigh family—one is to ally with brother Phineas, and the other to contain sister Veronica' wrath on her loss of her influence."

"A clear and blunt assessment."

"Colonel, I need to conclude this discussion. Our hunting party is about to leave."

"Are you an expert with the bow?" asked Luke.

"How condescending of you! I was brought up during the Civil War."

"And your brothers taught you to use a musket?"

"Exactly, and as a result I can shoot better than most men."

"That my lady may be an incriminating admission."

Caroline glared and walked away.

Luke left the meeting with new ideas running through his head. He had assumed that the shooter who killed Alexander and injured him was a man. Mark had remarked that the footprints were very light suggesting that the shooter was not a heavy person. Caroline was certainly light.

Luke found Jane and asked her about female footwear. He described the footprint found in and at the exit of the tunnel. She affirmed that such heels were more likely worn by women, but she had not seen any of the ladies wearing such a shoe. In the building, most wore higher heeled footwear, and an almost flat boot. The short rounded heel would be a useful all-conditions shoe.

As Luke returned to his apartment he was surprised to see Caroline on horseback being led back to the Abbey. He asked an attendant what had happened at the hunt. He replied, "It is continuing, but Lady Caroline was taken ill. She vomited and felt faint. The Earl ordered her to leave the hunt and rest."

Meanwhile a meeting was taking place that would have alarmed Caroline and Ranald. Veronica met her brother Phineas. Phineas was in a relaxed expansive mood. Before the return of the Earl, he was in a dominant position, which he was determined to maintain.

"To what do I owe this visit, dear sister?"

Veronica as blunt, "If we are to retain our positions of influence in this county, we need to unite our efforts."

Phineas laughed, "Sister, are you about to jump a sinking ship? You wish to join your son Nathan in an alliance that the Earl will shortly offer me. He cannot over rule us, but I will consider a partnership, if he agrees to several of my suggestions. You have been axed from his inner circle, otherwise you would not be here."

"The Earl ignores the support that Julius and I gave him for decades. He is captivated by his daughter-in-law whom I have never trusted. I am not the only one no longer consulted. The Earl and Caroline have sidelined Edwin, who I would not be surprised also pays you a visit. He is certainly upset about something."

"The Earl and Caroline may ignore Edwin, but Ranald continues to spend much time alone with him. Those two are very close, and Ranald has resisted Caroline's attempt to break them up. If I were the Earl, I would sideline Ranald, along with Edwin and yourself. I have to be frank with you Veronica. You are a political liability. If the Earl does not want your advice, for me to add you to my group, would make it more difficult for me to negotiate an alliance with him. The King wants a diverse group of officials in this county. According to the Colonel, he is most likely to appoint from both groups of Royalist gentry and retain some of the Cromwellians for good measure. Septimus Ingle has been offered a position on the bench of magistrates. It is time for you to retire from active politicking. Nathan is a worthy successor to Julius, and will be one of my nominees for a position of importance. Concentrate on winning support for your son. Your time in the sun is over."

Veronica was furious. She had never expected to be sidelined by the Earl and then rejected by her own brother. If she did not act immediately she would be a nobody. But what could she do? Who could she rally? As a mere woman, she little power to gain support compared to her brother and the Earl.

Then it hit her. She could only rise again, if she created a vacuum. She must destroy the credibility of the Earl and her brother. Then maybe her son could emerge as the new leader with herself as his adviser. Who currently at the Abbey had the power and authority to bring down the Earl and Phineas?

There was only one possibility—Colonel Luke Tremayne. She would provide him with enough unfavorable information to force his hand against her two predominant opponents. She would also try to develop an alliance with Edwin and whomever else was out of favor with Algernon and Phineas.

Veronica found Edwin walking in the garden and immediately raised her concerns with him. "You have been undermined in the Earl's eyes by your friend Ranald's devious wife. We should combine to show the Earl that Caroline is not to be trusted and that you and I are his longtime and most loyal supporters."

Edwin was disconcerted by the venom that drove Veronica's diatribe. He tried to placate her. "Nothing that the group gathered here decides will be binding or carried out. The King will make up his own mind, and that will be influenced by the report of Colonel Tremayne, which will not be very favorable to any of us. When you leave here Veronica forget about politics and power until the Earl dies. Although he is currently apparently reasonably well, his problems could reoccur at any time, and probably be fatal."

"If you have any information that can destroy Algernon and Phineas tell the Colonel. If he strongly recommends against both of them, the King would go along with it. That is why the King sent Tremayne here in the first place!"

"Don't show your bitterness too openly. There is still one or more killers loose in the Abbey, and you do not want to be the next victim," warned Edwin.

"I have to act now. I cannot wait until Algernon dies. When Ranald takes over, unless he is willing to divorce his wife, Caroline will remain the dominant woman in the county."

"Veronica, you are not only out to destroy Phineas, Algernon, and Caroline, but in the process destroy Ranald. Who could you possibly support as the senior politician in the county with all these people against you?"

"My son, Nathan with the advice from myself and Job, could carry out that role most effectively."

"Is Nathan willing to go along with your plans, my lady?"

"Of course."

"Have you spoken to him about destroying Algernon and Phineas?"

'No, but why would he object?"

"Because he greatly admires his uncle and wishes Phineas to be his social and political patron for years to come. Don't remain too close to Job. He is increasingly seen as a pariah whose behavior during the King's exile put other Royalists in danger. And the Earl believes he is the mysterious Cromwellian agent that Tremayne seeks to reveal."

Veronica could not conceal her growing anger. Everybody had turned against her. Despite what Edwin had said she would turn to the only person she could trust, her one time lover and alleged father of Nathan, Sir Job Elliott.

As she made her way to his room, she passed Ursula leaving the apartment of Ranald and Caroline. She politely asked whether Ranald and Caroline were well. Ursula who distrusted Veronica absolutely lied, "Yes my lady, both are fine. My visit was not related to my herbal prowess."

This only infuriated Veronica further. What else did Ursula have in common with Caroline? The only answer which jumped into her tormented mind was simple—their hatred of her.

37

Veronica, determined to bring down her former allies, visited Jane to ascertain what sort of information the Colonel would find most valuable.

Jane, immediately distrustful, was cautious. "His current tasks are well known. Uncover the murderer or murderers of Finch and Kemp. He is also interested on behalf of the King in two cold cases—the rape of Lucy Finch and the identity of the Cromwellian spy, high within Royalist ranks, code named Exodus."

"Has his investigation advanced far on any of those issues?" Veronica probed.

"Yes, he believes he is about to make an arrest concerning the murderer of Kemp."

Jane deliberately set the trap. "He only has to find the owner of a particular pair of shoes that left their impression at the scene of the shooting. By their description they belong to a woman. Given the Colonel's attitude, if he uncovers the Kemp murderer, it will be difficult to persuade him that the same person did not kill Finch."

"Look no further than the wives! Lucy Finch and Elspeth Kemp were never the happiest of women," Veronica snarled.

"To what end would they have their husbands murdered?"

"Both could improve their status with remarriage."

"Lucy's marriage to Winston was about to be annulled, so I doubt she needed to organize a murder, and no husband would give Elspeth the freedom that Alexander did. You were resident in the county throughout the King's exile and with your husband played a major part in Royalist politics during that period."

Jane deliberately provoked her listener and continued, "The Colonel has whittled down his list of female suspects to three—Caroline, Ursula and yourself. If you visit the Colonel, provide him with evidence that clears your name, and implicates the others."

Veronica was content. Jane had given her two names that she could easily blacken further. She would visit Tremayne and destroy both Caroline and Ursula.

Veronica met Luke and immediately began her destructive campaign. "My position in the county has deteriorated sharply since you first arrived here. You suspect me of being involved in one or more of the murders. I cannot defend myself as such, except to point out that others have stronger motives than I."

Veronica's anti-Papist prejudices boiled over. "Ursula Hall murdered Winston Finch—and possibly Alexander Kemp."

"Motive?"

"Very different in each case."

"What did she have against Finch?"

"Revenge for what happened over fifty years ago."

Luke's interest was sparked. This was new territory.

Veronica sensed her impact. "Colonel, it all goes back to the Gunpowder Plot and the Medlowe ancestor, John. He was murdered in the chapel by being stabbed repeatedly in the back to create an impression of the cross, just as Finch was decades later. Locals believed it was the result of an old curse delivered by the last superior of this Abbey when the Medlowe family usurped his monastery. It had nothing to do with any curse. John, Earl of Medlowe was about to be elevated to James I's Privy Council, which would have made him the most powerful aristocrat in the land. This was very unpopular in parts of this county, and especially within the city of London. The Medlowes at that time vigorously opposed the spread of the city."

"Surely conflict between the City and county aristocrats was not sufficient to provoke murder?" asked Luke.

"Probably in itself John's opponents would not have pushed so far, but the Gunpowder Plot erupted and anti-Catholic hysteria spread across the county," said Veronica.

"But the Medlowes were Protestant," commented Luke.

"Not all of them. John's wife was an Italian noblewoman—and a Papist. At the time it was widely believed that most aristocrats were crypto-Papists anyhow."

"How does all this relate back to Ursula Hall?"

"One of John's major local allies was a wealthy gentleman of Welsh descent, Sir David Jones. At the time John was murdered by hired assassins paid for by the London anti-Catholic plutocracy, they also paid mobs to plunder and loot any Catholic manor they could find. Sir David was killed by one rampaging mob, as were many of his servants. Other Catholic families managed to flee, as did Sir David's pregnant wife who was away visiting friends at the time."

"Ursula was that unborn child? I thought her birth name was Davies."

"Yes, her mother on returning to Wales remarried a Davies."

"All this is very interesting but how does the massacre of her father and fellow religionists fifty years ago, lead her to kill Finch and Kemp?"

"Two of the leading London families involved in the anti Medlowe campaign at the time of the Gunpowder Plot were the Finches and the Kemps."

"How do you know all this?"

"The county ally of the then Aldermen Finch and Kemp was my own Leigh grandfather. My marriage to Julius Petty, a Medlowe ally, a generation later, was part of my family's attempt to ameliorate the imbedded antagonism between the Leighs and the Medlowes."

"Why would Ursula wait all this time? If any of this is true, something must have re-activated a need for revenge."

"Yes, and Orlando is to blame. He made anti-Catholicism a political issue in the coming elections. Finch recently made it clear that he would support such an approach."

"Then why kill Kemp?"

"Maybe for the same reason, although you could never discover what Alexander actually believed or would support. More likely it was Ursula's motherly concern. She recently made known to Elspeth, and the rest of us that she was the woman's mother. Maybe she felt Kemp had not done the right thing by her daughter, especially in his forcing her to use her sexual appeal to men for his own selfish political gain. To free Elspeth from such a liability might be sufficient motive."

"I doubt that Elspeth's sexual adventures were forced on her by Alexander. Thank you Lady Veronica. You have certainly made me aware of matters of which I was in total ignorance. Anything equally negative about Lady Caroline?"

"What really annoys me is not that the political establishment changes its alliances. That is part of the game, but that loyalty of thirty years counts for nothing ."

Luke sensed for the first time that Veronica was very vulnerable as well as embittered. He decided to change his approach. "My lady since I arrived here, you stood out as one of two people with political acumen—common sense, logical argument and a necessary dose of pragmatism—unfortunately missing in most gentlemen seeking to serve the King. It must be a family trait as your brother is the other person clearly with such ability. He almost demolished the Ranald led Medlowe push single handed."

"Caroline doesn't have similar abilities?" Veronica snarled.

"I have no evidence of her strengths or weaknesses. All I do know is that she despises Lord Edwin, comes from a mixed political background and has an almost unhealthy relationship with her father-in-law. She was not at Medlowe Abbey to be the original Exodus, but in the last year or so of the Protectorate she could have become a second agent."

Veronica relaxed. "That Colonel could explain what the Earl and I noticed at the time. Up until a year or so ago the quality of information that Exodus sent to Thurloe was low grade. It was material that a good purse could pay for from people who were not central to our cause. At the time because he was throwing away money in all directions to improve his position in the county Algernon suspected that Exodus was Finch or, despite my objections, Job Elliot. Job is no traitor. His acts of Royalist defiance that may have appeared stupid came from the heart. In the months before the return of the King, Thurloe appeared to receive information that could only have come from the Earl's inner circle—Algernon, Ranald, Caroline, Edwin, Julius or myself."

"And from my perspective, I have no convincing evidence which one or two of the six it was."

"You can rule out Edwin. He was still on the continent when Thurloe's information picked up. Algernon already had good relationships with the Protectorate as can be seen in his closeness to Ingle. Julius was convinced years ago that the King would return and saw no need to curry favor with the government, as did I. Ranald frankly would not have the brains to maintain the secrecy that an agent such as Exodus obviously had. I understand that neither Thurloe nor the King had any idea who the agent or agents were."

"Consequently you are suggesting that the only person who could be part two of Exodus is Caroline?"

"Yes, and I have additional evidence pointing in that direction. Some of the information that clearly Thurloe had, was not known to Julius or myself nor Edwin or Ranald—matters discussed by Caroline and Algernon alone."

"Great! If you can give me the details of such information, I can question Lady Caroline on them. This could be the convincing evidence I need."

"It is difficult to remember as these things did not seem greatly important at the time. It is clear that your recommendations to the King will carry more weight than Ranald's pathetic attempt to put together an agreed list of suitable gentry, or my brother's much more professional team. At the moment with the Earl's return, no one seems to know where anybody stands. They have only a few days left. Will you recommend my son Nathan as a reliable Royal official or parliamentary member?"

"I have not yet probed into your son's stance on key issues, but his assessment that your brother rather than Ranald offered him the best opportunity to advance his prospects suggests he has some political acumen."

"Have you any other questions for me?"

"Yes, the most important of all. Can you give me any evidence that you are not the murderer or Exodus?"

Veronica was flustered. She had assumed that as the interview went on she had won over Luke's confidence. Had the whole exercise been a waste of time—and she remained a key suspect?

Luke continued to turn the screw, "From my point of view Lady Veronica you were the Earl's closest confidante during most of the period that Exodus operated. You were the one person in Medlowe Abbey who five years ago had enough political acumen to realize that the Cromwellian dynasty might be here to stay. To protect your position for the future to become an agent for Thurloe was a sensible and pragmatic decision. Finch may have discovered this, and you had him killed and dressed the incident up with daggers in the chapel to divert attention to Ursula."

Veronica said nothing.

"In addition your husband's attempt to seek an annulment on the grounds that Nathan was not his, could have caused you to act when you did. Maybe Kemp and Finch supported Julius, and you killed them or had them killed as an act of revenge. In that case the role of your Nathan, Job and Phineas would need further investigation."

This was too much for Veronica. "Rubbish! You are letting your imagination go berserk. There is absolutely no evidence that Finch or Kemp were in any way involved with Julius's plans. What Julius did to Nathan and myself would not be central to the Kemp Finch plans in any way. Politically Julius was seeking reconciliation with my brother, not a capitulation to the so called new guard of younger Royalists, most of whom had just returned from the continent."

"I have seen you enjoying the hunt on several occasions. Are you a good shot?"

"No! I had a proper education. Despite the Civil War I have never held a musket, carbine or pistol, let alone fired such weapons. But I am an excellent archer. And I note that nobody so far has had an arrow imbedded in their heart."

Luke was stymied—but was Veronica telling the truth?

"Have you been completely removed from the Earl's inner circle?"

"Yes, he now meets regularly with my brother."

"All the women have been dismissed?"

"I have, and Caroline is not well. She is pregnant."

38

"The Earl must be happy that a grandchild is on the way and the dynasty advanced into the next generation."

"Not necessarily. This may be another issue that requires your sleuthing abilities," commented Veronica.

"What do you mean?"

"Ranald is unable to beget children. Algernon discussed with me at one stage how to overcome this problem should James not return."

"Your solution?"

"The one taken by many aristocratic families in a similar position. Impregnate the wife by a potent source, and bring up the child as the legitimate offspring of the couple concerned."

"So Ranald is not the father?"

"Unless doctors or the clergy have worked a miracle, it is not likely."

"Who is?"

Veronica saw her opportunity to fire a lethal dart. "The only person who spent considerable time alone with Caroline both here and in the town house, was her father-in-law."

Luke was astonished.

The vindictive Veronica had conveniently ignored Vaughan's more likely paternity.

Heavy overnight rain continued into the morning, forcing Luke to delay his meeting with Mark and Miles at the gatehouse until early afternoon. As he approached the muddy surrounds to the gatehouse he noticed footprints in the mud leading from one of the gatehouse doors to an adjacent hedge on which washing had been belatedly placed to dry in the finally emerging sun. He stopped in his tracks. The footprint was identical with that of Kemp's killer.

He could hardly contain his excitement. He immediately found Bettina and asked, "Who placed your washing on the adjacent hedge?"

"Oh Colonel, you fancy some of the undergarments displayed there?" she asked cheekily.

"This is serious. Someone in this household could be charged with murder."

"Come, Colonel. I am not one of the fancy ladies in the big house. I do my own washing and place it on the hedge to dry—although given the heavy rain I have only just completed the task. What's so important about it?"

"Could you lift the hems of your skirt and petticoats six inches above the ground ?"

"I will remove both of them for you, Colonel," Bettina whispered, anticipating the long desired encounter with the still attractive soldier.

"All I am interested in at the moment are your shoes," was Luke's deflating comment.

"Why, my shoes?"

"They are the shoes of a murderer. And unless you can give me a satisfactory explanation I will arrest you for the fatal shooting of Alexander Kemp. Have you had those shoes for long?"

Bettina, quickly realizing her potentially dire situation, was immediately forthcoming.

"I only purchased those shoes a few days ago."

"Who from?"

"A maid of one of the ladies staying at the Abbey."

"How come?"

"Since the Abbey has been full of the rich, there has been an increase in the amount of still useable goods that they ask their servants to throw away, or that the servants steal. I quickly made it known to all that I would buy any suitable objects, and sell them on through Little Johnny at The Blue Dog."

"Whose servant sold you the shoes?"

"The Welsh witch, Ursula."

Luke smiled inwardly. All was fitting into place. He would take the shoes and confront Ursula. He cancelled his planned meeting and went straight to Ursula's rooms.

He was received by a pleasant Ursula who enquired whether there was yet another injured person for her to treat. "No my lady. Very serious charges have been made against you—in essence, that you murdered of Finch and Kemp."

"Why would I murder those two pushy local gentlemen?"

"Because their ancestors provoked a rampaging anti- Catholic mob that murdered your father as a cover for their killing of the then Earl of Medlowe."

"What rubbish! I was not even born when all that happened, and I was not aware of these details until the current Earl told me at the time I married Orlando. If I was so determined to exact my revenge, why did I wait over a decade to exact it?"

"You have become alarmed that another anti-Papist alliance is being created by your husband with Finch and Kemp against the Queen Mother, and the return of the Catholic peers to the House of Lords."

"Colonel, my only concern that is governed by my religion is personal, not political—the annulment of my marriage by church authorities. Orlando is attempting to derail this by parliamentary legislation. If I murder anybody it will be Orlando."

"Lady Ursula, I would like to believe you, but I have strong evidence that you shot Kemp at least."

"And what is that evidence?"

Luke extracted an item from a canvas bag, "This shoe, my lady."

"How does this shoe link me to the murder of Kemp?"

"It has an unusual heel and provided the distinctive footprints at the scene of the crime."

"But how is this shoe linked with me?"

"After I informed people that I was about to make an arrest of Kemp's murderer on the basis of a shoe print, you asked your maid to dispose of these shoes. Instead she sold them to Bettina the gatekeeper's wife who I discovered wearing them only an hour or so ago."

"Hand me the shoe, Colonel!"

Luke handed one of shoes to Ursula. She hitched up her skirts and petticoats, and proceeded to remove the shoe she was wearing. "Compare the shoes, colonel! My Welsh heritage has given me exceptionally large feet for a woman, I cannot fit into this shoe. It is too small. It is not mine."

Luke was flummoxed. Ursula did have comparatively large feet, and even at a struggle could in no way fit into the killer's shoe.

He recovered quickly and asked if he could speak to any of the maid servants who might have sold the shoe to Bettina. Three girls were brought before him.

"Nobody is in trouble, but one of you has been caught up in the middle of my murder investigations." Luke produced the shoes and continued, "Which of you sold these shoes to Bettina the gatekeeper's wife?"

Two of the girls looked bewildered, but the third looked discomforted. Luke focused on her. "You sold the shoe. Denying it will not help as all I have to do is to parade all three of you in front of Bettina, and she will identify the culprit."

"Abigail, tell the Colonel the truth. You are not in trouble, and what you say can help him a lot," intervened Ursula.

"Abigail, this is not your mistress's shoe. Where did you find it?"

"Each morning the waste from the various apartments is deposited in one of two places—a large pile that will be buried, and another that will be burnt. I took my lady's waste down the other day and there amongst the rubbish was a pair of hardly worn shoes. They were too classy for a servant to wear, and I had heard of Bettina's network and took them to her."

"So there is no way of knowing who discarded the shoes?"

"You could ask all the servants in the Abbey," suggested the now perky Abigail.

"In the circumstances I doubt that the lady concerned would have been stupid enough to give it to a servant to dispose of. And I would have buried it far from the domestic waste."

Luke left.

Ursula entered her bedchamber, threw herself on the bed and wept. She had seen those shoes before.

Luke had only just returned to his apartment when a servant asked him to meet immediately in the Earl's library. He entered the room to find the Earl, Caroline, Hector, the Earl's physician and the chaplain. They looked distressed.

"What has happened, my lord. Not another murder?"

The Earl whispered, "Ranald is dead."

Hector explained, "His lordship was gored to death by his favorite bull, Master Medlowe."

"Did anybody see it happen?"

"No. Ranald went into the pen, as he did daily. Those in the vicinity heard several screams, and entered the pen to find Ranald on the ground bleeding profusely and the bull stamping his feet and trying to gore him further," continued Hector.

"He was dead by the time I reached him," added the physician.

"Did you send for Ursula?"

"I wanted to, but Caroline forbade it," said Hector.

"Ursula works miracles with healing and control of animals. Why did you not invite her to help?" Luke asked of Caroline.

"Because she murdered Ranald."

"That is going too far, Caroline. Ranald was attacked by the bull," said Algernon.

"But why did the bull attack? Master Medlowe is the gentlest of animals, and he and Ranald had a friendly encounter every day. He spent more time with Master Medlowe than he did with me. Ursula bewitched the animal to attack him. I want her charged with witchcraft and murder."

Before Luke could answer, she stormed from the room.

He turned towards the remaining gentlemen. "I do not believe in witchcraft. It is a device to blame a scapegoat when no other explanation can be found. But Caroline has a point—why did a usually gentle beast turn into a killer. Where is Master Medlowe now? I hope he has not been killed."

Hector replied, "He is still in the pen. I will take you."

On his way to the cattle pen Luke said, "Despite Caroline's views, I need Ursula's assistance with this animal."

Luke collected Ursula and explained the situation—and Caroline's extraordinary accusation.

The beast was now quiet as the two of them entered the pen. Ursula went straight up to the animal and began whispering in his ear. She ran her hands gently over the bull which seemed to help the animal relax except when she fondled the area around the neck. Ursula examined the area closely and pointed out to Luke a series of dots of dried blood. Luke as a former cavalry officer knew from his experience with horses what this suggested. He asked out the assembled stockmen. "Did this bull have any sort of harness, or was he roped earlier?"

One of them replied. "Yes, when his lordship went into the pen, he had a thick leather collar which he put around the beast."

"Where is it now?"

"I don't know."

"I want all of you to look for that collar. It was probably imbedded with sharp pins or nails that pressed into the bull's neck, turning a gentle creature into a killer."

One herdsman saw the significance, "Lord Ranald was murdered?"

"Probably, and if we can find that collar, we may identify the murderer."

Luke returned with Ursula to inform the Earl. "My lord, Ranald was murdered, but not by any witchcraft of Lady Ursula. Someone who knew that Ranald spent most afternoons with the bull turned the gentle animal into a killer with a spiked collar."

"Thank goodness this clears you, Ursula. Caroline is obsessed with you at the moment." He turned to Luke, "Who murdered my son?"

"The same person who killed Finch and Kemp. If I can find someone who all three had grievously harmed, my task would be easy."

"At the rate people are being killed, and the speed of your investigation all the possible murderers will be dead before an answer is found," commented an undiplomatic Hector.

Luke turned to him with a gentle aside. "That is if you think the murderer is a male. None of my female suspects are dead."

39

Ursula spoke quietly to Algernon and Luke. "Upsetting Master Medlowe does not explain Lord Ranald's death. Ranald may have had his weaknesses, but he knew cattle. He and I were never close, but our relationship warmed, when we discussed or were with cattle."

"What are you implying?" asked Luke.

"Ranald would have noticed that the bull was agitated. It would not have gone from placid to goring someone to death in a minute or so. It would take some time for it to experience enough pain to strike out at Ranald. Why did Ranald expose himself to a dangerous bull, without taking common sense precautions? He didn't even have a staff with him."

"Knowing my son, he was probably drunk."

"At least. More likely he was drugged which seriously disabled him. I would like permission for the Colonel and I to examine the body," asked Ursula.

"Drugging Lord Ranald makes the murder attempt more believable. Provoking a bull and expecting it to kill Ranald is a little farfetched. Why open yourself to discovery for such a slim chance of the desired result? But if Ranald was not in a position to assess the situation correctly, and to act appropriately in the presence of an agitated bull the chances of success are greatly increased," said Luke.

Luke and Ursula's examination of the body was delayed until Caroline had temporarily left the Abbey, as Algernon did not want a confrontation between her and Ursula. Ursula concluded from the smell of his mouth that he had taken, in addition to alcohol, an unidentified herb that probably intensified the disabling effect.

Luke revisited the cattle pens and spoke to a few herdsmen who were not out in the fields. One of them had been present when Ranald came for his daily encounter. Luke asked, "Did Lord Ranald appear himself just before he went into the pen?"

The herdsman laughed, "It depends on what you mean *appear himself.* He was, as the saying goes as drunk as a lord. Even more so than usual. So much so that one of the lads offered to go into the pen with him. He refused but took up a collar to put around the animal's neck with an attached lead. Immediately he did this, Master Medlowe became agitated."

"Did his lordship notice this change in the bull's demeanor?"

"I wasn't there. We found the collar that the bull was wearing. I will fetch it."

The herdsman returned with the collar and commented, "There are holes in the leather where nails or pins may have been imbedded."

Luke thanked the herdsman for his information. It confirmed Ursula's and his hypothesis—and created the picture of a very carefully planned murder which nevertheless relied on a good deal of luck. It suggested to Luke that the murderer was a careful planner, but someone willing to take a chance—not the usual combination in the past murderers he had encountered.

Luke took advantage of Caroline's absence, and with Algernon's permission, and accompanied by Mark searched Ranald's apartment.

"What do you expect to find?" asked Mark.

"The obvious—that he had been drinking heavily. With luck some evidence of an additional herbal infusion. Who knows what else?"

They were about to knock on the door when a woman who was cleaning in the hallway volunteered that Lady Caroline had taken most of the servants with her, when she left a half hour earlier. In such circumstances Luke was surprised that the door was not locked. As he pushed it open he signaled to Mark to be silent. They both heard someone in one of the inner rooms.

"Probably a servant cleaning up," whispered Mark. "Let's surprise them!"

Luke and Mark burst through the inner door and were amazed to find a man on his knees rifling through the lower drawer of a tall bureau.

"What are you doing here, my lord?" asked Luke.

It was Edwin.

"I might ask you the same question," replied the peer.

"Clues as to why and who murdered Ranald."

"Ranald murdered? I thought he had been gored by his pet bull."

"It's a complicated story, but the bull had been deliberately provoked and Ranald drugged so that he could not respond to the agitated bull as he would normally do."

Edwin was disconcerted by the news and murmured, "Kemp, Finch, and now Ranald, am I next?"

"Why would you be? What did you have in common with those murdered trio?"

"That's the worry. Very little. Ranald and I were brought up together as schoolboys, but after we went to the continent I did not see him again until I returned here over a decade later. In that case the murderer has motives stemming from either our schooldays, or from the last couple of months. My only link with Finch was that he married my sister, a situation I could not understand until recently, and I had no contact with Kemp until he came here a few weeks ago."

"If you have so little connection with the murdered three, why do you think you might be next?" asked Luke.

"The five younger gentlemen present here, were Finch, Kemp, Ranald, Piers and myself. Is the old guard so desperate to maintain their influence that they are killing off the next generation?"

"A bit far-fetched! Now how do you explain your presence here, rifling through Ranald's possessions?"

"Removing some incriminating evidence! As a boy, and apparently since, Ranald was a prankster. Since the guests have been at the Abbey, Ranald has engaged in a number of pranks—disguising himself and tapping on the windows of the serving maids, and dressing as a women to see how far he could fool people."

Luke was elated. Kemp's killer was Ranald dressed as a woman. He asked Edwin "My lord, why would Ranald dress as a woman, and cause trouble. Was the disguise to protect his own identity?"

"Probably in part, but he had a more direct aim. He wished to discredit two women that he detested—his half- sister Elspeth, and her mother Ursula. He pretended to be a woman, when he directed the mild assault on Elspeth in her bed chamber. This campaign he confessed to me as a sympathetic aristocratic brother, eager to protect our inheritance and our Protestant faith. He always concealed from me another vendetta of his—punishing my sister and Finch's wife, Lucy."

"Why ?"

"It can only refer back to those early days of the royal court-in-exile because just before his death Finch suggested he had knew something that in my family's interest I might be willing to pay for."

"Any hints as to what that information might be?"

"I assumed that he was about to tell me that it was Ranald who had raped my sister."

"Had you suspected this yourself?"

"Ranald as a youth thought every young girl in the area was there for the taking. After talking to Piers and Finch about that period it had to one of those three—Ranald, Piers, or Finch."

Luke noted that as he spoke Edwin seemed distracted, looking vacantly into the distance. Was he about to have another fit? He continued his questioning, "Did you ask Lucy about it?"

"Yes, but she maintained the line she has used for ten years. She has no memory of the assault, but I do not believe her."

"Ranald and Winston are dead. Is Lucy taking her revenge? Is Piers next?" Or did he help her? She claims he has been more of a big brother to her than you."

Luke regretted his comment. Edwin looked upset by the statement but he responded, "If Lucy was involved, she certainly would need help. She has not got the strength of character or the personality to carry out such an enterprise."

"But with help from a brother she might?" Mark inserted unexpectedly into the conversation.

"My sister and I rarely speak. She has never asked for my help or support, but she has received much of this such since she has been here from two other people."

"Who?"

"Ursula and Elspeth. Lucy and Elspeth spend most of the day together."

"I can see Lucy and Elspeth combining to remove Ranald, but why also kill off their husbands?" asked Mark.

Luke commented, "It is possible that Ranald dressed in women's clothing to incriminate Elspeth shot at Kemp and myself. The footprints and shoes were created for me to find, and to reach the conclusions that Ranald had wanted—that I see no other motives than wifely revenge."

"It is still confusing. There are many motives for the killing of Finch and Ranald, but hardly any for Kemp," added Mark.

Luke turned to Edwin, "My lord as you are being frank about the late Ranald can you tell me how he felt about his wife, the undoubtable Caroline?"

"How does any cuckold feel?"

"Especially if the intruding party is your own father," commented Mark.

Edwin laughed, "Where did you get that ridiculous idea? Both Ranald and his father are no longer capable of begetting a child. It was even suggested just after I returned from the continent that I impregnate Caroline, so that the house of Medlowe could continue."

"You rejected the offer?" said Luke

"Not at all! I was very happy to oblige but Caroline absolutely refused to participate in what she considered a fraud. I suspect she was about to lodge a case for the annulment of her marriage, but then the severe illness of the Earl delayed her plans."

"Who is the father of her child?" asked an intrigued Luke.

"She is with him at the moment. That is why I knew there was no hope of my search being interrupted by her sudden return. She is at Whitehall with her lover."

"The King?" asked an amazed Mark.

"Not likely, but it is one of his new courtiers—a devious northerner who claimed to be her cousin. He stayed here for several weeks before you arrived. Why do you think Caroline has embarked on a vendetta against me? She has only known me for a few weeks. What could I have possibly done in such a short time to create such bitter opposition from her? It was because I informed Ranald and the Earl of her affair with Vaughan."

"I am surprised that she has chosen this moment to escape to her lover. With Ranald dead and the Earl capable of sliding back into serious illness at any time, she would have unlimited power to mold Medlowe Abbey according to her wishes, and be in an excellent position to deal with her enemies Veronica, Ursula, and Elspeth," commented Mark.

Luke probed more deeply. "Edwin do you think that Caroline with powerful courtly friends, dispensed with the idea of a long and costly annulment procedure, and had her husband murdered? The removal of Ranald required some knowledge and sophistication. Professional assassins hired by this courtly lover would fit the bill."

"Caroline certainly has the strength of character and determination to oversee such a project."

"Thanks my lord for your valuable insights. Continue your search, while Mark and I try to discover what Ranald ate and drank just before his death."

"Try his study. Nothing has been cleared or cleaned since he left it on his last walk to the cattle pens."

The evidence was so neatly displayed that both Luke and Mark immediately suspected it had been set up A half empty carafe of Bordeaux red, and a smashed glass goblet, and even more unconvincingly a half empty bottle of a tonic, which Luke confiscated to take to Ursula. It had the same odor that Luke had noted in the mouth of the deceased.

Mark turned to Luke, "Has this scene been set up by Caroline to incriminate Ursula especially with the bottle of tonic, or was it done by Edwin for reasons we have yet to discover?"

"Or was it genuine, and Caroline was so glad to be rid of Ranald, she took no steps to defend his reputation by removing the wine and the tonic?"

Luke took the bottle of tonic to Ursula. She was gravely disconcerted. "What's wrong, my lady?"

"This bottle is mine. I prescribed a tonic for the Earl just before he was moved to his town house."

"So what's the problem?"

"The contents are not my tonic. In fact it is a very strong combination of a sleep inducing and major hallucigenic drug. Ranald not only was not rational when he confronted the bull, but he may have seen some frightening creature rather than his favorite and gentle animal. Our murderer was taking no chances. Ranald probably thought he was confronting some diabolical monster. How's your investigation going? Have you had any luck with the shoes?"

Ursula tried to conceal her anxiety. She knew who owned those shoes.

"The shoes were worn by Ranald, partly dressed as a woman possibly to incriminate your daughter Elspeth in the murder of her husband."

Ursula gave Luke a big hug.

"What was that for?"

"I have a confession Luke. Those shoes belong to Elspeth, but disappeared at the time she was attacked."

"It all fits. Ranald pretended to be the woman directing that assault, and probably stole the shoes at the same time."

40

Luke's conviction that Ranald had been murdered by professional assassins on instructions from his wife was immediately challenged by Mark, who argued that Lucy and Elspeth, maybe with help from Ursula, were the more likely perpetrators.

Luke would question Lucy. There had been a remarkable change in her personality since the death of her husband. The docile, timid woman had been replaced by a lively outgoing female who gave Luke a warm reception.

"How can I help my favorite Colonel?" she purred.

"I'm trying to establish who murdered Winston. May I peruse any of his papers that you might have?"

"Waste of time! Winston committed very little to paper. That was part of his success. What exactly did you hope to uncover?"

"Evidence that he was Exodus, and how this might have related to Ranald."

"While Winston committed little to writing he did save letters written to him in case he could use them in later negotiations. I came across a small bundle of them hidden in a pair of boots I was about to donate to the poor."

Lucy left the room and returned with a bundle of less than a dozen letters. Luke suggested he read them in her presence so that she could answer any questions he might have. He was immediately struck by the powerful positions the letter writers once or still held. There were letters from the King in exile, the Lord Mayor of London, Sir Septimus Ingle the leading Cromwellian magistrate in the county. One letter sent Luke's heart racing. It was unsigned and its apparently meaningless message was clearly in code.

Luke recognized the handwriting.

It was that of Cromwell's head of intelligence, John Thurloe. Winston Finch had been Exodus. Luke was well aware of the codes used by Thurloe as he had used several of them as head of military intelligence.

Luke addressed Lucy. "My lady this letter all but confirms that Winston was the Cromwellian agent."

"I am not surprised. Winston liked to cover all options. Five years ago it looked as if Cromwell would be King, and Charles never likely to return."

"I will take this letter and have it decoded. Can you think of any link between Winston and Ranald? Why was Winston really meeting Ranald in the chapel?"

"Winston had many areas in which to pressure Ranald into accepting him as the Medlowe's candidate for election to one of their family boroughs, or any royal appointment in the county. He was very keen to become Commissioner for Sewers so that he could control the drainage of the water lands along the river which formed most of his estate. It would increase his wealth fivefold."

"Did Winston accuse Ranald of raping you, all those years ago? You recently confessed to him that you thought it was Ranald?"

"Over the years we concluded together it could only have been Ranald. I knew for a variety of very personal reasons it was not the royal brothers, Winston nor Piers. Like some of your investigations how can one prove beyond doubt what you suspect? In his youth Ranald was a notorious seducer and assaulter of women but in those days he had confined his assaults to wenches of the lower orders. Winston might easily have claimed that I had proof that my attacker was Ranald, and tried to use it against him."

"If that was the case and Ranald killed him, then your life would have also been in danger. Did you seek the help of Elspeth and Ursula to remove Ranald before he had you killed?" asked Luke in an attempt to derail Lucy's confident responses.

It failed.

"Colonel, don't expect me to incriminate myself. I was not in fear of my life, because I believe the weapons that Winston used to exert pressure on Ranald did not concern ancient history, but related to the more recent past. Two years ago Winston returned from a visit to Medlowe Abbey, rubbing his hands together and proclaiming he had the heir to the Earl of Medlowe completely in his power."

"His leverage?"

"At the time Winston was heavily engaged in the illegal import of Irish cattle and despite claiming otherwise Ranald had purchased a large number of them. As you are aware the import of cattle is one of the major issues confronting landowners at the moment. It is quite ironic that Master Medlowe, the murderous bull, was one of these illegal Irish purchases."

Luke returned to his apartment at Whitehall to consult his code books of the previous regime. He quickly translated Thurloe's short missive to Winston Finch. He could have danced for joy. It simply thanked Winston for involving such a key family figure at Medlowe Abbey in becoming his associate as Exodus. The added warning that the wife of this recruit was not to be trusted, identified the new agent as Ranald, as other family possibilities were not married, or their wives were distant from the abbey.

Ranald probably killed Winston when the latter threatened to reveal Ranald's role as a Cromwellian agent. No wonder the quality of information improved. towards the end of the republican regime.

Before Luke left Whitehall he received a request from the King to visit him as soon as possible. Luke was pleasantly surprised that his presence had been noted. "Your security must be very effective. Ashcroft should be congratulated. I thought I had entered the premises undetected."

"Enough small talk. I thought you were solving or preventing a series of problems emerging from my county gentry. Instead one of them flees your influence and throws herself on me with an incredible tale of violence, seduction and kidnapping. Lady Caroline Medlowe claims she is being held a virtual prisoner here by one of my Gentlemen of the Bedchamber, Lord Vaughan who I was led to believe was her cousin. She claims she was beaten by her late husband and in seeking solace when she was looking after the Earl in the Medlowe town house was seduced by Vaughan who, promised to marry her when she obtained an annulment because of Medlowe's inability to breed children. She became pregnant to Vaughan, and when her husband died, she discovered Vaughan was already married. She came here to sort the situation out but Vaughan refused to let her leave. She has asked me to have her escorted back to Medlowe Abbey, and have me declare that her unborn child is in fact the legitimate heir to the Medlowe title and estates. What is your assessment of her situation?"

"Your Majesty, do not believe a word that Caroline has said. I suspect working with Vaughan she contrived the death of her husband. It was well known that Caroline had cuckolded her husband for some time. Vaughan was reasonably well known at Medlowe Abbey. He apparently stayed there with his cousin for several weeks before she moved to the town house."

"At which point his accommodation here as a Gentleman of the Bedchamber was arranged. He obviously saw a lot of Caroline during her stay in the town house. I had hoped to order him back to Medlowe Abbey so that you could assess his suitability as one of my courtiers, but the plague made that impossible."

"Perhaps you should question both of them regarding their exact relationship. Caroline lied in pretending Vaughan was her cousin, and had no hesitation in sleeping with him. The relationship started when he was at Medlowe Abbey. Maybe Caroline was seduced by Vaughan with the prospect of marriage, but I imagine she has also realized that if the child is declared a Medlowe it will inherit the vast wealth and power of the Earls of Medlowe. I am sure she thought she could convince Algernon that this is the only way of continuing the dynasty."

"I have Vaughan and Caroline waiting in separate rooms. I would like you to assist me in their interrogation."

The King did not mince words with Vaughan. "You are dismissed as a Gentleman of my Bedchamber, and unless you can present a reasonable defense you will be consigned to The Tower at my pleasure. You lied to me and the Medlowe household regarding your relationship with Caroline. You abused the hospitality offered at Medlowe Abbey by cuckolding the son and heir, and your behavior towards Caroline since seems to have been dominated by lies and coercion. Colonel Tremayne, who sits beside me, suspects that you may have played a part in the murder of Ranald."

Vaughan who remained kneeling during this avalanche of charges was signaled to stand. "What have you to say in your own defense?"

"I did not technically lie. I am distantly related to Caroline. Our great grandfathers were brothers. When I moved into Medlowe Abbey it seemed discreet to pretend we were much more closely related. This became imperative as my boyhood feelings for Caroline returned, and she responded with unbelievable passion. She told me she was seeking an annulment of her marriage as Ranald had been unable to provide her with a child. She immediately saw the opportunity of marrying me as soon as the annulment went through."

"You did not tell her that you were married?" asked Luke.

"No, because in the beginning, I thought I might do something about my own marital situation."

"Did you contribute to the death of Lord Ranald?"

"How could I? For several weeks the Abbey has been quarantined, and I have been busy here serving Your Majesty."

"Unfortunately the men under my command have been stretched to the limit, and I am well aware that several people have left and returned to the Abbey undetected, including Caroline. You could have been smuggled in one night and helped organize the spiked leather collar," said Luke.

"I could have, but I didn't. For one simple reason. My ardor for Caroline has waned—and I did not want to jeopardize my position here."

"What created the current stand off?" asked the King.

"The death of Ranald, her pregnancy and the revelation that I was married unhinged Caroline. She arrived here unannounced and claimed she would not leave until I had put the situation right."

"And how did she expect you to do that?"

"Her harebrained scheme was that I should ask you for a diplomatic post and she would go with me as my wife, until I removed my existing spouse. When I refused she stormed off, claiming that I had abducted her, seduced her and now kept her prisoner."

"Vaughan, in your rural existence in the far north, are you mainly concerned with sheep or cattle?" said Luke changing the topic.

"My estate has only horses and cattle."

"Did you at any time instruct Caroline into the behavior patterns of cattle or into their management?" continued Luke.

Vaughan was silent for some time. "At the time I thought nothing of it, but on at least three occasions she and I visited the cattle pens and observed the cattle in the fields together. She was very inquisitive, suggesting that we northerners knew a lot about cattle that we could teach to those living on the edges of London."

Luke could not wait to interview Caroline, whom he had never liked.

41

The King asked Luke to interview Caroline alone. She was surprised and taken aback that the man who entered the room to question her was not the King, but Colonel Luke Tremayne. "Don't be amazed to see me here. I am the King's special investigator into a series of issues surrounding your ladyship."

"Such as?"

"Your role along with your accomplice Lord Vaughan in the murder of your husband."

"I was never near the cattle pens, and detested the animals."

"That is not Lord Vaughan's recollection."

"You cannot believe a word that perfidious nobleman says. He must blacken my name to save his."

"You administered the drugs that made it impossible for Ranald to adjust to an agitated animal. I discovered a bottle of such a drug in your apartment."

"Ranald was taking all sorts of concoctions. If he was full of drugs at the time of his death, they were self-administered"

"Where did he get these drugs?"

"From Ursula Hall, obviously."

"Why did he take them?"

"Since my threatened annulment, he was trying pathetically to make himself more of a man."

"Did it work?"

"No. He became worse in many ways. Either Ursula's concoctions were a fraud or she deliberately gave him something to befuddle his mind and slow his reflexes. If he took too much he fell into a trance."

A flicker of doubt crossed Luke's mind. Maybe Ursula was behind the murder, not Caroline. "Even if you played no part in his death, you are not unhappy with his demise?"

"You will misinterpret this, but I am overjoyed. Ranald was an evil character. I was married to him sight unseen, and I soon discovered he was an unpleasant person. He claimed to have raped many a servant girl without remorse, and devised devious pranks to embarrass and frighten many of the female servants. I was appalled when he confessed that he raped Lucy Symes years ago at the King's court, and was very proud of the act—and the fact that he had got away with it. He loved dressing in women's clothes and gatecrashed many a meeting of women. All this because he was impotent, and unable to sire children. The last straw was his irrational fear that his father would divert much of his inheritance to Elspeth. He then began to slowly poison his father. That is why I moved Algernon to the town house."

Luke seized his opportunity. He knew from the investigation carried on by one of his unit that this was probably a lie. The King's doctors had proved that the Earl was slowly being poisoned by his favorite daily meal of mushrooms. Ranald continued to send the daily supply to the town house unaware that Algernon had been moved to Whitehall. These daily supplies were intercepted by Luke's men and after examination were shown to contain some toxic varieties of fungi. A country woman of Caroline's background would have some knowledge of which varieties are edible and which are not.

On second thoughts he would not challenge Caroline's version of the attempt on the Earl's life. She appeared to have no motive other than implicate Ranald in the death of his father. He decided to assume for the moment that Caroline was innocent, and concentrate his questioning on the hours before Ranald's death.

"If I assume that you did not tamper with Ranald's tonic before he visited the bull, and that Ursula had not provided a debilitating drug in the first place, did anybody visit him that morning, or the day before?"

"I can't tell you as I was not there much of the time. Ranald and I led separate lives but his valet Robert is here with me. Question him!"

"Thank you my lady. The King will shortly deliver his decision on the situation between you and Lord Vaughan, and your request for your child to be considered a Medlowe."

Luke reported to the King who expelled Vaughan from the court, forbade Caroline from any return to Medlowe Abbey. He exiled both to their home county in the north west of England where any issues between them could be sorted out by their respective families. The King refused to legitimize the coming infant as a Medlowe. It would be Caroline's bastard, sired by the already married Reginald, Lord Vaughan.

Luke found Ranald's former valet, Robert, preparing to leave Caroline and return to Medlowe Abbey along with all of the other servants, except for one maid who would accompany her to the north.

Given the circumstances Luke did not question Robert until the next day after both had settled back at Medlowe Abbey.

Luke explained, "I am interested in who visited Lord Ranald the day and a half before he died, in particular who may have had access to his tonic. Did he receive a fresh supply every day?"

"No, for several months his lordship received three bottles of a tonic prepared by Lady Ursula once a week. The only persons allowed near his tonic were himself and the mistress."

"So nobody else could have tampered with them?"

"The morning before he died his lordship had many visitors. Sir Job and Lady Veronica arrived very early. They stayed for over an hour."

"Was it a social visit?"

"Far from it. There were raised voices, threats and counterthreats."

"What was the issue?"

"Nathan Petty! His lordship and Petty have had many a conflict over recent years which was only contained by the intervention almost constantly by their respective fathers, the Earl and the late Sir Julius."

"Had anything brought this conflict to a head in recent weeks?"

"Yes, a major property deal. Nathan, as Julius's heir will inherit a large number of properties which Ranald wanted. Apparently Ranald had stopped the transfer of the properties to Nathan on the grounds that he was not the legitimate heir of Sir Julius, but fathered by Sir Job Elliott. As such his claim would lapse, and Ranald would be in a stronger position to usurp the properties."

"So Ranald resurrected the Julius plan to have Nathan declared illegitimate ?"

"Yes, and he had canvassed many of the gentlemen here to support this should they become members of Parliament."

"Surely the Earl did not agree with this move?"

"No, but since the Earl returned to the Abbey, Lord Ranald and his father have hardly spoken. Lord Ranald has always been haunted by thoughts of a returning elder brother which would leave him without many assets. Under the guidance of Sir Winston Finch, Ranald began to buy property, apparently borrowing large sums of money from Sir Winston to do so."

Luke was delighted. Ranald had killed Finch, but the motive which at first appeared to be their joint role as Exodus, could be the removal of a massive debt which Ranald owed Finch.

"During the visit of Sir Job and Lady Veronica were they left alone with any bottles of tonic?"

"On several occasions, but not for any period that would have enabled them to adulterate the tonic."

"But long enough to substitute a similar looking bottle for one of the tonics?"

"Yes."

"I searched this room a few days ago to find evidence concerning his murder. Did Lord Ranald have a secret drawer in which he may have hidden valuable papers or other items?"

The valet smiled. "He had two. One of which he allowed Lady Caroline to discover and then filled it with information and other strange items to send her into a real dither. His lordship loved to play pranks. He even forged a letter purporting to come from Lord Vaughan professing undying love and a promise of marriage for Caroline, which he displayed in his not so secret drawer."

"And the second hidden drawer?"

"It is in this cabinet, but I can't open the normal drawers let alone the secret ones."

"This is a modern French cabinet with which I became very familiar when I worked for a French aristocrat six or seven years ago. Give me time and I should be able to open it. Is there anything else I should know about Lord Ranald's last days?"

"His other visitors after Lady Veronica and Sir Job were the ladies Elspeth and Lucy."

"Was it a friendly visit?"

"It appeared to be. I do not know what was discussed."

"Who else came?"

Lord Edwin arrived. He appeared very cross. He certainly argued with the late master.

"How did Ranald appear after that visit?"

"Distracted, he appeared to swing from elation to depression in a continuous series. The swings were intensified as he consumed a considerable amount of wine, and almost a whole bottle of his tonic, just before he headed to the cattle pens."

Luke dismissed Robert and began his meticulous dismantling of the complicated French cabinet. He sent for Mark and Jane.

The three agents of the King were delighted. Here was a man who kept detailed notes, letters—and a diary. The latter clearly confirmed that in association with Finch he was Exodus and that as he struggled to build up a property portfolio he had become deeply indebted to him. The entry for the day of Finch's death was illuminating. *Everything has been done to incriminate Elspeth and the conniving Papist.*

Further searching in the most secret of the drawers revealed a bejeweled ceremonial dagger with the thinnest of blades—the murder weapon that had killed Sir Winston Finch. And then Luke found dozens of tightly packed small bags—full of Finch's ready cash.

Luke divided the dozen letters between the three of them.

Within minutes Luke was on his feet, clapped his hands, abused the late Ranald and declared, "We may have some good news for the Earl." This is a ransom demand that must have been received by Ranald when he was acting for the then very ill Earl. He clearly concealed it from the rest of the family. It is from some old acquaintances of mine when I was Ambassador to the Islamic states of North Africa. The corsairs of Benbali captured a Venetian admiral during a sea battle in the Adriatic. He claims to be an Englishman, James, Lord Medlowe. There is a short note from James to his father."

The three of them burst in on the Earl who was in the library with one of the Ramsden twins. "Explain this uncivil intrusion!"

"We bring you excellent news." Luke handed over the ransom demand and James's letter. The Earl asked the Ramsden twin to leave.

The Earl was overcome. He eventually rose, kissed Jane, and hugged both Luke and Mark. "I will take immediate steps to meet the demands. His captors are not aware of the extent of the Medlowe wealth, or they would have asked for much more. Can we trust these infidel?"

"I know these people. They will strike a hard bargain and are ruthless when crossed, but they will keep their word."

"You just saved me from making a major mistake. In order to save the Medlowe dynasty I was just about to ask Hyacinth to marry me to produce a male heir as soon as possible. With James returning that is no longer necessary."

Luke wondered about the Earl's alleged impotence. Perhaps a surrogate father was planned.

"James may already have children of his own," suggested Jane.

Luke, Mark and Jane retired to Luke's apartment. He brought the others up to date on his recent interrogations concluding, "We have solved all the issues that confronted us except the latest—who killed Ranald? The guilty party was whoever replaced his tonic with a toxic mind bending drug. It could have been Caroline, Veronica, Job, Lucy, Elspeth, Ursula or Edwin, although the last appears to have the least motive. We will never know. My intuition is that it was a plan devised and carried out by Ursula, Lucy and Elspeth."

"You have an unfortunate tendency when in doubt to find a scapegoat among the female suspects. You have a problem Luke," responded an annoyed Jane.

Before Luke could reply a servant arrived and said he was required at Lord Edwin's apartment immediately.

When he arrived at the door he was confronted by a tearful Elspeth who announced, "Edwin is dead. He had a fit, went into a coma and died. His sister Lucy was with him at the time. She is still in there with him and the Earl's physician."

"If he died from his shrapnel injuries, which was not unexpected, why have you called me in. Is there any possibility that he was murdered?"

"No, he knew that the next one or two fits would be his last and two days ago when we enjoyed a delightful romp together he made a major confession to me, which on his death I was to relay to you."

"And what did he confess?"

"That he murdered Ranald. They were no longer friends. In the last few weeks Edwin became aware of several of Ranald's appalling acts. Apparently after drinking far too much Ranald boasted to Edwin that it was he who had raped his sister Lucy a decade ago. He showed no remorse, and could see nothing wrong in telling the girl's brother about it. This played on Edwin's conscience. If he had obeyed his father and joined his sister at the court-in- exile he would have been there to protect her. Later Ranald confessed he had murdered Finch to free himself from a massive debt, and Kemp simply to implicate me in the murder. The last straw was last week when Ranald told Edwin that his elder brother was alive but that he had hidden a ransom request and James would probably die in an Islamic prison. If Edwin had survived this last attack he intended to confess to you before you left Medlowe. He knew he would be dead before the law could run its course.

Luke declared his mission at an end.

On reflection he had doubts concerning Edwin's confession. Did Edwin knowing he was near death take the blame to divert attention from his sister Lucy; or did Elspeth fabricate the entire confession to hide her own guilt?

Epilogue

A week after Edwin's death Luke concluded his mission at Medlowe Abbey and returned to Whitehall to await his next assignment. He submitted a list of recommendations regarding the suitability of the local Royalist gentry to the King which was accepted totally. A month later Sir Job and Lady Veronica announced that they were to be married, and were migrating immediately to Virginia.

Elspeth was sent to Italy by the Earl to deliver the ransom, and meet her now released half-brother James, who introduced her to his Italian wife and two sons. The great social event of the following year was the marriage of Lucy to Nathan Petty who with the death of Edwin and his marriage had become heir to the lands and title of Viscount Symes.

The King on Luke's advice had created a broad alliance of able people of diverse views to run the county led by Algernon Earl of Medlowe, Phineas Leigh, Nathan Petty and Septimus Ingle.